UNREAL

BOOK #1 IN THE UNREAL SERIES

CINDY GUNDERSON

Button Press

PART 1
CHANNEL

MARCH 8, 2161 - MARCH 27, 2161

CHAPTER 1

MY NAME IS CHANNEL, and I'm Unreal. Before you feel pity or whatever else you Real people feel, let me assure you: I'm beyond thrilled to be living in Paradise 3 Community. I've read the history, and I've heard the stories. I don't ever want to see the world as it was. Or still is, I guess. I highly doubt it's changed that much in the last hundred years. What is it they say? It takes over *a thousand* years for a landscape like ours to truly regenerate? And we weren't even on the same continent as Campi when it erupted. Sorry Europe.

Yeah. I'm good here. With one minimally invasive upgrade—retinal implants—my visual reality is permeated with color and beauty you can't even imagine. And what is *reality*, anyway? If my brain is interpreting electrical impulses to create the world I see, isn't that precisely the same as what's happening in your brain?

But—being Unreal—I'm *choosing* my input. I'm opting for the diverse and picturesque while you're stuck with whatever mundane, monochromatic drudgery this scarred rock has to offer at any given moment. So what if my input is coming from within my visual-neural pathways, and yours is coming from the reflected light around you? Our brains can't tell the difference, so why would I settle for less? As far as I can tell, non-augmented reality isn't a reality worth living.

"Channel!" Mom calls from the kitchen, interrupting my writing.

"In here!" I shout back.

"Can you be *in here* with me, please? So I don't have to yell?"

"In a second!"

I quickly swipe away my dashboard, though my personal preferences are still uploading for the morning. Should've started that process yesterday when I was on break. Standing, I smooth my cyan blanket over the bed and fluff my pillow. My pictures dance in their frames on the wall, and I smile at my cheery, tidy room. Turning, I wave my hand lightly across the open space of my doorway to disable the privacy screen, then walk into the hall.

"Nice hair," Mom says, raising an eyebrow as I walk into the kitchen.

"It felt like a purple kind of day."

She tilts her head, interested, though I doubt she has any clue what I mean. Her hair has been the same every day since I can remember: light brown with golden highlights that shimmer in the sunlight. Pretty. And boring. Sometimes I wonder if I'd recognize her without augmentation from the Edge—the software built with algorithms that determine what I see and what I don't. How much is she choosing to change?

"Did you finish your capsule?" Mom asks.

I shake my head. "Almost. Still working on my letter to the Reals."

"Ah." She nods knowingly. "Have I ever shown you mine?"

I look at her, incredulous. "*You* wrote a capsule letter?"

Mom laughs, the joyful sound filling our utilitarian space to the brim. "Capsules haven't changed since my day, Channel. How old do you think I am?" She swipes her hand, and the projection hanging in the air over the countertop disappears. "Ready for another week?"

I nod, walking behind her and opening up the cupboard. Our kitchen is small and efficient. Everything has a place, and since it's just the two of us now, we don't have many things to find places for. There's no need for them. At any time, we can change the decorations, color scheme, style—anything we want. 'Things' are so 2030.

"Any other ideas for your World Build project?"

Taking a packet from the breakfast shelf, I turn, allowing the door to close softly on its own. I shake my head, avoiding her eyes as I take a seat on the stool across from her.

Mom raises an eyebrow.

"Don't judge, okay? I'm not—" I sigh, unable to communicate a fully-formed thought as I rip open the packaging.

"I'm not judging. I'm just...surprised, I guess. Third-quarter, it seemed like you had a plethora of ideas to choose from."

"They weren't good ones," I mutter under my breath, then pull out the pressed breakfast bar. I'm not totally sure what's in these things, but today the sweet scent of banana permeates my senses. At least something I recognize. I take a bite.

"You think that's true?" Mom puts a hand on my shoulder. I hate when she does this. Asks a question while making it perfectly clear that there's only one acceptable answer. At least only one that won't catalyze a lecture on self-doubt.

"Kind of," I hedge, then wait for the inevitable response.

"What about—"

"I know, Mom, you don't have to keep bringing it up. That win was pure luck—I practically stumbled onto that upgrade."

She folds her arms across her chest. "I don't think it was luck."

"Well, it was. And all of my ideas last quarter have basically been integrated into the Edge already."

Mom is silent for a moment while I eat. Finally, she stands, pulls a glass from beside the water dispenser, and fills it.

"We're at that point, I think," she says softly, lifting the glass to her lips.

"What point?" I brush the crumbs from my lips and snatch the glass from her hand, sneaking a drink.

Mom scoffs in mock-horror, and I giggle as she wipes the splashed water droplets from her hand. She waves me off when I offer it back to her, then turns to fill another cup.

"We're at the point where we need a breakthrough," she says, her back still turned. "Haven't you noticed the pattern? Technology ebbs and flows. One massive innovation hits unexpectedly, and then we ride the wave for a while. The sea's been calm for too long."

I drink the last sip of water, then toss my breakfast packaging in the compost, leaving the empty glass on the counter.

"Well, I highly doubt that brilliant idea is coming from me."

Mom laughs. "Why *not* you? You're one of the most critical thinkers I know—"

"You need to get out more," I say, walking to her and kissing her cheek. "Love you."

"Love you, too. Have a great day, and say hi to—"

"Will do, Mom!" I rush down the hall and pull a jacket from the hooks next to the door.

"Clear your dishes next time, Channel! And aren't you going to take your mask?"

"Don't need it! I'm going straight to the Grid and home after!" I call, then bounce into the bright morning sunlight.

. . .

"Lex, load Capsule Letter, sinistral," I instruct and watch as the words I created in my room earlier populate my left field of vision. The words hover in the air, and I turn my head to make it look as if they're written on the bricks in front of me. The glow is intense today. It warms my skin as I stride down the walkway, quickly passing the few people on the path in front of me.

"Initiate voice transcription," I say, then begin narrating when a small green light blinks at the top of the text.

"This is what you Reals don't get," I say, continuing where I left off. "The feeling of the sun on my skin? Real. Touch? Taste? Smell? Sound? Real. It's all real. I get to experience complete 'reality' in all my senses with the added benefit of visualizing something more stimulating."

My breathing quickens as I walk with more intensity. This always happens when I try to narrate while I walk—especially when I don't have extra oxygen. Not that Mom was right about the mask. It's challenging to narrate with it on, and my capsule presentation is directly after World Build—I'm not even close to being finished.

"Right now," I continue, "I'm looking at buildings that wouldn't exist anywhere on this planet if World Builders hadn't preserved them in this reality—*my* reality. A mix of ancient Gothic and Renaissance architecture, mixed with New World elements and improvements. I get to walk to work along stones that existed thousands of years ago. And the best part? Next year it'll be something different. Some other piece of forgotten history or previously unknown beauty." I take a deep breath. "And next year...I might be the one building it."

Something catches my eye, and I stop in my tracks. Rushing to the window of my favorite shop, I nearly shriek with delight. I'd posted requests on the network for weeks—practically begging that the next painting rotation be Carol Marine. But of course, you never expect your opinion to be the one that wins out. And yet, *here they are*. Floor to ceiling. Paintings of people doing whatever people did before the Communities. When everything was still vibrant and colorful, and...not dead.

Seeing my request in real life sends a shiver down my spine. I close my eyes, forcing the images to momentarily disappear. Sometimes I think it would be exhilarating to keep my eyes closed and still see the world around me—especially convenient when my corneas get dry and irritated by low air quality. But more often, I'm glad the Edge is triggered off when my eyelids shut—because then I can do *this*.

I snap my eyes open again, and the juxtaposition of the black nothingness against the colorful paintings makes them even more stunning and delightful. One in particular catches my eye. Three women in conversation, their facial expressions somehow obvious, yet blurred at the same time. I don't know how she does that.

The blue skirt of the girl on the left intrigues me, and I inspect every inch of her. Her tanned skin, athletic legs, and high cheekbones look nothing like mine. My skin is pale and my shape not nearly as elegant. The shoulder-length dark hair, though. That we have in common. Huh. It looks good on her.

I sigh, my eyes drifting over the rest of the paintings. Couples, friends, even flowers and old cups. More than anything, I want to be the one building this. I want to be the one to decide which requests are granted and what direction we go in our Community design. I want to have creative flexibility to make things more beautiful and seamless for our entire Community. But that's not going to happen unless I find some way to distinguish myself. Some way—

"You're going to be late," a voice says behind me, and I spin around.

I relax, grinning. "If I'm late, then so are you," I say, walking forward. Aave's brown hair is tousled and, if I didn't know it was purposeful, I'd think he'd just rolled out of bed. He turns. I begin to follow, then stop, blinking.

"Close capsule letter," I say hastily and hurry to match his stride.

Aave laughs. "I hope my incredibly witty comment made it into your dictation."

I roll my eyes. "Because I definitely wouldn't just delete it." His voice wouldn't activate my system anyway. Our retinal displays only have the capacity to augment the visual world around us, but the bracelets on our wrists allow us to connect to the Edge through voice command. Mine is set to private, and Aave knows it.

Aave shrugs. "How was your Rest Day?"

"Not at all restful. You?"

"I slept." He swings his hands almost giddily, flashing a smug smile.

"Of course you did," I grumble. "How is it that your parents somehow understand the need for adolescent sleep, whereas my mom thinks articulated shoulder bridges at first light are the answer to my 'ornery disposition'?"

"Wait, she thinks your attitude is changeable?" Aave laughs. "Has she even met you?"

"Ha. Ha," I reach out to smack him, but he dodges. We approach the open-air gates of the Grid and lift our braceletted wrists for the scanners.

"Did you bring something to experiment with today?" Aave asks, smirking because he already knows the answer.

"Did you?" I ask, toning down the annoyance in my voice, but only slightly. It bugs me that I can't come up with an idea.

Something has shifted in my world the past few months, and as much as I'd like to blame it on the Community—Mom, Aave, everyone else I come in contact with—I know it's not *everyone else*.

As we walk into the protected glass dome, I take a deep breath. My lungs fill with fresh, clean air, and the tightness in my chest dissipates slightly. The familiar pressure will be gone entirely after I flush my lungs a few more times.

Sometimes I like to imagine I'm one of those kids in the Real world—wearing a backpack, stepping off a bus at their school building, and walking into a classroom where a single teacher stands in front of the group to impart their wisdom. It was an inefficient learning model, to be sure, but the idea of sitting together in a room just listening and talking about interesting subjects with my friends sounds idyllic.

I can't complain, though. Our project and subject rotations maximize the benefits of social learning while minimizing distractions and wasted time. And the Grid is much cooler than a boxy schoolhouse. The massive brick archways create a line to the left of us, signifying individual ports. Sunlight streams through the vast dome above us, creating small strips of rainbow light on the walls.

I follow Aave through an archway to our station and step onto my port. Glyn's already linked up. The timestamp directly in my field of view seems to be judging me with its glowing digits. Whoops. I guess we're a few minutes late after all. I'll have to catch her on the inside.

I place my hands in the drivers. The sensor recognizes my slightly elevated heart rate but doesn't complain. Stepping forward, I rest my head on the padded metal bar, close my eyes, and in seconds, I'm standing next to Aave and Glyn, their now fully digital selves reflecting off the smooth, black walls surrounding us.

"This is what we're doing now?" I say, unimpressed with the monochromatic color scheme of the simulation.

"Hey, you two weren't here yet. I'm not the creative one, remember?" Glyn answers defensively. With slicked dark hair and three facial piercings, her form is reminiscent of a goth musician. Skintight onyx pants and platform boots complete her ensemble—anything but subtle.

"I can get on board with minimalist," Aave says, scanning the room. "Save all the good stuff for the coding."

"Speaking of which, I have something I want to try today," Glyn says excitedly. "It's not sexy, but it hits an Edge glitch point."

"Which one?" I scoff.

Glyn gives an annoyed look, obviously wishing I was more excited about her announcement. "Lag Compensation," she says.

"A worthy adversary," Aave says dramatically.

I'm immediately skeptical. "Do you even notice lag anymore?" I ask. "I know it's a thing, but—"

"It's *totally* a thing," Glyn cuts in. "It drives me crazy. Every single time I'm playing that stupid game with my brother, it looks like he hasn't even hit the target. But then, all of a sudden, his points show up!"

Her passion surprises me—I hold up my hands in defense. "Okay," I laugh, "you've convinced me. Lag is still a major problem."

Glyn folds her arms across her chest. "It seriously doesn't bother you?"

I shrug.

Aave laughs, putting an arm of solidarity around Glyn's shoulders.

"You know I can't feel that," she says, glancing at him sideways.

"It's the thought that counts?" Aave grins.

"Are you going to keep hanging on me, or can we start working on the algorithm?" she says.

"I can't work in this environment," I tease.

Glyn rolls her eyes. "I'm convinced this could move us up the ranks for the World Build. It's a problem that nobody has tackled—"

"Because other groups haven't been successful," I cut in.

"Right, but they weren't using the correct model," Glyn says excitedly.

"Wait," Aave says, pacing across the floor, his body reflected on the smooth surface beneath him. "My understanding of lag is that it's a problem with the server. If we want a lower ping time, doesn't that have to start with them?" he asks, pointing skyward.

"Yes, the amount of time it takes for our user input to travel to the Edge and bounce back to create the visual world around us is definitely on the World Builders," Glyn agrees. "But—as far as I know—a server update hasn't been deemed 'necessary,' so that means it's on us to provide a solution for now. If we can write an algorithm that would predict future actions—"

"But we *can't* predict the future, Glyn," I say. "At least not perfectly. Remember Carrow's group last year? They attempted it and ended up with mediocre results at best."

"That's because Carrow's an idiot," Glyn says, grinning. "There has to be a way to solve it. Something more than just prediction has to be an option. If we could mix two different models—"

"I don't know," Aave sighs. "Not that I don't love the idea—I do, Glyn. It would be seamless if we could all experience the same thing simultaneously in every circumstance—especially gaming. But I don't know if this is big enough to win the World Build. Every winner in the past has done something to solve a quality of life problem—a real one, not a convenient one," he says, holding up a hand before Glyn can argue. "I'm talking about something major—that impacts food production or body maintenance. What is this useful for?"

Glyn, in obvious frustration, stares bleakly at the blank wall in front of her.

"Hey," Aave says gently, "I'm not shutting it down. Just because Channel and I don't see the big picture doesn't mean it isn't a great idea." He looks at me meaningfully.

"Aave's right," I say, attempting to come up with something comforting but failing miserably.

Aave gives me the '*is that the best you could do?*' expression, and I shrug apologetically.

"It should only take a couple of days, and...maybe it will lead us to something bigger," Glyn says.

"We're a team," Aave says resolutely. "Channel and I just need to trust you."

Aave's words trigger a memory strong enough to tug me out of the present moment.

"Channel, it's a storm. It's going to be okay," Dad says, sitting on my bed and allowing me to snuggle up under his arm.

"Why is it so loud and scary?" my seven-year-old self asks.

"Because warm and cold air is swirling around up there in the heavens."

"That's why it makes those sounds?"

Dad nods.

"You have to trust me, Channel. Even when things seem scary, you have to remember that I'll always be here to take care of you and your mother. I'll be here to protect you."

The last time someone told me to trust them? I jumped in wholeheartedly. And it broke me.

"Pull up the game info," Aave says. "Let's see what we're working with."

I watch half-heartedly as the code appears, and Glyn begins pulling sections out for further inspection. If we can pull this off—which is highly unlikely, even if Carrow is an idiot—every P3 gamer would be praising our names. But winning the World Build without a life-altering code? Not exactly likely.

"Hey," Aave's voice sounds in my ear.

I look over, but his avatar is still standing next to Glyn, his eyes trained on the task at hand. It's a private message. In the simulator, we can see and hear each other with simple commands because of our connection to the sensors. One of the many reasons working here is more efficient than collaborating over the Edge at home.

"You coming?" he asks.

I press both thumbs down to reply, then speak. "Yes, sorry, just thinking."

"I think this will be a good thing. And you don't have anything to prove, Channel," Aave says gently. "You've already—"

"I haven't 'already' anything. Please stop trying to make me feel better."

"You're just putting too much pressure on yourself, and I—"

"I'm good," I say, cutting him off. I know he's trying to help, but he doesn't get it. Working as a group is hard enough for me these days. I don't want to rely on anyone else, and—more importantly—I don't want them to rely on me. Turning off my private communication, I push my avatar forward to join them.

At lunch, I sit on a bench behind the meal dispensary and carefully unwrap my food packet. A light breeze brushes my cheek as I admire the flowers along the path in front of me. They sway rhythmically, arching their delicate petals to the sky overhead, drinking in the day.

Looking down, I choose the orb in the middle of my food packet first and bite into the crisp outer layer. Though we eat the same thing for lunch most days, it always looks different. I wonder how much of our gustatory experience is visual, which then makes me wonder what this food actually looks like without augmentation, which *then*—

<I wish we could have an implant for our tongues>

The message appears in my field of view, startling me. I look over and see Aave sauntering my direction.

"I thought I turned that off," I say.

"Guess not," he smiles.

"That was a super weird message."

Aave laughs out loud. "No, it wasn't! It's completely relevant. Wouldn't it be incredible if we could taste anything we wanted instead of this same mush every day?"

"It's crispy today. What are you talking about?" I say blandly, biting into orb number two.

"But it could be way better, right?" he says jovially, taking a seat next to me. "We could make it taste like anything—invent flavors nobody in the Communities—in the world—has ever experienced."

I swallow before I respond. "First of all, I don't think that technology will ever exist. Second, those flavors would probably be gross. Third," I pause, "just because we can make new flavors doesn't mean our body will magically evolve to like them."

Aave looks at me quizzically. "What is it with you? You used to be the one imagining crazy possibilities, and now you shoot them all down."

His comment—though I know it wasn't meant to—cuts. I stare at the stones beneath my feet. He's right. It's like the happy-go-lucky Channel died the second she realized what was at stake this year. And I'm having trouble getting her back.

"Hey, Channel, I didn't mean—"

"No, you're right. I'm negative and—and completely unhelpful in our World Build project. Everything feels impossible because—"

"Because you're stuck on this *one thing* and can't see other possibilities?"

"There aren't other possibilities, Aave! World Building is *all* I want to do! If I can't do that, then what's the point? I can't end up stuck in food preparation or sanitation for the rest of my life!"

"You're not going to be stuck in—"

"How do you know? Someone has to do it, and if I'm not exceeding expectations in the coding department, then why not me?"

Aave stares at me in frustration, pursing his lips.

"I'm sorry," I say, forcing myself to relax. "I know I'm emotional these days, but I really can't see another suitable option. Theoretically, I know my life won't be over if I don't get this placement, but..."

Aave leans back on the bench and takes a deep breath. His hair lightly rustles in the breeze, and my eyes linger on the angles of his jaw.

"No, I get it," he says. "I've felt like that. I still do sometimes."

I'm intrigued. "You? Mr. Positive?"

Aave nods, peering up at the blue, cloudless sky. "Of course. You think I'm thrilled to be leaving a predictable post-pubescent life to jump into a new one I know nothing about?" He looks purposely pathetic, and I laugh. "But we can't control everything, Channel, and I don't think we're supposed to."

"Here we go," I sigh good-naturedly. "Go ahead, therapist Aave. Give me the lecture."

He feigns offense and pulls me close, throwing his arm around my shoulders. "What!? It's true! Those feelings are entirely fear-based. I feel frozen when I worry about becoming an adult, but if I let go...."

"Easier said than done," I say, resting my head on his shoulder.

"Hey," he says gently. "I'm not criticizing. I get it. Having more responsibility sounds both exciting and the worst."

I laugh, nodding in agreement. "I mean, how could they trust people like *us* to be in charge of keeping this Community running?"

He shifts his head back so he can look at me. His blue eyes narrow. "Is that why you want to World Build?" He speaks gently as if he doesn't want to break this new, fragile thought or scare me away by voicing it.

"What do you mean?"

"Do you want to World Build so you won't have any major responsibility?"

My heart pounds. "World Building is a major responsibility."

"Not really. It's a creative pass where you have free rein to explore and discover. Anything that's not open-ended is basically network maintenance—which you already have the skills to tackle—with predictable steps and results."

As he speaks, I bundle up the rest of my food, clench my jaw and try to hold back unexpected tears. Without even having to think about it, I know he's right. I'm gutted and a complete coward. And I can't decide whether I'm more upset about the fact that he called me on it or the fact that I wasn't able to see it in myself first. I stand and turn back to the Grid quickly, angling my face away from him.

"Channel—"

"No, I'm good. I'm going back in to have a look at that equation before Glyn's lunch break is over. See you in there," I say, giving a small wave behind my back as I jog quickly away from him, throwing the remnants of my lunch in the bin.

CHAPTER 2

At home, I reset my privacy settings to take myself offline. I don't go into incognito mode often, but when I do? I feel like one of those undercover agents from an ancient super spy novel. I read a bunch of them during my primary years—sneaking past my restrictions because Mom knew they gave me nightmares. But they also gave me power and hope. If those characters could solve impossible puzzles, maybe I could, too.

"Heading out for a bath!" I call toward Mom's bedroom as I grab a drying sheet from the dispenser. She doesn't answer, but I'm positive she's already aware of my plan. I always shower post-Grid. Even though I'm not physically exerting myself there, being in the simulator always makes me sweaty.

Stepping outside, I turn left and take the three-minute path to the bathhouse that serves our section of the Community. I can hear the water running from outside the front entrance, and I groan, hoping there's an open stall. It always used to be empty at this time of day, but lately, I haven't been so lucky.

Entering the building, I smile triumphantly. Success. Green lights along the right wall indicate at least two open stalls. I quickly strip off my shoes and clothing, throw them in the sanitation slots, and turn toward the second set of doors.

My feet slap against the tile as I walk back into the shower room. Scanning the stalls, I look for another green light and walk toward it—weaving past the other patrons marked as grey, offline columns moving between the stalls. I'm not sure when everyone decided to go entirely offline instead of using a placeholder image, but the anonymity certainly makes my life easier. The last thing I want is for someone to notice me and strike up a conversation while I'm in the middle of washing my armpits. Plus, undercover agent fantasy. Very important to keep that intact.

I turn on the water and shiver as the warm stream hits my chest. Rotating, I allow the spray to cascade over my head and form rivulets down my face and body. Someone's singing to herself in the stall across from me, and it makes me smile.

Without taking too much of my allotted time, I quickly scan my body, looking for anything that could be of concern. I do everything I can to avoid looking at my Real self most of the time, but augmentation isn't active in the bathhouse. I understand why. If I never look at myself, I might not notice a problem. Though it seems like my annual physical check-up should be sufficient.

My soft composition isn't anywhere as impressive as my toned body in the Edge. My thighs are wider, my breasts smaller, and my dull, shoulder-length brown hair leaves much to be desired. Mom talks a lot about shifting beauty standards, but the fact is: augmentation looks really good on me.

Today, I notice a bruise on my left shin. No wonder it's been sore. Must've happened when I tripped over the bench in the backyard the other day. Natural skin is so...messy. And hairy. Gross.

Turning toward the wall, I hit the button and hold my hand out to catch the soap tablet. Rubbing it between my hands, I use the lather to wash my hair, then rub the soft foam over the rest of my body.

I rely on these showers to be moments of peace—moments where I can be completely alone and let go of my worries. But today—though I'm doing my best to force it—my brain simply won't sit still.

Time is running out for me to build enough of a portfolio for placement consideration as a World Builder. I know this. I think Mom knows it, too, even though she continues to bring up my few small successes. Granted, a few small successes are better than nothing, but World Building is too competitive to simply be average. I don't want to hope I get lucky. I want to know beyond a shadow of a doubt that I'm at the top of the recruiting pile.

Which is why I can't stop thinking about our current build. Glyn said we needed to develop something beyond prediction—to write a powerful enough algorithm to correct the lag in our retinal programming. And she's right. But nothing beyond prediction exists. Which, I guess, is the point. That's our job—to come up with something revolutionary. But usually our revolutionary ideas are more in the realm of enhancements, not a complete overhaul of a traditional model.

My mind runs over option after option—the same pathways I've been considering since the simulator—and I always end up at the same dead-ends. It's a dead-end project. We could write the most powerful predictive algorithm, and it still wouldn't be up for the task in all circumstances. But what could possibly—?

I freeze mid-thought. The water streams over my body, rinsing the final remnants of soap from my skin down into the drain. My heart rate quickens. I hastily rinse every part of me under the water one last time, then press the button for the dryers. My hands shake in nervous anticipation, willing the fans to work faster. Finally, the antibacterial mist hits my skin, and I walk as quickly as possible to retrieve new, clean clothes.

I have to get to the simulator. Now.

. . .

"I thought you said this was only going to take a couple of days," Aave says to Glyn with a grin. His speech is slightly muffled by his mask, just like the rest of us, though none of us ever choose to show it in our visual form. Masks are necessary but not appealing.

"I may have minimized it slightly," Glyn laughs, pushing him forward along the path. "But it wasn't my fault. Channel's the one who decided to shift the project."

Today, Glyn's dressed in black—again—though her signature short bob haircut is a new stunning color of electric blue.

"Okay, stop here," I say. "I think this will work."

We pause at the edge of the field behind the Community Center. The green grass rustles in the breeze, and the red glowing sun hangs low in the evening sky.

"Do you think the code is good enough to put it in a real-world simulation?" I ask. Despite hours of collaborative effort over the past three days, we still haven't been able to get rid of a few significant bugs. Lag-time in an algorithm built to eliminate lag-time? Not ideal.

Glyn shrugs. "Why not? If it doesn't perform, at least we'll be able to see the issues in the light of day. And if it does—"

"You won't have to listen to us complain anymore," Aave finishes for her.

Glyn nods with a grin.

"Risky," I tease.

Glyn waves me off. "Lex, load Target Match, invite players in proximity."

"Accept," I say as soon as the invitation appears in my field of vision.

"Accept," Aave mirrors, pressing his auditory sensor to his temple.

I reach into my pocket for mine, quickly setting it in place above my cheekbone before targets and barriers appear across the field.

"Parameters?" Aave asks, his voice now vibrating through my sensor.

"First one to five loses," Glyn says.

"Targets count as—"

"Negative one. Each minute that passes adds a point to your roster. Targets have a one-minute kill time. We're starting without the code addition. So watch for lag."

I nod, adrenaline pumping through my body. I haven't played this since I was a kid.

A green light appears in the sky, and I bolt to the nearest barrier, sliding out of view behind it. Glancing down at my hands, I find them empty and flick my wrists. Small, digital firearms appear, and I position my pointer fingers to pull the triggers.

I can't help but smile as the antiquated music fills my ears. It hasn't changed, and I love it. Peeking around the edge, I spot a target and carefully aim. Before I lock, a shot whizzes past the right side of my face, and I lurch to safety.

That was too close. My eyes dart left and right. Without pausing to analyze, I launch myself forward—exposing my body momentarily before taking shelter behind a barrier with a more protected view of the target. I hesitantly lean out and aim, then fire, hitting the target squarely in the center. Another shot sounds, and I pull back only to see a point appear on my tally count a full second after I was in the open. I thought I protected myself, but the game algorithm determined I'd been hit. Lag. This is what Glyn was talking about. It makes the game seem arbitrary and unfair.

A minute and a half passes while I'm analyzing the situation, which means I've gained a point despite my target hit and late damage canceling each other out. I need to move and find another safe zone.

With as much fire as I've been attracting, I decide to move toward the back of the battle zone and hit the targets there. I'm not sure who was firing at me, but since the bullets seemed to be coming from two different locations, my guess is both of them. If I can extricate myself, maybe Aave and Glyn can keep each other busy while I lower my point count.

Keeping close to the ground, I dodge around the first barrier I'd used and clamber behind a rock to the left. The lack of audible gunshots gives me courage, and I flat-out run to the next obstacle further back. A target comes into view, and I shoot it, keeping my score at one despite the timer passing minute number two.

At this point, I can wait a minute for the kill time to pass and hit this same target again. It's cheap, but technically not cheating. It's tempting, mainly because as a kid, playing offensively was never my strong suit. But I'm not a kid anymore, and sitting here seems like a cop-out.

I sneak a glance to the left and catch a blur of movement across the open space behind me. Turning the other direction, I slowly creep to the edge of the barrier and poke my head around the corner. It's Aave. I can just make out the edge of his shoulder.

I doubt I'd be able to hit him from here with such a small target area, and I don't want to scare him off. But...if I stood up and took a step out, I'd have a completely clear shot. Worth the risk?

Taking a deep breath to calm my heart hammering in my chest, I stand up and step out, raising my weapon and firing without hesitation. I fire again before he can move, and the simulation dissolves.

Aave throws up his hands in frustration, and Glyn laughs, standing up from a slow crouch.

"Did you notice it?" she asks.

"Uh, yep," Aave says. "That last hit shouldn't have counted. I'd already shifted out of Channel's view, and yet somehow she still hit me."

"Annoying, right? But you *were* actually hit—the information is delayed on your end, not Channel's. She saw you where you were at the time, but the algorithm takes time to process the information."

"I know how it works," Aave mutters, breathing hard.

"It's frustrating, for sure," I add, "but where would this have real applications besides a game arena?"

"Think about it," Glyn says excitedly. "When you give someone access to your reality, the Edge is constantly adjusting things to ensure a seamless, integrated experience for both of you."

"Like when my mom pulls up a projection," I muse.

"Exactly. That information has to show up on both of your retinal displays at the same time, but if you're moving and she swipes, you've got that lag. I know it doesn't sound like a huge deal, but at a minimum, I see it eliminating all of these day-to-day inefficiencies in the system. Who knows what we could do with that extra bandwidth?"

I nod, impressed. "So, are we going to try this thing and see if it works?"

Aave snorts. "I don't care if it works. I want a rematch."

"So I can beat you again?" I laugh.

"It was a cheap shot," he mutters.

"This algorithm I came up with," I start, suddenly feeling nervous, "it uses prediction *and* joint rendering. The idea is that it will give unlimited users a baseline timeline—instead of rewinding time to create accurate results. The Edge should theoretically create a reality that could be accessed simultaneously between users so all of us could access the same information at the same time."

"It sounds great on paper," Aave says.

"I have no idea if it's going to work," I say.

"The code looked good when I mastered it," Glyn says with a smile. "I had to adjust a few different formulas, but other than that—"

"This is not a time for monologuing," Aave says with a grin. "Let's play."

Glyn rolls her eyes. "Lex, load Target Match Restructured."

Again, the targets and barriers appear, this time in a different config-uration.

"You're going down," I tease, running past Aave and hiding behind a stack of logs.

"It's not perfect," Glyn says, her digital avatar staring up at the endless strings of numbers and symbols on the wall in front of us.

"But it functions," I say in awe. "Beating Aave in Target Match over and over—"

"Would you say 'relentlessly'?" Glyn laughs, and Aave groans.

"I would, Glyn. That is the perfect adverb, thank you. Beating Aave *relentlessly* in Target Match proved that we've worked out most of the major issues over the past twenty-four hours."

Aave sighs, defeated. "I'm so proud of us."

Glyn bites her lip, and I can see the worry on her face. I'm not the only one hoping to make a mark on this competition.

"That's all we can do," I say. "We did our best."

Glyn nods. "It's Rest Day tomorrow, and they aren't taking any other submissions after that," she says, almost to herself. She pulls a piece of code out to analyze it. "I at least wanted to give this a little—"

"Stop! None of the World Builds are perfect—are you kidding me?" I tease. "If ours were, we would've already been recruited."

"Wrap it up," Aave says. "Let's finish this convo on the outside."

Glyn shrugs reluctantly, and the code disappears.

Pulling my head from the sensors, I blink and step out of the simulation. I stretch my fingers and tip my head side to side to relax the muscles in my neck. Within moments, Aave and Glyn are standing next to me.

"Submitted?" I ask.

"Yep," Glyn says nervously, shoving her hands in her pockets.

"You did good," I say, throwing an arm around her shoulders. "This far exceeded my expectations. I'm sorry we gave you such a hard time when you first brought it up."

Aave walks around to Glyn's opposite side and joins our awkward celebratory hug as we walk together past the ports toward the main scanners.

"Are you saying trusting Glyn was a good idea, Channel?"

I laugh, and Aave's eyes dance. "Do you think we'll hear about it when the Real-world adopts our algorithms?" he asks.

Glyn pushes him sideways. "Whatever, don't get ahead of yourself. It's not *that* good."

"Luckily, it doesn't have to be *that* good for them to want a piece of it," I laugh, stumbling to hold on to her as Aave dramatically teeters on one foot.

"Still, it'd be cool to hear about it," Aave says, dropping his arms and leading us toward the exit.

We walk in silence for a few moments, and my mind spins, imagining what it might be like to have our upgrade *out there*.

"I doubt there's even that many Reals to impress these days," Glyn says nonchalantly as we approach our meeting point.

I chew on my lower lip, and my stomach sinks. *Are* they still out there? If so, what is their reality like? Do they regret their decisions and wish they could be here with us?

Why I care about Real people who chose to stay in a broken world, I have no idea. But I do.

CHAPTER 3

"CHANNEL, are you almost finished? Sanitation will be here any minute," Mom calls from the living area.

"Yep, almost done." I glance over at Dad and smile. He's sitting next to me on the bed where he always sits.

"Looks like Mom needs me," I say apologetically. "Thanks for being here." I feel silly saying the words out loud. He had no choice in the matter—I can bring his form here anytime I want with a few taps—but it still feels like the right thing to say.

I ache to be held by him, the way I was as a child. I've been bringing him here for years, and it never makes me miss him less. You'd think I'd learn. I yawn, give him a small wave, and swipe away the projection.

"Why is sanitation coming so early today?" I ask, trudging out of my room.

Mom sits on the paisley sofa, patting the cushion next to her. "They always come in the morning."

"But not till—" I stop short, noticing the time in my field of vision. I laugh sheepishly. "Ah. I guess I've been watching longer than I thought."

Mom raises an eyebrow knowingly. "It's your Rest Day, no judgment."

I sit next to her on the couch and lean my head on her shoulder. "Since when is there ever 'no judgment?'"

"What were you watching?" she asks, ignoring my sarcasm.

I shrug.

"You know I can just tune in."

Scoffing, I lift my head. "I had my privacy screen on."

"I could still get in if I wanted to. I have parental access."

"You wouldn't."

"I might," she laughs.

"It was nothing," I say, letting my head drop.

"You were talking with him again, weren't you." Her tone is gentle, not accusatory, but I sense the underlying disappointment. "You have to let him go," she says, reaching out and playing with a tendril of my hair. "That digital version of him isn't real."

"I know," I nod, looking at the floor. "But it is *kind of* him. He's built out of pieces of the real thing."

"It's only memory of things he's already done or said. Nothing new, Channel."

"It's still comforting to remember."

Mom sighs, "I know. I really do. I miss him every day. But I've found the more I dwell on him, the harder the days feel. It's good to move on. Hard, but good."

I ponder her words, enjoying the soft tug of her hand on my hair.

"Channel, do you wish you had...someone?" she asks, and the question surprises me.

"What do you mean?"

"I think it's normal at seventeen to want to have a relationship—"

"Mooom," I groan, pulling away from her.

"No, I'm serious! You've never really taken an interest in anyone—like that—and I just wondered..." she trails off. "I don't know. Maybe it would be good to build a new relationship."

"So I can forget about Dad?"

"It might help," she admits. "What about Aave?"

"What *about* Aave?"

"Well, it seems like you spend a lot of time with him—"

"Yeah, and Glyn. Because we were partnered together for the World Build."

"But even before then, you two—"

"Mom! Stop, okay? Aave is one of my best friends. It's not like that."

Mom holds up her hands. "Fine, I guess I misunderstood."

I sit up and roll my eyes. "I'm going to meet *Aave and Glyn* for a bit," I say dramatically.

"Uh-huh," Mom laughs. "Ooh, before you go—there's something I wanted to show you. I can't believe I forgot. Lex, pull up my inbox, please."

I sit back down as she taps the projection to open a document.

"What is this?" I ask, reading the first few lines, then turning to her for an explanation.

Mom's eyes remain trained on the words in front of her, and she motions for me to keep reading. She's trying hard to treat this casually, but the tightness of her jaw belies real anxiety. It spooks me.

"Why didn't this show up on my console this morning?" I ask, moving closer to the text.

"Not sure." She swipes left, and I begin to read the specifics on the second page. I go over it twice—making sure I understood it correctly—before speaking.

"Mom, this isn't a 'hey, I have something to show you' kind of thing. This is a massive deal." When she doesn't respond, I continue. "Has an update like this ever happened before?"

Mom shakes her head. "Not in my lifetime."

She scrolls to the next page, and I suck in a breath.

"*A three-day recovery time?* Does that mean it's actually—they're planning to—"

"Go in?" she finishes pensively. "Definitely."

"Why?"

She swipes to the next image, and my heart stops.

"But...this is a *brain*," I whisper.

Mom nods, and I'm practically catatonic, staring at the implant site.

"This isn't a retinal implant update, Channel," she says, putting a hand on my shoulder. "The Communities are launching a full replacement."

I take a deep breath and hold it a moment before releasing the air slowly. We all knew this was a possibility. Someday. Like when my theoretical kids have theoretical kids. Some amorphous day far in the future—because there's no way our technology has come far enough to do something like this, right? I mean, we barely updated our software's tracking capacity during last semester's World Build. How could something like this *actually exist?*

"What does this have to do with us?" I ask softly, my stomach flipping beneath my rib cage.

Mom chews on her lower lip. "They want us to attend an informational meeting."

"Are we—"

"I don't know, Channel," Mom sighs, swiping the projection closed. "Just try to keep an open mind, okay?"

"Do we have an assigned slot?"

"Tomorrow. Eighteen-hundred."

I nod, forcing myself to keep my mouth shut.

"We can talk more tonight," she says, reaching out a hand and touching my shoulder. "I'm sorry. I didn't mean to spring that on you. I guess I didn't know how to bring it up gracefully." Her eyes glance to the right. "Ooh, you have to get going."

"Because my world didn't just completely shift," I mutter. "Let me just go hang out with my friends like normal after reading all that."

"Channel—"

Pulling my lips into a tight smile, I step back and turn, walking toward the front door.

"Love you," I call.

"Love you, too!"

Flashing my wrist at the sensor, I grab my mask, step outside, and head toward the park without another word.

"Is this the first time we've made good on our threat to get together outside of Grid hours?" Aave teases, waving as I approach. He's sitting on our bench, and just walking to this spot makes my mood lighter.

"Why is this bench always empty?" eleven-year-old Aave asks.

"*Probably because we're always here,*" I laugh.

"*Do you think we scare people off?*"

"*You do,*" I tease, and he rubs his knuckles on the top of my head. I giggle and push him away.

"*I think we should officially call this the Aave and Channel bench!*" Aave declares, standing on the seat and throwing his fist into the air.

"*Should we make a sign?*"

"*Watch this,*" he says, moving his fingers in front of him. When he's finished, he stands back to admire his work.

"*I can't see it,*" I say.

"*Right, just a sec—*" He enters his settings and gives me access to his creation, and there it is. '*Aave and Channel's bench*' written in small green neon letters, as if etched into the wood itself.

I clap my hands in delight. "*I love it!*"

"*Now it's officially ours.*"

The letters are still there, though Aave's shoulders are covering them slightly. Glyn stands a ways off, her hair pulled up into a tight bun on top of her head and wearing utility pants with a hot pink tank top. Aave's dressed in his typical outfit—grey t-shirt and black slacks. He's almost as dull and predictable as Mom.

"First time in fourth quarter, maybe," I say. "What's the plan?" Without waiting for a response, I turn, watching a group of younger children playing Target Match across the field. I can't help but grin at how ridiculous it looks when I don't have visual access to the barriers and targets they're seeing.

Aave waves a hand in front of my face and catches my attention. I smack him away playfully.

"We don't have to have a plan today," he says, "so we're not going to make one."

"Ah. I see. We're playing 'restless, spontaneous youth' this morning," I chide, but despite my badgering, Aave's excitement is contagious. *What about Aave?* Mom's question pops up, and my cheeks burn.

At Aave's declaration of freedom, Glyn's face finally shows a glimmer of something other than disinterest. She's always somewhat standoffish, but this morning she seems particularly broody. Probably worried about the build, and I don't blame her.

"I'm in," she says. "Let's walk any direction—Aave, you choose first—and then whenever we get to a cross-street, I'll run my randomizer, and we'll go whichever direction it tells us to."

"Easy. That way," Aave says, pointing north.

I laugh, grateful for the distraction. "I don't think that's going to work. What if your randomizer just sends us back and forth."

"New rule, we can't go back the direction we just came. I'll only put in three options," Glyn says, and I nod.

The soft breeze brushes against my skin as I rush to keep up. "I have to be back in a couple of hours, so we can't go too far."

Glyn groans. "As if we could go far enough that you'd be late. Community boundaries are only a twenty-minute walk."

"Yeah, *Channel*, but by all means, keep poo-pooing our ideas," Aave says, feigning disgust. He winks at me to make sure I know his comments are good-humored. Though I can't say the same about Glyn. Something feels off with her, and I can't put my finger on it.

Scanning the street, I can't help but see things differently. From one day to the next, my reality went from cutting edge to obsolete. This augmented world is going to be outdone by a full sensory experience. *Virtual reality, not visually augmented. A complete brain implant.* Do my friends know about this?

I quickly shove the unwanted thoughts deep down and force a smile to my face. Even if they do know, I absolutely *do not* want to talk about that now and have it sully our day off. I kind of don't want to talk about that ever.

Glyn holds out her arms perpendicular to her body, barring us from moving past her. "Okay, stop. Lex, pull up a randomizer for left, right, or straight." She scrutinizes the air in front of her. "Right."

We follow her down the street and weave around other people window shopping and strolling amiably along the path. Usually, I love Rest Days. No hurry, no rush. This should all feel peaceful. But of course, it doesn't. Any calm has been forever obliterated by the dull ache I feel in my stomach when I think about that message. Or the strange, new hesitation that hits me each time Aave opens his mouth. Why would Mom bring these things up today of all days?

"Winners for World Build will be announced in two weeks. Are you nervous?" Aave asks, breaking me from my thoughts.

Glyn shrugs.

"What, don't want to get your hopes up?" Aave teases.

"I think it's too late for that," I say.

Aave grins. "Having your hopes up is never a bad thing."

"Until your heart gets ripped out and crushed with disappointment," Glyn mutters.

"Whatever, just project a smiley, gracious face to everyone that night, and you'll be fine," I tease. "Make sure to upload it beforehand so nobody witnesses your indignation."

Glyn grimaces. "I'm going to turn off 'all-access.' Then everyone around me will only be able to see my placeholder image."

"Choose a weird one," Aave says.

"That's probably an easier option," I admit. "Ooh! Question—"

"Wait! Next turn needs to be decided," Glyn says, cutting me off.

Aave and I wait patiently as she reruns the sequence.

"Straight," she commands, and we obediently follow. "Your question?" she asks.

"Right. Did you two know our parents can bypass privacy screens?"

Aave's head snaps in my direction. "What?"

"My mom said she could tune in to what I was watching earlier if she wanted to."

"No way," Glyn says. "She was kidding."

I shrug. "I'm just saying. Be careful out there."

Aave looks visibly shaken by this information, and I stifle a laugh. Glyn runs her randomizer at least six more times over the course of the next five minutes, and we find ourselves walking the block leading behind the Community Center.

"There's no way that's true, right?" Aave says.

"What's true?" Glyn asks.

"The privacy thing," he says.

"Wait, you're still thinking about that?" I laugh. "What do you have to hide?"

"Nothing, it just seems wrong that they could do it."

"Uh-huh. I want to see your history," I tease.

"New subject," Glyn says, obviously annoyed by our bantering. "What do you think the chances are that everyone will forget about the Reveal at the World Build celebration?"

I groan. "Is that happening this time? I always forget which quarter it's in."

"How can you forget?" Glyn asks, obviously annoyed. "It's always fourth."

"Not true," I shoot back. "One time we did it in second, remember? They switched it because of—well, I don't remember why, but they did! And then there was that—"

"We get it, Channel," Glyn says, "but it's almost always fourth quarter."

Fair. "Aren't you used to it by now?" I ask.

"How could we get used to it?" Aave asks, aghast. "Are you used to it?" He looks at me, horrified.

"I guess."

"You guess?"

"Yeah."

Aave stops on the street. "How can you be *used* to seeing the Real World? It's the stuff nightmares are made of. I've begged my parents not to take me; I've faked illness, I've tried to injure myself, all so I wouldn't have to show up for the Reveal each year."

I blink.

"Explain," Aave says, planting his feet and refusing to budge.

I look between him and Glyn. "I guess I'm just braver or something?"

Aave doubles down. "You're telling me that the pitch-black doesn't terrify you? Or the dull eyes in your parents' faces? Sorry," Aave says quickly, looking down, "your mom's face? Or the—"

"I've never seen it, okay?" I blurt out.

Aave and Glyn stare at me, their eyes wide.

"Ever since I was little...it was too scary. So I just closed my eyes."

"You *closed your eyes* for over half an hour straight?" Aave asks, incredulous.

"Every year?" Glyn asks.

I nod.

"You were never curious?" Aave continues.

"Of course I was curious. I was just...more terrified."

Aave laughs in shock. "So you've never had nightmares like us?"

"I've had plenty," I shoot back, feeling my hackles rise. "It's not like I haven't heard people describe it! Which is why I never wanted to see it—"

"But don't you think it would be better to know? Instead of letting your imagination go wild?" Glyn counters.

She has a point. Especially considering the thoughts I've been having lately. We walk in silence a moment, and I step purposefully—one foot in front of the other—trying to take my mind off the topic by walking perfectly along the line where the edge of the street meets the walkway.

There isn't much to see here on a typical day, let alone Rest Day. With no interesting shops in this part of P3, the streets are dead. Lush greenery peeks out behind the brick buildings and above even the tallest rooftops. They're far enough away, though, that if you walk closer and closer, you'll hit the Community boundary before you can reach out to test if the trunks of the trees are there or not. I know they're not.

"This year, you have to open them," Aave says. "You have to, Channel. It's the last time you'll be a part of it. Who knows if they let you do that once you're an adult."

I shrug.

"Promise me?" he says, lowering his face to force me to meet his eyes.

"What will you give me for it?" I ask stubbornly.

Aave waggles an eyebrow.

"No! I didn't mean it like that," I laugh, pushing him away. "Fine, whatever. I'll open my eyes, but only for a second."

I feel slightly guilty about the white lie I just told my friends. I didn't close my eyes because I was scared. I mean, initially, yes. When I was younger, it seemed terrifying, and I refused to open my eyes. My dad and mom would both take a hand and stand with me during the opening ceremonies of World Build. Dad told me the year I was nine that next year I'd definitely be strong enough. Next year, I'd be able to open my eyes and see him for Real. Three months later, he was gone.

And if I couldn't see him for Real, I didn't want to see anything.

A blue butterfly flutters around the flowers in a planter next to us, and I follow it, marveling at the brilliant iridescent wings and erratic flight pattern. That's impressive code right there.

Suddenly, a hand grips my arm and pulls me off the path—away from the butterfly and closer to the building on our right. When I begin to protest, Glyn puts a finger to my lips and motions down the street. I turn and nearly gasp before catching myself.

An image is flickering in and out of focus. Despite being too far away for full rendering, I squint—attempting to make sense of what I'm seeing. Two men are dragging what looks to be a heavy sack—but, wait, I see shoes peeking out from under the fabric. I suck in a breath.

"Shhh," Aave says, and I cover my mouth.

When my head starts to feel fuzzy, I force myself to exhale and breathe slowly. We watch—frozen together in a tight huddle—until the image fades entirely, and we're left staring once more at an empty street.

CHAPTER 4

"What was that?" Glyn asks, breathless.

"I have no idea," I whisper, still catching my breath. "Did you guys see—"

"They were dragging *a person,*" Aave finishes, and I freeze. I didn't just imagine it.

Glyn shakes out her hands. "I couldn't see who they were—their clothing kept pixelating. It didn't look like Community workers."

"It looked like medical staff to me," Aave says. "They were wearing tags."

"Maybe it was that," I say hopefully. "Maybe someone expired, and they were taking them for body disposal—"

"Out the back door of the Community Center?" Glyn scoffs.

"True," I say, deflated. It's not like we know where they take people who expire. I was too young to know what happened to my dad, and I don't think either of these two has lost someone yet.

Glancing down the now fully empty street, our game doesn't seem fun anymore.

"I thought stuff like that only happened in the Real world," Glyn says softly, shoving her hands in her pockets.

"We shouldn't jump to conclusions. Just because we've never seen anything like that before doesn't mean there isn't a good explanation," I say.

Glyn looks at me, her eyebrows furrowed. "So how do we find out? Are you going to march in there and ask why people were dragging a body out the back door?"

Her sudden intensity startles me, and I step back.

"Let's just head back to the park," Aave says. "We can ask our parents or something."

Glyn looks back toward the Community Center, then reluctantly pulls herself away and follows us down the street. It's a straight shot back to the park, thankfully, because nobody seems to have much to say. Before we get there, Glyn waves noncommittally as she splits off to head down a side street—a quicker way home—which means I'm left alone with Aave for the last awkward half a block.

The discomfort of not speaking is painful enough that I'm willing to broach the only subject on my mind besides the body in the alley.

"Hey," I say, clearing my throat. "Did you hear about the update?"

Aave slows and looks at me quizzically.

"I'll take that as a 'no,'" I laugh, almost giddily. I convince myself I can counteract the heaviness of the topic with over-the-top levity.

"What are you talking about?" Aave asks, seeing right through my anxious humor. "Doesn't the Edge update as needed?"

"No. I mean, yes—it does, but this isn't an Edge update." I stop, grabbing onto his sleeve and pulling him backward to stop in front of me. "Aave. It looks like they're developing—they've developed—a full sensory implant."

He stares at me blankly.

"It's like we were joking about the other day. A tongue implant, right? But more than that. It's implanted in the brain and can oversee all executive processing." *It's the next step*, I think. No big deal, just the natural next step.

His mouth drops open slightly.

"Wait," I laugh, "Are you speechless? Did I finally land on something that—"

"What do you mean?" Aave blurts—completely ignoring my needling comments—and it sobers me immediately.

"I—I don't know much, but we had a message this morning. There's an informational session—"

"You've been selected to participate?"

I shrug. "I'm not sure. Maybe? I only looked at the schematic for a minute before I left. I didn't have much time to inspect—"

"When is it?"

I blink.

"Your time slot," he clarifies, walking forward again.

I rush to catch up. "Tomorrow at eighteen hundred."

Aave nods then makes a beeline across the street for our bench. Today it's painted a pleasant blue with shiny black legs folding into the ground.

He sits.

I sit next to him and fold my arms across my chest. "You don't have to act all mad. I'm only the messenger."

Aave runs his hands through his hair. "I'm not upset. It just took me by surprise, that's all."

"Yeah," I nod. "I got that."

"Did you see the specs?"

I shake my head. "I only saw the message and then the image—"

"What did it look like?"

"It showed the implant site in the brain stem. But there are these—I don't know what you call them, tendrils, I guess?—that reach out to specific contact points."

Aave shakes his head. "That's insane."

"I know. I can't begin to imagine the possibilities."

Exhaling audibly, Aave shifts and meets my eyes. "I think that's the problem. I'm *beginning* to imagine the possibilities. When it seemed impossible, it felt fun and exciting, but knowing it could actually happen? That it is happening?" He leans forward and rests his arms on his knees. "With an implant like that, someone could literally be left in a bed with zero external stimulation, and they could think they were—I don't know, flying or something."

My face scrunches up at his comment. "No way. There's *no way* we're ready to go full sensory VR."

Aave looks at me, unconvinced.

"I know," I say. "The whole idea sounds crazy to me, too. But I don't think our tech would be at that level yet. Especially with a Gen 1 implant. They've got to start small, right?"

Aave nods.

"But if it was full VR..." I shake my head. "We'd be able to experience *anything*. No more simply viewing it or linking up—we'd be able to *experience* it." A thought occurs to me, and I suck in a breath. I could be with my Dad. For real. I could hug him and be with him whenever I wanted. Yes, it would still be replicated from previous digital interactions, but...maybe it could go beyond that. Maybe we could use predictive models to—

"Could they make one that's removable? Like, we could just put it on and take it off?" Aave asks.

I look at him quizzically, trying to catch up. "The implant?"

"Yeah, it'd be super convenient."

I laugh out loud. "Who knows, maybe that's what it is!"

"Just put a little trap door back here," he says, moving his hands to the base of his skull, pretending to open it up, take something out, and put it tenderly in his pocket.

This only makes me laugh harder.

When I can finally breathe again, I stand up and stretch my legs. "I'm sure Sanitation's done by now. I should probably get back."

"Enjoy," Aave says with a goofy grin. "It might be your last night fully as yourself."

I roll my eyes and take a step backward. "Yeah, because they're definitely going to just roll us in for surgery after their brief presentation."

"Just be careful." He smiles at me, attempting to keep the comment casual, but his expression is anything but.

I wave—my heart full of excitement and renewed hope—and turn back toward home.

CHAPTER 5

"READY?" Mom calls from inside the house. "We need to leave!"

"I know, I'm coming!" I call, rubbing my eyes and forcing myself to sit up. Naps are my new favorite thing, especially when it's warm enough to lie outside in the afternoon sunshine.

"You haven't even eaten yet," Mom scolds as I walk into the kitchen.

"Why don't they just stream these meetings, so we don't have to go anywhere?"

Mom throws me a mask. "Because we do actually benefit from social gatherings, despite your constant efforts to avoid them."

I follow her out the door, and we walk in step toward the Community Center. "I was very social this week," I argue petulantly.

"Glyn and Aave don't count."

"How do they *not count*?"

Mom sighs dramatically. "Fine, they *kind of* count, but it could be good for you to branch out a little. You're going to be eighteen in—"

"Wait, are you continuing to insinuate that I should start looking for a partner?" My face contorts involuntarily into a look of disgust.

Mom purses her lips. "No," she says slowly, "but haven't you at least thought about it?"

"No. No, I have not," I lie. Of course I've thought about it.

"It's your life," she says with a slight edge to her tone. "But I know from experience that it isn't a lot of fun to do this solo."

I groan internally. Classic Mom move to bring up a subject that obliterates any chance of rebuttal. Sick of my argument? Just bring up dead Dad. Conversation over.

"What is 'this' anyway," I say, pivoting to attack the only piece of her comment that's still in play.

"Ugh, don't start this again, Channel. The meaning of life isn't going to be discovered on our way to this meeting."

I stifle a laugh, and Mom notices. Her eyes flash, but I see a slight grin begin to form on her lips before she hastily turns her head away.

As we approach the building, we hold our bracelets up to the sensors and walk through the large double doors into the expansive foyer, already packed with people waiting to enter the auditorium. Without any warning, my mind flashes back to the scene we witnessed in the street behind this building yesterday.

I shudder. "The doors aren't even open yet. I could've slept for five more minutes at least."

Mom rolls her eyes. Then, turning, her face lights up, and she smiles. She waves at a friend across the room.

"I'm sorry," I say with difficulty. "I know I haven't been in the best mood lately. And I'm trying."

Mom looks at me knowingly, a friendly smile still on her lips. "I doubt it has anything to do with the end of an era combined with unknown information that could potentially turn our lives upside down?"

"Couldn't be that," I say, and she reaches out to pull me close.

"Listen," she says. "Whatever happens in there, we're in this together. This is only informational, and once we have said information, we'll take it home and discuss, okay? Nothing has to be decided right now."

I jump as a metallic scraping noise cuts through the buzz of conversation around us. Two doors on either side of the hall open up, and we follow the stream of people into the seating area. Mom chooses a seat near the aisle, and I slide into the open chair next to her.

Not for the first time, I wish I could somehow surreptitiously turn on a game to quell my anxiety while I wait. Since that's been my strategy to avoid assignments all year, however, Mom is far too tuned into my air taps at this point to get away with it. There's no way she wouldn't notice.

Instead, I take in the room around me—the golden scrollwork, the maroon panels, the rotating ceiling. Quite a change from the last time I was here. It's visually stunning, and that helps take the edge off.

The lights begin to dim, and my attention drifts back to the front of the room where a Community leader stands on stage. Her red blazer sets her apart from the other Community workers in blue sitting to her left. I hold my hand up and pretend to squish her between my thumb and forefinger. Mom swats my wrist.

"Welcome," she says, and I immediately recognize her voice but can't place it.

"Who is that?" I whisper, and Mom moves her head close to mine.

"Cass. She does all the announcements."

Realization dawns when I hear her name, and I remember the countless times I've seen her in announcement messages. There are only about twenty-eight thousand Community members, so you'd think I'd know more people personally. Apparently, Mom is right about me needing to branch out.

"I'm sure you all have plenty of questions, and we'll have a Q and A session both in person and virtually after this session, but first, let me see if I can cover the basic information."

The same three-dimensional image I'd seen the day before appears and hovers in the air above our seats.

"I know you've all seen this," Cass says, "but I wanted to talk about it in more depth. First of all, you are likely well aware that it's been over forty years since our last innovation in retinal implants. I'm sure you've at times wondered why the World Builders haven't come up with something revolutionary during that time. I know I have," she teases.

"Well, *this* is why. At a certain point, there simply wasn't much more to accomplish with retinal imaging. Yes, during each World Build we've been able to update the Edge—thanks to some brilliant coding by our youth." She pauses and claps her hands, waiting for people to join her in applause.

When the sound dies down, she graciously continues. "We've all enjoyed increased resolution, dynamic light play, creative gaming, and incredible flexibility with personal enhancements, just to name a few innovations. But resolution can be only *so good* before our brains struggle to differentiate a meaningful difference."

She pauses and scans the room as if gauging how to phrase her next words. "Right here in North America, there are five hundred million people. There are over four billion people in Communities like this one— that's over half the world's population. Let that sink in for a minute. Over *half* of the humans on this planet are experiencing life at a level never before imagined because of our retinal implant technology.

"I'm sure you've heard this a million times before, but it's powerful, so I'm going to say it again. Our retinal implants have allowed us to create the world we crave. And not only that, augmented reality has created a world where resources can be used on necessities instead of unnecessary luxuries.

"Can anyone recall the amount of money spent on, I don't know, let's choose clothing—fashion—before the Communities?" Cass looks for a hand and finds one raised a few rows back from the stage.

"Over a trillion dollars," the woman says, her voice shrill as she attempts to project.

Cass nods. "Right on. Over a trillion dollars. Annually. Within the Communities, that statistic has dropped to next to nothing. Because it doesn't matter what our clothing looks like. We wear something comfortable and then create our own fashion in the Edge. And when *over half* the world's population cuts out a need for resources like that?" She shakes her head. "Well, that builds all of us a better world. And that's only one example. We could spend all day listing the global inefficiencies we've abolished in Community living, but I don't need to hash that out. You know all this." She smiles. "So why am I repeating it?"

I'm annoyed with her unending perkiness, but I'm also riveted. The brain map still spins in the air above our heads, and the room feels electric—all of us on the edges of our seats. I have to remind myself to breathe.

"I'm repeating it," Cass continues, "because this week, we are making the first substantial leap forward since the Communities began." She pauses, waiting for this information to land fully. "This week, Paradise 3 is one of *ten* Global Communities selected to be a part of the initial rollout for the Cerebrolink."

The room erupts with applause and cheers, and goosebumps lift on my skin.

"The Cerebrolink is sleek—barely taking up enough space to cover the tip of your finger—and is implanted in the brain stem."

The image above us lights up, and a minuscule silver disc appears at the base of the brain.

"From there, sensory stimulation can be catalyzed by the Edge in a series of preprogrammed experiences, or directly by the individual."

My brows furrow, and I lean close to Mom. "Did she say we'd be able to control it? In the moment?"

"Shhh," Mom says, holding up a finger.

"These fibrils will be unique—built by the Cerebrolink specifically to match your brain chemistry—and will learn and adapt as electrical input is received and integrated over time."

Cass swipes the projection away, and the lights dim slightly, leaving her illuminated in a singular spotlight.

"This technology," she says with intensity, "as with any tool this powerful, will require a linking between the individual and the artificial intelligence. It will be like learning to ride a bike. Except this one can literally take you anywhere."

Or bring you anyone, I think.

Cass pauses again, the air in the room thick with anticipation. "And when you achieve symbiosis? Your brain will look like this."

The image reappears, this time with delicate strings of light stretched in arcs across the cerebral cortex, each of them ending with a tiny glowing bead pressed against the fleshy folds. There are thousands of them.

After the presentation, Mom and I walk down the darkened street toward home. I can't think of a single word to say; my thoughts are jumbled into one massive pile of shock, disbelief, possibilities, and worry.

"That was something," Mom says finally.

I nod.

"What'd you think?"

My mind continues to spin, and it's impossible to form a cohesive sentence. Being able to experience literally whatever I want is tantalizing. And unbelievable. An implantable artificial intelligence that can learn from and bond with your brain? Who wouldn't jump at the chance to live in a world with no boundaries?

And yet...something deep inside me swirls with hesitation about the entire endeavor. Is it fear of the unknown? Fear of allowing someone to access my body and mess with my brain? Fear that I'll end up living in my past and not moving on like Mom says? All of these thoughts crash against each other, and I'm officially overwhelmed.

Mom sighs. "She's a fantastic public speaker."

How is she so calm and collected, as if we just went out for a nice lunch? Again, I nod in agreement as we cross the street to our living quarters. When we reach the front door, Mom scans her bracelet, and we walk in, closing the door behind us.

"Can you believe we're one of *ten* communities chosen to roll out the Cerebrolink? I wonder why they picked us," Mom continues to ramble, hanging her jacket on one of the hooks on the wall and setting her shoes on the floor underneath it.

My thoughts compete to get out, and when one bubbles to the surface, I can't hold it back any longer.

"What are people living like in the Real world?" I blurt out, and Mom blinks at me.

"What do you mean?" She turns and walks toward the kitchen, and I follow.

"Cass said over half of the world population now lives in Communities like ours, right?"

Mom nods, reaching for a cup and filling it with water.

"So, then, why? What about the other half? Why don't they live here too?"

"I'm sure they wish they did," Mom says, taking a sip, "but it's been a process trying to convert such a large population. I mean, think about it. Implants for eight billion people all at once? And infrastructure to support the Edge?"

"Yeah," I nod, "I guess that would be a massive undertaking."

"Massive is right. And," she takes a deep breath, "I know there are some purists out there who are completely against the Communities, but from what I've heard, they're dwindling out quickly. It's bad, Channel."

"Like how bad?" I ask.

She looks at me quizzically. "Don't you remember what it looked like at the last—"

"Of course," I lie preemptively, "but it sounds like it's gotten worse since then. And, even if I can see what it looks like here, I don't know what it looks like somewhere else. Outside the Communities."

Mom accepts my explanation with a slight nod.

"Do they have to wear masks, too?" I ask.

Mom scoffs, planting both hands on the counter in front of her. "Of course they do. Can you imagine? Walking outside every day, not having air-mitigated buildings—so you have to wear your mask at *all* times outside of the house—being met by bleak views everywhere you look." She shakes her head. "Even within their own homes, there isn't always an opportunity to make things livable. It would just be...depressing."

I try to imagine this. Masks all the time. Bleak. Colorless. No safe spaces.

"What if it's not," I say softly, sitting down on a stool and leaning on the countertop.

Mom's eyes narrow, and she smiles. "You're doubting?" she says gently.

"Maybe a little," I say, jutting out my chin. "Is that bad? I'm just facing some pretty intense decisions. My chances of having a family of my own are slim to none—"

"What? Where is this coming from Chan—?"

"—*and* I'm putting all this time and energy into building algorithms and fixes for software that might be completely obsolete at this point! If the Cerebrolink works? Everything we've done is for nothing. What's the point of World Building? We could just live in whatever worlds we want to create for ourselves." I slump over and press my head into my hands.

Mom walks toward me and rubs my back. "Why in the world do you think you have slim chances of starting a family?"

"You said it yourself. I've never really found someone I want to get together with. And who knows if that will even be an option with all this. I mean, why do it for Real when you could have a virtual family without all the pain?"

Mom nods. "That does sound appealing."

"Hey!" I complain, and Mom laughs.

"This Cerebrolink won't be the end of the species, Channel, if that's where your mind is going. The goal is to improve life, not to end it."

I nod.

"And you are smart, charming, fun to be around—I'm sorry if I made you feel pressured. I have no doubts you'll find someone when it's time."

I have doubts, but I decide to keep quiet on that point.

"And your hard work wasn't for nothing. How do you think the Cerebrolink came to be? It was because of thinkers like you! People working together to come up with something new and better, to give us more opportunities to learn and experience life."

"But are we experiencing it?" I ask, lifting my head. "Or are we just finding ways to escape it?" I know that's partially what I'm doing.

Mom sits on the stool next to me, pondering my question. "I guess I would ask—as a counter-question—what is our purpose here?"

"That's exactly what I'm asking."

"No, you're asking if—as a society—we're choosing to blind ourselves to the way things really look and feel."

It's true. I'll give her that.

"So what is our purpose here? What is the point of life?"

Her question terrifies me, and I want to squirm out from under her hand and curl up in my bed.

"I don't know," I whisper.

"Well, that's comforting because neither do I," she laughs. "But I would argue that there isn't any overarching meaning to our existence. And I know how that sounds—hear me out. I do think there is *value* to our existence. I believe we *do* have a moral obligation to our species to make life better for each other. That is a truth that sits deep within each of us."

She sighs, leaning her elbow on the counter and turning to face me. "I guess what I'm trying to say is...why would we purposely force ourselves or anyone else to suffer if they didn't have to? And I guess you could argue that suffering is relative," she says, raising an eyebrow.

I laugh in spite of myself.

"But," she continues, "I would say that withholding a more pleasant experience is always suffering in some way. Especially because we can't pretend a better way doesn't exist."

I meet her eyes. She looks serious, intense.

"So maybe I can do that," I say.

"Do what?"

"Help convince people to join the Communities. Help people suffer less."

Mom beams at me. "That's my girl."

. . .

"Channel, Aave, what are you two doing?" Dad asks, amused.

"We're pretending to be Real!" I announce, throwing my nine-year-old fist into the air dramatically.

"Yeah," Aave says. "We have to make all our own food, and everything around us is a barren wasteland."

Dad chuckles. "So, how are you going to make food?"

Aave's small shoulders deflate. "I didn't think of that. We might starve to death."

"No we won't," I say excitedly. "We can grow things in the dirt. If we give them enough nutrients—"

"What about the air," Dad asks, pointing toward his mask. He always shows when he's wearing one to be a good example.

My brow knits together. "Well, then we'd have to build them a filtered house. A house just for the plants."

Aave beams at me. "You're so good at solving problems, Channel."

Dad grins and reaches out to ruffle my hair. "That's my girl."

CHAPTER 6

THE NEXT MORNING, my body is stiff. Even though I know I slept, I must have been a subconscious ball of stress because every muscle in my body screams at me as I stand up. Not cool that I'll be sore for the first day of celebrations. Not cool.

Twice a year, we take time off to rest, recoup, and celebrate our accomplishments as Young Builders. My stomach twinges as I realize this is my last World Build celebration. Ever.

Sure, I'll still participate with the rest of the Community after that, but it won't be the same. I won't be the one competing. I'll be placed as a Community worker somewhere—no, I'll be a World Builder. *Positive self-talk, remember?* Which means...I'll get to judge the submissions. A thrill of excitement passes through me...until I remember the Cerebrolink.

Questions again fill my mind. Will that be a draw for people to join the Communities? Will people want to jump straight from Real life to that? Am I even sure this whole virtual reality thing is a good idea? I know nothing about people on the outside. I know nothing about people on the inside, either. I can't even make up my own mind about all this. And if I can't code...I basically know nothing.

I mope into the kitchen for something to eat and see Mom out in the backyard. Grabbing a breakfast bar, I walk out to join her.

"Hey," she says, smiling and turning her head. Her hair is cropped short today, and it takes me by surprise. "I didn't want to wake you. It's a big day."

"Thanks." I sit on the end of her wooden lounge chair. "Did you sleep okay?"

"I did."

"Wait, aren't you supposed to be at work?"

"It's the first day of the celebration. I'm not missing your *last* World Build celebration, Channel. I'm going with you."

I try to hide my smile unsuccessfully. "Okay, then. I'll go get changed."

I pull up my profile and—feeling lighter than I have all week—choose my style for the afternoon. Mom took off work to attend with me? It seemed like she thought I was making too big of a deal about my *last* everything, but maybe she does get how important it feels to me.

I settle on black faded jeans, a pale purple top, and a black leather jacket. With long wavy hair and black nail polish, I look very intense. And very adult.

"Wow," Mom says when I walk into the hall. "That's a little dark, don't you think?"

I roll my eyes. "It's empowering, and don't say anything else about how I'm taking this too seriously, or I'm going by myself."

Mom stifles a laugh. "I won't, I promise. You look amazing."

We walk out the door and head to the Grid but take our time noticing how the center of town has been completely transformed. Colorful bricks have replaced the building facades, and people are already streaming through the streets. Music filters through the air, and I can't help but begin to walk in rhythm with the steady beat.

"The accomplishments of the rising generation are the best reasons to celebrate, don't you think?" Mom says with a smile.

"How do you know we have any accomplishments?" I say.

"Oh, no, I wasn't talking about you. I meant the kids who weren't all washed up and ready to be adults. The ones who still have dreams and think the world is their oyster."

"Ah," I laugh. "They are definitely worth celebrating."

Mom nudges me gently with her elbow. "You know, you still haven't told me about your submission."

I shrug.

"I know it's something good. And," she clears her throat, "I also know that you came up with the algorithm."

I stop, turning toward her. "Who told you that?"

"Aave," she says, stopping a few paces ahead.

"Since when do you talk to Aave?"

She motions for me to keep walking and links her arm with mine. "Aave and I secretly meet at night after you've gone to bed. He tells me everything about your life that you refuse to tell me."

"You do not," I laugh.

"You think he's your friend, but really he's mine."

"Mom, stop!"

She laughs, tickled with herself. "I happened to see him when I was walking through the park yesterday. He told me how brilliant you are."

"Aave said that?"

She nods. "I'm dying to hear about this, Channel!"

"Okay, okay, but the reason I'm not talking about it is that I combined two different models to create a new one. Even though we've tested it, we didn't have enough time to try it under different circumstances or in different situations. I have no idea if it will work."

"I don't care," Mom says. "Tell me about it."

I grin, and it's impossible to resist the surge of excitement that bubbles up. As much as I hate to admit it, I do think my algorithm is excellent. I do hope it wins. But saying that out loud is terrifying. I take a breath and start from the beginning.

Mom and I stand in the clearing at town center, surrounded by what feels like the entire P3 Community. I know it's not that bad. I'm just not feeling particularly jazzed about being surrounded by random people at the moment. Or my friends, to be honest. I'm glad that tonight will just be her and me. I can do all the socializing starting on night two when I've hopefully worked through a few more things.

I clench my fists and recognize my stress for once. Taking a moment to acknowledge the tension in my body, I actively release it. Shaking out my hands, I realize I have a choice to make. I can focus on all the things I dislike about this situation, or I can focus on the fact that I'm here with someone who loves me. It seems like such an easy path. *Just be okay with not knowing. Be patient. Do all the things that people keep telling me I'm afraid of.* I'm so tired of fighting things all the time, but stepping over that line fills me with dread.

The celebration begins with psychedelic colors streaking across the sky, and I gratefully latch on to this break from my cognitive dissonance. Cheers and shouts lift into the air around me, and I surprise myself by joining in. I might not be able to fix myself tonight, but I can have a good time.

I keep my eyes trained straight ahead until the feeling of someone's eyes on me becomes too powerful to ignore. Glancing to the side, I catch Aave looking in our direction. How he found me in this mass of people, I have no idea. He's mouthing something, but he's far enough away, I can't catch his meaning. I shrug, lifting my hands to show my confusion.

A message pops up in my field of vision. I tap the air in front of me to accept.

"Turn that off," Mom says, "you're going to miss this."

"It's Aave," I whisper, ignoring her.

<Keep them open>

I roll my eyes, flick the message away, and turn back to look at him. He gives me a thumbs-up and a goofy grin.

I'd somehow managed to forget about the Reveal until this moment. My heart flutters, and I ball my hands into fists. Again. I'm not going to open my eyes. Or should I? I can't. I—

"Channel, look at that!" Mom says in complete awe.

Ahead of us, a swirling circle of gold sparks begins to swell and grow until it seems to envelop the entire evening sky. An ethereal voice begins to speak.

"Our world is abounding with beauty and adventure."

The center of the spinning disc opens into an inky pool, and I suddenly feel unsteady. I grip Mom's arm as the darkness transforms into lush rainforests, then bleeds into ancient ruins, boundless deserts, and finally plunges into the tourmaline water of a tropical sea.

. . .

"See it. Taste it. Touch it."

Leaving the reef, we are launched through the blue sky, past the clouds, and high into the starry night. I wiggle my toes and take a purposeful breath.

"Experience life without limitation. Experience Cerebrolink"

The golden orb begins to shrink—our portal to the planets slowly dissolving into dusk.

"Wow," Mom says.

"I've never seen resolution like that," I whisper. "It was like—"

"We were there," she breathes.

The voice sounds again.

"During each World Build, we take a few moments for children and youth who have yet to find their placement within our Community. A time to remember the world before Paradise 3 and Communities like it existed. A time to show gratitude for those who came before us and to renew our commitment to building the best version of ourselves and our world."

My breath begins to come in short bursts. I don't want to do this. I do, but I don't. Somehow without realizing it, my secret ritual had become a scrupulosity of sorts. If I don't open my eyes, my world can stay the same. The world where things are predictable and beautiful. The world where

I can hide behind settings and preferences and never have to let anybody in if I don't want to. The only world where my Dad still exists.

"In thirty seconds, this year's Reveal will begin. Please keep your masks safely on as we guide you through our opening ceremony."

I don't have to keep my eyes open. I know that. Facing Aave and Glyn afterward would be annoying, but I could always pretend I saw.

Peer pressure is *not* the reason I keep my eyes fixed on the world ahead of me. I have to do this for myself. If I don't know what the Real world is like, how can I ever truly convince someone that my world is better? How can I ever fully believe it for myself?

I wait, my heart pounding in my chest.

You can do this, I keep repeating in my head. *It can't be as bad as they say.* And then my world goes dark.

CHAPTER 7

I GASP, and Mom reaches for my hand.

I was wrong. It's absolutely as bad as they say. Pressing my free hand to my chest, I force myself to take a breath.

The world around me looks like an alien landscape—completely foreign. I don't recognize anything or anyone around me. Hazy sunlight bathes the rocky earth in a dull orange glow, and I'm surrounded by an army in grey.

"Here," Mom says, handing me the thin metal tube she always gave me during Reveals. I know to press the button on the handle as she's instructed me countless times before, but in the past, I hadn't seen what happened next.

A stream of light bursts from the end of the rod and illuminates the space around me. Lights blink into existence all over the clearing, better illuminating the barren space and filling it with ghostly silhouettes.

"How long do we have?" I ask, my voice low.

"Hmm?"

"Mom, how long before they turn it back on." I purposefully stare straight ahead, not ready to see her Real face. *I've never seen my mother's Real face.*

"It's like always. They'll give you a few moments to acclimate, and then we'll go on with the ceremony. Usually about twenty to thirty minutes, I think."

"I want to go home."

"Now? But Chan—"

"No, I don't want to leave—I just want to see our home. How it really looks."

"I don't think that's the point; it's more—"

"Mom, I need to see it," I plead. "They won't even know we're gone. We can go quickly and come right back."

Mom sighs audibly. "It's your last year. I want you to know that's the only reason I'm entertaining this." She pulls on my arm, and we quickly make our way through the people around us, back to the walkway.

It's not a walkway. Well, it is. Just not the walkway I thought it was. Nothing is like I thought it was.

The buildings are dark and ominous—not cheery and full of character like I'm used to. Even in the dark, I can tell our houses are solid grey blocks, sitting in a perfect row. The direction of the streets makes sense to me, but everything else is disturbingly different. I turn my light back and forth, taking it all in.

What I thought was soft green grass at the park is some substance I don't recognize. Definitely not green. My stream of light stretches far enough that I should be able to see the trees, but they don't appear. Tiny specs of something float in the air around me, distracting me from the horizon. Dust? I can't believe I've walked out here without a mask on. It almost makes me gag.

"Hurry," Mom says, walking briskly. Without meaning to, I notice her hair. It's dark brown and shoulder length. Darker than normal, but not different enough to seem out of character. This is more comforting than I could've imagined. Looking away, I put the light down and focus on keeping up.

She has to stop me when we get to our house because I don't recognize it. It looks identical to the ones around it, with no distinguishing factors.

"Five minutes," she says nervously.

I walk in quickly, using muscle memory to navigate the visually unfamiliar space. The walls are dark grey. Smooth and cold. I walk straight into the kitchen and flash the light around. The stool I sit on—with its sleek metal legs and shiny black top—is grey, too. Everything is grey. Blank and colorless.

I turn in a circle, taking it in. The cupboards are light brown and completely plain—no detailing like in real life. Well, my real life.

Spinning around, I walk to my room and desperately shine the light through the doorway. It's empty except for a basic metal bed with dull blankets. This view takes my breath away. My colorful walls, the pictures I've hung—my cyan blanket and my favorite pillow with the flowers on it. They don't exist.

I sit down on the bed and pull the modest pillow to my chest. A tear rolls down my cheek, and I hastily wipe it away. I knew this. I knew theoretically that this is how things were, but somehow...actually seeing it...

Clutching the light, I reluctantly set the pillow down and walk back to the front door. Hesitantly, I step outside, shining my light into the street.

Mom. Standing directly in front of me. Relief floods over me when I realize every part of her looks almost exactly like she usually does, except...

"What happened?" I breathe, moving toward her and reaching out a hand. She winces when I touch the left side of her face.

"You've never asked me about this before."

"I've never looked."

She looks at me, concerned. "Never?"

I shake my head.

"Even when—"

"Never, Mom."

"I thought you were just playing a game, that you didn't want me to see you with your eyes open..." she trails off and takes a breath. "I fell. When I was a kid. Hit the side of a table."

"Does it hurt?" I run my fingers along the stretch of puckered skin stretching from her hairline down to her cheekbone.

"No," she shakes her head. "Just a little more sensitive, I guess."

I look down at our clothing. Grey. Plain. No surprise there at this point. I step back and shine my light over Mom's shoulder.

Beyond the houses, there's just nothing. As far as I can see. Nothing but rocks and earth.

Movement catches my eye, and I turn, startled. I shine my light directly into a boy's face, and he quickly covers his eyes with his hand.

"Are you two okay?" he says, and I gasp. Aave.

CHAPTER 8

I STARE at him as he blocks the light. Wavy, light hair just long enough to be tucked behind his ears. Eyelashes that cast shadows on his cheeks. His face surprisingly still recognizable but softer somehow—more boyish.

"Can you lower that, please?" he asks.

"Sorry," I say, quickly pointing the light away from his face. "What are you doing here?"

"I looked over and saw you were gone," he says. "Since this was—wait, did you tell her?" he asks, pointing to my Mom.

"Tell me what?" Mom asks sternly. "Channel, what is he talking about?"

I roll my eyes. "She's kidding, I told her."

Mom laughs, and Aave's shoulders relax.

"Sorry," she says. "I know I shouldn't be teasing you, but the opportunity was too perfect."

He takes a deep breath and tries to laugh it off. "Since it was your first time seeing...all of this," he motions around him, "I worried it might've been too much." He walks closer. "I wanted to make sure you were okay."

This is Aave. The boy who knocked on my door every day when we were kids, asking if I could play. The boy who made me laugh for the first time after my Dad died. The boy who's still always watching to make sure I'm doing alright.

My light is pointed to the side, but there's enough ambient illumination for me to view his features clearly. His *Real* features. His eyes are dark, but not completely. I can see a little blue—no green. Maybe a mix? I find myself inspecting him openly, and then my heart stops. If I can see the real him...he can see the real me.

I quickly whip around and face Mom. "I think it's time to get back, right?" I ask hastily. "We've already been gone too long."

Mom takes in my alarmed expression, and her eyebrows furrow. Even now, I can't stop staring at her cheek.

"Yes, we should get going—"

"Thanks for checking on us," I say hastily to Aave, turning to go but angling my face toward Mom. "See you later when we meet up with Glyn?"

"Sure," he says, disheartened. "See you then."

Walking quickly past him, I don't allow myself to look back.

I breathe out slowly, feeling much more comfortable now that I can hide behind my algorithm. After Mom and I return to the clearing—though we missed a few parts of the presentation—we are just in time to watch the Edge gradually come back up. It's incredible. My vision is divided into segments and each one is methodically loaded in sequence.

At one point, half of the Community is augmented, while the other half is Real. The contrast is stark and breathtaking. I try to enjoy the moment instead of geeking out about the code I know is running behind the scenes. Sometimes all I see in my head are strings of numbers. There's probably something very wrong with me.

I find Aave and Glyn after everything is back online. We still have an hour before the celebration officially kicks off. Mom said I could catch up with my friends only if I promised I'd come back to our spot at least ten minutes early.

"Tonight is about family," she'd insisted. *"You'll have the rest of the week to hang out with your friends."* She's continuing to take this last celebration thing extremely seriously.

Aave sits next to Glyn on the ground in the clearing, and he's reverted to exactly what I'm used to seeing. I can't help but feel disappointed. I find myself sneaking glances, hoping I'll somehow catch a glimpse of the face I saw earlier.

"So, what did you think?" Aave asks, catching me off-guard.

I swallow hard. "Of what?"

"Ha. Ha," he chides. "You know what."

I shrug. "The Reveal? I don't know. I can't say I'm glad I saw it, but...I think I needed to. I think lately—" I pause, considering my words. "I guess I've had a lot of questions, you know? Have you ever wondered if everything we've been told is true?"

"Of course," Glyn scoffs. "All of us have wondered, but *we've* been brave enough to see this every year, remember?" She motions between her and Aave.

I roll my eyes, and she laughs good-humoredly. "Plus, it seems pretty obvious we're still in crisis. Every time I forget my mask and I'm out for too long, I'm reminded real quick," she says.

"Yeah, I guess that's true," I say, remembering my tight chest and tired lungs.

"But you're not weird for questioning," Aave says hurriedly, noticing the look on my face. "I'm glad you got some closure."

Closure. This night feels like anything but closure.

"How did the meeting go?" he asks me.

"What meeting?"

"What meeting!? What is wrong with you, Channel? For the sensory implant!"

"Oh!" I laugh, "I kind of forgot about that. Feels like a lot has happened since then."

Aave shakes his head.

"It was intense, actually," I press on. "The technology is mind-blowing. They implant it, and it completely syncs with your brain over time. It's supposed to be seamless eventually."

Glyn's eyes light up. "It's incredible. That scan they showed—"

"I know!" I say excitedly, cutting her off. "Can you imagine all those connections in your brain?"

"I didn't realize you were at the presentation, too," Glyn says.

"*You* were there?" I ask.

"What, that's surprising? I don't know if I was at the same one, I guess, but I attended one," Glyn says, scowling slightly, then stands and stretches her arms over her head as if she couldn't care one way or the other. Aave and I stay sprawled comfortably on the ground.

"Huh," Aave grunts, suddenly overly interested in the group of people happily chatting across the path.

"Are you okay?" I ask.

"Yes," he answers too quickly, not even looking toward us.

I raise an eyebrow and let the silence sit.

"No," he sighs finally. "Honestly, it's just taking me a minute to process that I wasn't on the initial list."

The expression on his face shows hurt and confusion, and it leads me to wonder. Why wasn't he included? Were the meetings scheduled geographically?

"Maybe they're just doing one neighborhood at a time. That would make sense," I say.

"No, there's got to be a reason," Glyn says matter-of-factly. "Channel, help me. Let's figure out what's wrong with Aave. Why wasn't he chosen for the first round of meetings?"

Aave waves us off, but I see a smile threatening to break out at any moment.

"I think it's his terrible sense of humor," she teases.

"Ha. Ha," Aave says. He pulls a snack from his pocket.

"Do you always have food in there?" I laugh.

"*That's* it. His metabolism's too high," Glyn says.

"*Your* metabolism's too high!" he shouts obnoxiously.

I can barely understand his words through the food in his mouth, and I laugh at the ridiculousness of it. Knowing I might be mocked, I reach into my pocket for a nutrition gel packet. I don't care if Glyn ribs me too. Watching him eat is making me hungry.

"Gross," Glyn says, looking disgusted as she watches me slurp it down. "I'm heading back," she announces. "See you tomorrow. And don't stay out too late, Aave. You're being weird."

"*That's* what's wrong with me," he says excitedly. "I'm too weird! Thank you for the analysis. It's good to finally have answers!"

Glyn rolls her eyes, shoves her hands in her pockets, and walks down the path.

As soon as she retreats from view, my carefree mood is tempered slightly. I've spent plenty of time with Aave alone, but tonight feels different.

Vulnerable. I lay back on the non-grass, cushioning my head with my hands, and stare at the starry sky.

"So you're really okay after everything tonight?" he asks gently.

"I mean, 'okay' is a strong word."

"Yeah. It's pretty intense." He leans back and rests his head on the ground next to mine.

"You're avoiding me," he states matter-of-factly, and it takes me off-guard.

My face screws up in confusion. "No, I'm not! I've spent every possible second with you guys tonight."

"Yeah, but that's not what I'm talking about. See?" he points. "Even now. You won't look directly at me."

"Because I'm looking up at the stars," I argue, then look straight at him to prove it. He's closer than I thought. My heart beats faster, and I know he sees something unsteady in my expression.

"I've seen the real you, but that's the first time you've seen me," he states calmly.

I watch him closely, again wishing I could see more of his Real eyes and face. "You've seen me before?" I ask, and my voice is a whisper.

He nods. "Since you were a big coward and had your eyes closed, you probably didn't notice I was there."

I laugh softly, turning back to the sky. I didn't like the feeling of him looking at the Real me tonight. I've changed so much about myself because I don't want those things to exist, and I don't want to be reminded they still do.

"So. You were spying on me," I say, feigning annoyance.

Aave leans his head back and laughs. "Yep, you caught me."

I roll up the empty gel packet still in my hand and stuff it in my pocket.

"It's weird, though, right? I know I don't look exactly like this," he says nervously, motioning to himself.

"But you look good," I say reflexively, then immediately regret it when I hear him chuckle.

"Oh, yeah?" he grins, turning to me.

"Whatever, stop," I laugh. "I was only being nice." My cheeks flush, and I've never been more grateful to hide behind my preferences. This is why I can't be Real. My body constantly betrays me.

"So you're not worried about the Cerebrolink anymore?" I ask quickly, changing the subject.

"Of course I am." He lets out a slow breath.

"It sounded like you wished you had an opportunity to do it."

"Not to *do* it, but yeah, being considered would be nice," he says. "I still think the whole thing is crazy. But that's just because I'm not as trusting as you."

"I'm not trusting," I mutter.

"Not in a bad way," he laughs. "Wow, Channel. You're so defensive lately! Lighten up. I tend to worry about people taking advantage of things. Or even *myself* taking advantage of things. I wouldn't trust myself to make a better, more difficult choice if there was an easier option. You're more...sure of yourself."

"No, I'm not."

"Okay. Are you going to argue with everything I say?" he asks.

I ignore the comment altogether. Trusting him and Glyn in the World Build still feels uncomfortable to me. Yes, maybe it's easier to trust Community leaders, but even that makes me squirm a little if I think too hard about it. Aave doesn't know me as well as he thinks he does.

"But why would it matter?" I ask. "Who cares if we take the 'better' path. What makes it *better*? If we can experience these incredible things without life being as difficult anymore, why not?"

Aave ponders this a moment. "I don't know, honestly. It feels utterly wrong to me. To only experience things neurologically without engaging our bodies? I know we don't have longitudinal research on all of this yet— how could we?—but it just seems like there would have to be negative consequences. I mean, we're in bodies for a reason."

I shrug. "Maybe we're not. Maybe we only have bodies because there wasn't a better option."

"And you think this is it?"

"Evolution, right? Why couldn't this be the next step?"

Aave grins. "You never know. I wish we could skip forward and see the end result."

"You're telling me," I laugh.

Aave nudges me with his shoulder, and the touch feels electric. It feels as though my stomach drops to my knees, and my laugh instantly dies in my throat. This swooping feeling has been happening more frequently when I'm around him, and it makes me anxious. It's not a bad feeling, just a new one. I don't know how to handle it.

"So, have you been thinking the same thing I have with all this going on?" he asks softly.

My throat feels thick, and I stall. "Hmm?"

He rolls to his side and props his head on his hand. "About our World Build?"

Relief floods over me, but it still takes a minute for me to catch my breath.

He sits up fully and brushes a crumb from his lip with the back of his hand. "I've just been thinking about the fact that none of our work is going to even matter once that update comes out. Possibly. I guess some things could be rolled over."

I nod, sitting up. "Definitely. But who knows when it's going to happen? They haven't called off the Build, so the rewards must still be on the table."

"I really want access to the Game Cube—I'm not going to lie."

"You would."

"Not all of us have won before," Aave teases.

"It was one time! And it was a total fluke!"

"There it is. Keep arguing with me," he says with a grin, egging me on.

I shake my head, then look past him at the glass dome behind us. I can't help but wonder what *that* looks like in real life. Is it just another grey box?

The Grid has been my second home for the last four years. Coding, experimenting, problem-solving—honing skills that were supposed to make our reality better. All skills that might be completely useless now.

"What do you think this is all going to look like when we're adults?" I sigh, pulling my knees close and wrapping my arms around them.

"You mean in less than a year?" Aave chuckles wryly.

I nod, clenching my jaw to keep tears from forming in my eyes. "What if —" I start but can't finish the sentence. *What is wrong with me?* My emotions are all over the place and so close to the surface. I can't seem to reign them in.

Aave is silent next to me, obviously sensing the shift in my mood. When he speaks, the edge is gone from his voice entirely.

"I guess it doesn't matter, right? Either we'll move on to Community posts or..."

"Or our reality will be upgraded." I chew on my lower lip. "It's not the worst, right? I mean, think of the incredible things we could do with a simulator that powerful. We could do...literally anything. Be anyone."

Aave turns toward me and raises an eyebrow. "You've always wanted to visit other planets."

I nod, looking down at the ground.

"You're kind of excited, aren't you?" he asks.

I nod, unable to keep a smile from my face. "Your concerns make sense— I'm not arguing with that," I say pointedly, "but there are so many things that would be better. And easier." I hesitate. "Aave...I've been spending time with my dad."

"You have?"

"Uh-huh. I know it's not really him, but it feels nice to talk to him." Saying this out loud to Aave makes me feel childish and silly. Maybe I am. Maybe I'm not quite ready to grow up yet. "With Cerebrolink, I could actually be with him, you know?" I sigh, my shoulders slumping as I rest my chin on my knees. "Mom says it's a bad idea. That I need to move on."

Aave is silent. He puts a hand over my shoulder, and for once, I don't flinch away. His skin against mine feels nice—comforting. Why do I need to move on? Move on to what? If this makes me happy, then isn't that what I should be moving on to?

"I'm so sorry, Channel. I know how hard it's been without him."

What if I don't have to let him go?" I breathe, leaning into him. "Why would it be bad for me to have him around? Cerebrolink could make it so nobody would ever have to fully lose someone. Isn't that a good thing?"

"I don't know," Aave says. "It sounds great to take away everything that's painful, but I still don't feel good about it. I can't really put it into words."

"I know. I feel the same way." And I do. It feels too easy.

I rest my head on his shoulder and close my eyes. Every other sense is heightened as I feel his body breathing next to mine. I feel his warmth and smell the light scent of citrus on his skin.

"I guess now we know how everyone felt before," he says.

"What do you mean?"

"The first members of the Community," he explains.

I yawn, the worry and excitement of the past two days catching up with me. "How could we know what they felt? Their life was miserable." I lift my head.

"Maybe that's what people hundreds of years from now will say about us," he whispers. "*We* were miserable. *Of course* we would've jumped at the chance for a sensory implant. We didn't even have disgusting new food flavors."

I snort, a surge of giddiness rushing through me, and I push him away. Aave's eyes dance with amusement as he pulls me back. His hand barely brushes my cheek, and my skin tingles.

I walk down the dark street—barely illuminated by a pale moon hanging low in the sky—and my head darts side to side. Particles of something— ash? dust?—float eerily in the air around me, and it's almost interesting enough to make me stop to inspect it. But I can't stop. I have to find him. Aave is in trouble, and I'm almost at his house.

I'm sure this is his, even though all the grey boxes look the same. I can feel that he's inside, and I rush to the door. I lift my wrist out of habit, then realize it's not necessary. I'm in the Real world.

The house is so dark, I can barely make my way down the hall to his room. I feel along the wall, my heart pounding. I can't see a thing. Finally, I turn the corner and see a faint blue light emanating from the doorway a few steps ahead of me. I rush through the door and freeze, my blood running cold.

An emaciated unclothed body lies on a metal platform. Tubes protrude from his chest and a mask covers his nose and mouth. He's breathing—his bony ribs rise and fall weakly.

He's alive, but just barely. That's when I start screaming.

"Channel? Channel!"

My eyes fly open and I slam upright, knocking Mom off the side of my bed. My head is fuzzy, and my breath comes in spurts. I swing my legs out from under the covers and lean over, trying to calm my heart rate.

"I'm sorry," I spit between gasps. "I'm sorry."

Mom lifts herself off the floor, rubbing her head. She sits next to me and puts her hand on my shoulder.

"Are you okay?" she asks tenderly.

My erratic breathing slows and regulates. I take a deep breath, holding it for a second before answering. Sitting upright, I nod slowly.

"I'm sorry, I overrode the privacy—"

"No, Mom, it's fine. I think this situation is exactly why that option exists." Reaching behind my head, I massage the muscles in my neck, attempting to release the tension. "I had a horrible dream. I'm sorry I knocked you over."

She waves me off as if it was nothing. "Want to talk about it?"

I shake my head, and she slumps over, resting her elbows on her knees.

She speaks under her breath. "Why did you wait so long—"

"What are you talking about?"

"To open your eyes!" she blurts out, turning on me.

"Are you blaming me for—"

"No, Channel, I'm not blaming you for your bad dream—I'm just frustrated, okay? I knew this was going to be hard on you, and now—" She runs her hands through her hair and squeezes her eyes closed.

"Now what? Now I had *one* bad dream? And it had nothing to do with seeing the Real world!"

"How did it not?" she says, and her voice oozes with motherly guilt and worry.

"It was about something Aave said." I run my hands over my face, wiping the damp hair from my forehead. "About the Cerebrolink."

"What did he say?" she asks, lifting slightly.

My eyelids feel heavy, and I yawn, letting my head fall onto her shoulder. "I don't know. He was talking about how it could be dangerous to only use our brains like that—to be physically disconnected. That we shouldn't be cutting our bodies out of life."

"Hmm. Aave said that?"

I nod against the soft cotton of her shirt.

"He's a smart kid," she says, grinning.

I sit up. "You agree with him?"

"I didn't say that. But I've definitely wondered about...I don't know. All of this." Her eyes drop to the floor, and she fiddles with her hands. "The older I get, the more I wish..." She stops, and I wait with indefatigable interest. What does she wish? I know she wishes Dad were still here, though she refuses to spend much time talking about him. I know she wishes I would get in line and show excitement—not worry—about my placement. But beyond that, I don't know what wishes my mom has.

"What?" I ask.

"It's pointless even to go there," she smiles wanly. "It's the middle of the night. I'm not thinking clearly."

"Tell me," I whine. "I probably won't even remember in the morning."

Mom stands and drops her hands to her side. She's too exhausted to withstand my pestering, and I know it.

"Sometimes, I wish we could've been born at a different time," she whispers. "And I know that sounds crazy because I'm fully aware of all of the hardships people had back then. And the negative things that were happening in the world, but...what if we could've found a small corner of peace? Where everything was still simple and beautiful. Before the Communities. Before the masks—"

She stares past me as if seeing something right there on the wall next to my bed. I follow her gaze but only see my pictures flickering.

"See?" she says, shrugging. "Silly. Goodnight, Channel. I hope you sleep better for the next few hours."

"Mom," I say softly, and she pauses next to my door. "I don't think it's silly for what it's worth."

She turns, flashes a small smile, and disappears into the hall.

CHAPTER 9

"DID YOUR MOM HEAD HOME? Day two was too taxing for her?" Aave asks, and I look at him, annoyed.

"Why? Did you want to tell her more about our submission?"

Aave's eyes grow wide. "What? I only told her about how great your code was. Is that somehow a bad thing?"

"Save it," I say with a grin. "I'm kidding. But it is a little strange that you talk to my mom when I'm not around."

He looks relieved. "You're mom's cool—what can I say?"

I roll my eyes.

"This whole celebration is boring so far," Glyn says, pretending to yawn for added drama.

"Only because we had to do all of the official stuff yesterday," Aave says. "That's always how it is. The rest of the week will be all ours."

Glyn looks restless. "Want to try those shiny filaments over there?" She points to a long line leading up to a booth where a worker is handing out sticks covered with tufts of whimsical, luminescent strands.

Though day two of World Build isn't living up to her expectations, for me? It's been my best yet. Mom and I have tried everything—even the basic games created by the youngest entrants. They were kind of impressive, to be honest. I couldn't have created code like that when I was twelve.

Somehow, she's succeeded at taking my mind off our submission, which is no small feat. She's been a perfect distraction without even realizing it. Aave's right. My mom is pretty cool.

We watch as a woman takes her treat excitedly, plucks one strand free, and places it on her tongue. Her eyes widen, and she immediately rushes to get back in line for another.

"What do you think they taste like?" I ask.

"We'll never find out if we sit here ruminating!" Aave grabs my hand and pulls me forward, but Glyn runs full tilt and—since she doesn't have a person in tow—beats us to the line. Though there are over fifteen people in front of us, we move quickly and it isn't long before I'm holding my very own World Build featured food experiment.

"Remember the one last year that turned my tongue black?" Glyn asks, laughing as we stare at the glowing tendrils in front of us, dancing against the night sky.

"That one was *so* delicious. Totally worth the bitter aftertaste," Aave says.

We walk across the street and sit on our favorite bench. The sudden quiet is almost jarring. After being surrounded by celebratory people of all ages in line and in the clearing, the still air seems ominous.

"Mmmmm," Glyn sighs, letting the first piece melt on her tongue. "It's like—how do I describe it?"

"Like joy," Aave says, closing his eyes. "Tastes like pure joy. And maybe pineapple? What do you think?" He looks at me expectantly. "Channel! What are you waiting for?"

I take a deep breath. "I don't know. My brain won't stop buzzing."

"Delicious food will help with that," Aave says.

Glyn's eyes narrow. "About what?"

"About everything. About how this is our last World Build ever, about how we might be going completely different directions in the next few months. About this new implant..."

"Yeah...about that," Glyn says blandly, plucking off another tendril. "I'm going to do it." She inspects her tufted stick, obviously avoiding direct eye contact.

"What do you mean?" Aave asks, and I look at her, puzzled.

"I've been offered a slot," she says matter-of-factly.

I share a look with Aave. "*What do you mean?*" I repeat.

Glyn shrugs. "A Community worker called us in yesterday. Said they were taking top-tier Community members first. I qualified."

"Top-tier?" I ask skeptically. "What—is there a ranking system we're not aware of?" I laugh. That would be ridiculous, especially when they're clearly working on getting the information out to the entire Community.

Glyn glances down at her shoes. "Yeah. Rankings. You know they're always paying attention, especially now when we're up for placement."

I study her, attempting to keep my face blank. Aave shuffles his feet, suddenly even more absorbed with the food in his hand.

"I know what you're thinking," Glyn says coldly. "How could I be ranked higher than you, right?" she says with a sardonic laugh. "When you've won a World Build and had parts of your code integrated already. Yeah?"

My cheeks flush. "No, Glyn—"

"Here I thought you'd be happy for me."

"How can I be happy for you?" I ask, incredulous. "We've barely known about this implant for, what, a week and a half? We don't even know what this entails, and you're ready to jump in and have your head cut open? Sorry we're not jumping for joy."

"When is this happening?" Aave asks, suddenly surfacing from his snack.

"Three days."

"Three—? So you're not even going to wait to hear the results of the World Build?" My voice rises in intensity. "Glyn, why would you—"

"I already know the results, okay?" Glyn shouts. "My submission won."

I stare at her, my eyes flashing. "You mean *our* submission? Why didn't they message us and—"

"*Because your names aren't on it,*" she snaps, taking a few steps away from us. "I had no chance of a good placement, and you and Aave? You'll be fine. I needed this win."

My eyes widen in shock, and my hands clench into fists. My palms sting as my fingernails cut into them.

"Wow," I taunt. "Classy."

"So you completely cut us out?" Aave asks angrily.

Realization dawns, and I drop my swirling treat on the ground. "Is this why they offered you the Cerebrolink? Because they think you created that code?"

Glyn shrugs. "Either way. With the implant, it's not like this code matters anyway. I probably did you two a favor." She spins on her platform shoe and walks toward the edge of the grass.

Rage builds in my chest, and I'm positive that if I can get close to her, my hands will involuntarily wrap around her scrawny neck. I storm after her, but sturdy arms catch me and pull me back.

"It's not worth it," Aave whispers.

"I trusted her, Aave. You told me to trust her—"

"I know, I'm sorry." He repeats this over and over in my ear as I continue to struggle against his strength.

I watch Glyn's form flicker and disappear. "Thanks for being a fantastic friend!" I shriek into the air ahead of me. My whole body shakes as I turn, and Aave pulls me close. I don't push away when he wraps me tightly in his arms.

"Shhh," he says, stroking my hair. I want to stay here, to calm down. To let the bile in my throat disappear and the throbbing in my head subside. But I can't. *I trusted her.* I gave her my work, and she used it as her own, shamelessly.

"Channel, I'm so sorry, but your Dad—he didn't make it," Mom says.

"What do you mean he didn't make it?"

"The growth in his brain was too large. They tried to remove it, but—"

"But he said he'd always be here for me. He said I could trust him," I whisper, watching tears stream down her face.

"I know, I know. And he'll always be with us in—"

"How can he be if he's dead?" I spit the words into the air between us, and Mom flinches. I want to apologize, but my throat is thick.

"I'm so sorry, Channel," Mom repeats, and I run to my room.

"No! Don't 'shhh' me!" I explode, pushing on Aave's chest and ripping myself out of his embrace. "How can you act like this isn't a huge deal? I spent an immense amount of time and energy perfecting that code, and she just claimed it as hers? And now she's first in line for this—this thing that's probably going to completely revamp our entire way of life?"

"Channel—"

"She was right about one thing. Everything we've worked for—all the coding I've done, all the skills I have? They're useless. With a full sensory implant—"

"There will still be a need for code, Channel! Clearly! Just because it's all-encompassing doesn't mean they won't need new innovation. Take a second and calm down, okay?" Aave drops his arms to his side, still holding firmly to his joy filaments.

His jaw clenches. "You're making assumptions that don't have any basis in reality. We don't have enough information to know how this will impact our future yet. And yes, what Glyn did was selfish and hurtful. But losing your mind and allowing that to ruin your last celebration would be idiotic."

My heart is still beating wildly in my chest, but the look on Aave's face...If I could trust anyone, it would be him, and I'm sick of him taking the brunt of my eruptions.

With some effort, I calm my temper. "So you're calling me an idiot now?" I say, raising an eyebrow.

Aave smiles gratefully. "I'm saying that if someone *hypothetically* lost their mind in this moment and refused to enjoy the second night of the World Build celebration, *that* person would be an idiot."

I chuckle—softly at first, but it quickly transforms into a full-blown laughing fit. I clutch my ribs and force myself to breathe.

"Wow, Channel. You're kind of all over the place the last few days," Aave laughs. "Are you really okay?"

I nod, wiping the tears from my cheeks. "It's ridiculous. I thought she was our friend, and then—"

"People do crazy things when they're desperate."

"Don't make excuses for her."

Aave shrugs.

"Do you think she was always planning to tell us? Or was she just going to let us hear the results with no warning?"

"Maybe she thought she was doing the considerate thing by telling us tonight. She's probably been thinking about it non-stop since—well, since whenever she completely sold her soul to the Community leaders."

I snort.

"Hey," he says, reaching for me. I walk closer, this time allowing him to slip his hand into mine. "I know what she did was brutal. You deserved credit."

"So did you!" I say indignantly, lifting my head and looking at him. Again, his closeness startles me. Aave and I have been friends since we were little kids, and I'm still not used to this new turn our relationship is taking. Every nerve is on edge. I feel the heat from his side and the soft skin of his hand under my fingertips. Goosebumps lift on my arms and neck as I notice his eyes are a deep green today. Almost his natural color.

I awkwardly step back.

Aave shoves his hands in his pockets. "It's okay," he says, clearing his throat. "Even with that win, I know my skills aren't strong enough for a placement like yours."

"Don't say that."

"It's true, and I'm okay with it. There are plenty of other good placements, Channel."

I nod.

"So. Are you up for checking out the other activities? End on a good note?"

I smile. "You might be terrible at Target Match, but you have a gift for positivity."

"I'll take that compliment," he grins.

I follow him over to the featured games with my hands still shaking. Out of residual anger or attraction, I'm not sure. How could Glyn do that to us? And for what? A potentially better placement? To be first on the list? And I was entirely in the dark—I never questioned her. If I didn't see that coming, what else am I missing?

I walk into the kitchen the following day to find Mom waiting expectantly. "What are you doing here?" I ask grumpily.

"Good morning to you, too," Mom says with a grin. "Good sleep?"

I flash her an annoyed look and walk to the cupboard.

"What's wrong?" she asks, concern thick in her voice.

"Maybe you should ask Aave. He seems to be your best source of information these days."

"Channel, seriously?"

I don't look at her as I pull a breakfast bar from the shelf.

"Did something happen last night?"

My eyes sting, and I busy myself filling a cup with water so she doesn't see the emotion on my face. When I'm able to compose myself, I turn.

"Weren't you supposed to go to work this morning?" I ask.

"I was planning on it, but then I woke up to that message."

"What message?"

"You haven't checked your board?"

I shake my head.

"They're meeting with families individually over the next week about the Cerebrolink and wondered if we could come in at some point. I know you don't have anything scheduled until this evening, and tomorrow I have a mandatory maintenance session to oversee, so I thought—"

"During World Build? And why do they want to meet with *us?*"

Mom cocks her head quizzically. "I think you know the answer to that, don't you?"

My eyes drop to the ground. "Well, apparently you have to be highly ranked to be given a Cerebrolink spot. I don't think I qualify at this point." I pull the bar from its sleeve and take a bite.

"Have you taken some time to process all this?" she asks.

No, I think. I've been avoiding it with every ounce of my being. Except it all keeps getting shoved down my throat when I least expect it.

"Yes, a little," I lie.

"And?"

I swallow.

"I'll wait," she says, folding her arms across her chest.

I take another bite. "I'm hungry, I'm not avoiding the question."

"Mmhmm."

Chewing purposely slowly, I eventually swallow and meet her anticipatory gaze. My conversations with Aave play in my head.

"I don't know, Mom. I don't think anything. Parts of it sound exciting and then parts of it sound…"

"Terrifying?"

I nod.

"Then I don't understand why you're fighting these meetings so much!" she says, exasperated. "This is how we find out more—this is where we can ask questions and get information that could help."

"But what if we go to meeting after meeting, and then suddenly—"

"What, you're indoctrinated, and you can't think for yourself anymore?" she says sympathetically.

"No!" I groan. "What if I like it! And I want to do it! And then—"

"Then what, Channel?" Her voice is soft, and tears well up in my eyes.

"I don't know," I whisper. "I already want to do it. Everything in my life has taken a major turn."

Mom laughs through her tears. "Is that actually why?"

I shake my head. "No. I want to do it because it sounds better. I could actually be with Dad anytime I want—"

Mom gives me a warning glance.

"I know. I get why you think that's a terrible idea, I do, but you said people should suffer less, right? This would help me suffer less! I could do exactly what I want and create a world I want to live in."

She nods, thinking for a moment. "Then why are you so conflicted?"

I sigh. "I don't even know. Up here," I say, pointing to my head, "it all sounds great, but here," I lower my hands to my stomach, "I feel sick about it."

"Anything to do with Aave?"

"Maybe? Probably?"

She sits up and reaches for me, pulling me close. My head rests on her shoulder, and she squeezes me tight.

"Channel, let's be honest. If there's one thing I'm *not* worried about, it's you suddenly jumping into something without doing your due diligence," she says, and a laugh bursts out of me. I try to pull away from her, but she holds on. "Let's ask the questions. Then see how you feel, okay?"

I take a deep breath and nod. I don't know when I stopped hugging my mom like this, but I miss it.

. . .

"Stop tapping your foot," Mom says, putting her hand on my knee. "And was it really necessary to dress like that?" she adds, her voice low.

"You've never cared about my fashion choices before."

"I don't," she sighs, eyeing my electric purple pants and fringed top. "I mean, I do care. I love your flair."

"Clearly," I mutter.

I've never been to this part of the Community Center. Even though I pass this building almost daily, I've only been inside a handful of times—and each of them was for some sort of presentation. This hallway and set of rooms sit behind the auditorium, and the entire area is formatted more rigidly than I'm used to. Straight lines. Flat colors. Not what I'm accustomed to seeing, and definitely not what I would choose.

"Quin, Channel?" a woman calls our names, and we stand.

"How are they even meeting with everyone individually?" I whisper as the woman motions us forward. "Doesn't that seem like overkill? Think of the infrastructure—"

"Shhh," Mom hushes me, and we walk through the door into a richly adorned, boldly colored meeting room. Juxtaposed with the waiting area, the effect is jarring.

The woman walks behind a desk and sits. Her nearly white hair is cropped close to her jawline, and her violet, bird-like eyes follow me as I take in the room.

"You like it?" she asks with a smile.

I nod.

"I know it can seem a little intense at first, but I figure if I'm spending most of my time here, the decor may as well agree with my sensibilities."

"I get that," I say. "What inspired this?"

The woman's eyes light up. "Are you familiar with the ancient Zarif Mustafa Pasha mansion in Turkey?" Seeing the blank expression on my face, she waves the comment off. "It's magnificent—definitely pull it up when you have time."

"I will."

"My name's Vera. I've been assigned to your geographical area of the Community as a Cerebrolink advisor."

"What does that mean, exactly?" Mom asks, and I can tell she's only asking for my benefit.

"It means that I'm here to answer any questions you may have, as well as help you schedule pre and post-operative care if you choose to go that route."

"Do we have a choice?" I ask, and Vera smiles, her peach-colored lips shimmering.

"About what? My help or the Cerebrolink."

"Either," I shrug.

"Of course." She smiles widely, amused.

"So if we choose not to undergo the procedure, what happens?" I ask.

"Initially, nothing," Vera says confidently, interlocking her fingers and leaning forward over the table. "Your life will continue as normal. Over time, if you prefer to remain unlinked, you will likely need to relocate to a neighboring Paradise Community. As more and more of your Community members choose to link, it will be more beneficial for you to be in an environment that suits your preferences."

Mom nods. More beneficial. Meaning I'll be mostly alone.

Vera smiles gently, leans back in her chair, and locks eyes with me. "Where are you at with all of this? Is there anything I can help you with?"

Her gaze seems to pierce my soul, and my heart begins to pound.

"How do we know this is safe?" I blurt. "If we're the first to be testing this, how do we know we won't end up with serious complications years from now? And what if we hate it? What if we want to unlink? Is that even poss—"

"Hold on a second," Vera chuckles. "Those are fantastic questions, but let's take them one at a time." She pulls up a projection between us. "First, you asked about safety. This chart shows our initial trials. As you can see, this technology has been in the making for years. We've tested different versions of this as far back as 2120. Of course, that was more for neurological disease management, but regardless, the results are relevant." She waits a moment, allowing us to pore over the numbers in front of us.

"The Community Builders would never be willing to introduce something that wasn't in the best interest of members," she concludes, and I have to admit, the numbers are compelling. Over forty years of data.

"There are people living right now who are already linked?" I ask in awe.

"Mmhmm. Thousands of them."

"Can I talk to them?" I say without thinking.

Vera looks at me in surprise.

"Not all of them," I laugh nervously. "I just thought—maybe if I could talk to someone who is living it, that could help me feel more comfortable," I stammer.

Swiping away the projection, Vera looks at me with interest. "I'm sure that could be arranged. I'll need to get approval. It could take a few days."

"That's fine," I say, attempting to hide my excitement.

"Quin? Anything I can do for you?" Vera asks, turning to Mom.

"No," Mom says, shaking her head. "Thank you."

"Channel, I didn't forget about your other question," Vera says. "You wondered about removing the Cerebrolink if you didn't like it."

I nod.

"There is a period of time where the Cerebrolink could be removed— within the first three weeks or so. But once enough links have been made, it is considered permanent. You can imagine how difficult it would be to remove all of those connections, especially when each individual is unique in their linking."

Vera inspects my face, then continues, "You should know that in all our years of testing, we've never had one person ask for it to be removed." She slides her chair back and stands.

"Not one?" I ask skeptically.

She shakes her head. "It's that good, Channel. I know it seems scary to jump into the unknown like this, but based on what I've seen? You won't regret it." She smiles, leading us to the door. "I'll be in touch."

Mom shakes Vera's hand gratefully, and a little bit of magic seeps out of me as we leave her colorful sanctuary and walk back into the austere hall.

CHAPTER 10

IT'S BEEN three days since I received Oren's information from Vera, but I still haven't made contact. I haven't been able to think of a good way to start this conversation.

Hey, Oren, I'm a random girl from P3 who's too terrified to sign up for linking. Would you like to talk to me?

Or,

Hey, I know we don't know each other at all, but please. Tell me every intimate detail about your Cerebrolinked life.

Pretty pathetic. But *not* talking to Oren is almost worse. I wasn't able to enjoy the kick-off to World Build, and Aave was definitely disappointed by my obvious distraction. Especially because we didn't have Glyn to buffer our interactions. I knew I wasn't fooling him, but no matter how many times I tried to focus on the puckering flavor of sour gelatin bubbles or the kaleidoscopic backdrop, I kept getting sucked back into my subconscious conundrum. And I might have also been avoiding any kind of closeness after getting stabbed in the back by Glyn. There's also that.

The situation didn't improve the next day either, and so far, today is no different. My questions are screaming at me, and my desire to avoid everything about World Build has only grown exponentially since Glyn's announcement. You'd think after watching every dream I'd been clinging to so desperately disappear out of thin air, I'd have nothing left to lose. You'd think I'd be able to let go and open up—stop worrying so much about nothing. Somehow it's had the opposite effect. I only want to distract myself more. Hide more. Disappear more.

Yep. I'm fully aware I'm pitiful. But today is the last day I'm going to give in to cowardice. I've opened my eyes and seen the Real world, for goodness sakes. I can do anything I put my mind to!

I know. My pep talk is super dramatic. But cheesy stuff like that might be the only way to work me up enough to go through with this. Because when I opened Oren's profile two minutes ago to send him a delayed message, that option didn't exist. The only choice was a live connection.

With sweating palms, I press the button in the air above my desk that says 'call.' And then I wait.

A small circle with Oren's smiling face pulses in front of me, and I inspect his features. His dark hair sweeps across his forehead, completely covering his right eye. The other eye is a brilliant tourmaline blue.

Abruptly, the circle disappears, and my heart stops. Text appears in front of me, and I breathe a sigh of relief.

>Hey, this is Oren. Can't talk directly right now, but I can live chat.

I hastily turn on voice dictation before I lose my nerve.

"Hey, sorry to interrupt your day. I'm Channel. I live in P3, and we have been invited to receive the Cerebrolink. I wanted to talk to someone who had experience with it to see if it's something I'd like to do."

That wasn't half-bad, I think, pressing send. Where was that two days ago?

>Ha, I was nervous, too.

"Why did you do it?"

>That's kind of a long story, but the short answer is that it was a way for my family to get into a Community. I was pretty young.

Oren wasn't in a Community before linking? *He'd lived in the Real world?* The questions begin to pile up in my mind, making it difficult to decide what to send next.

"How long have you been linked?"

>Almost eight years.

My eyes widen. Eight years. That would've been when he was nine or ten—didn't his profile say he was my age?

"Was the procedure painful?"

>No

.   .   .

Perfect. At least I can check that off my list of worries.

>Kidding. It was excruciating. But I was out for most of it. It's really only bad for a few hours before the Cerebrolink begins to take your instructions.

"Thanks for that. I felt hopeful for about two seconds."

>Glad I wrote back quickly.

"The Cerebrolink takes your instructions? What does that feel like?" I wait for his response to come through, staring at the blinking light indicating he's talking.

>I'm not sure how to describe it. At first it's kind of like a conversation. I would think, "I don't want to feel this pain," and then I'd hear—no, more like understand—that my request was being taken care of.

"And now?"

>Now? I don't know. It's just all me. I think what I want, and it happens.

Seamless. That's the word Cass had used.

"Can you think anything?"

. . .

>Yes.

"Like *anything* anything?"

>Yes. Yes.

I laugh out loud. "What is your life like?"

>That's a broad question.

"Fair point. What does a typical day look like when you're linked?"

>It's fairly normal, I think. I wake up, spend time with my family in the morning while we eat breakfast. Then I meet up with my pod.

"You eat breakfast?"

>Of course I eat breakfast.

I take a deep breath, thoroughly confused. "I know this might be a weird question, but what happens to your body while you're linked?"

His response doesn't appear immediately, so again, I wait, rereading our messages until it comes through.

. . .

>My body is exactly the same as it would be without the Cerebrolink. I still walk around, I still eat, I still do everything the way I usually would. It's just way better. Everything feels better, tastes better, I never have to feel pain, and I can choose to experience anything I normally wouldn't be able to.

I take this in. If bodies are still utilized with the Cerebrolink, then it really is the best of both worlds. Whole sensory experience without the downsides. No more cold. No more uncomfortable masks. No more pain when you hurt yourself or get sick—

"Wait, if you don't feel pain, how do you know if your body is safe?"

>I didn't say I don't feel pain, I can just choose not to. I can check in on pain anytime I want. But it's way easier to view my diagnostic levels.

I laugh again, this time due to a surge of excitement. Of course they'd have a built-in health monitor. *Of course they would've thought about how to keep us healthy.* I saw the data. Aave's concerns seem to be unfounded, and I couldn't be more grateful.

"Seems easier, for sure," I say, and watch the text appear.

>To each their own, I guess.

"What's a pod?"

. . .

>A group of friends. We adventure together. That's actually why I'm not available right now.

"You're with them?"

>Yep, we're deep into a Challenge.

"Sorry, I should let you go."

>No, it's okay. I'm scanning the ocean floor right now. Haven't found what I'm looking for yet.

"Seriously? That's incredible."

>Found it! Sorry, got to go. I'll connect with you later if that's okay?

"Sure, thanks for the info."

I wait a few moments—just in case—for a response that doesn't come. Searching the ocean floor? With friends? The idea is thrilling. Oren's been linked for eight years, and he spends time with his family. He explores the world with his pod. Maybe this is exactly what I need next in my life. No more fighting for a place, I can build my own. I'll be World Building *for myself*.

This thought sends tingles down my spine. I hop up and run out into the hall.

CHAPTER 11

>THAT'S SO WEIRD.

"What's weird?" I ask, laughing at Oren's obliviousness.

>So you have a week where you celebrate—what exactly?

"Okay, that's enough. I know we're basically lesser humans in your mind, but World Builds are actually pretty intense."

>I know, I'm messing with you. I'm just jealous because I didn't ever get to experience one.

"Never?"

>Nope. I didn't live in the Communities, remember?

"Right. I keep forgetting. What was life even like for you?"

>Boring.

"You're not going to give me any specifics?"

>Nope.

"I'm going to keep bugging you about it."

>Be my guest.

"You're really stubborn."

>Thank you.

I laugh out loud, then clap a hand over my mouth. I'm supposed to be sleeping, and as far as I know, Mom has no clue that I've spent nearly every waking hour over the last two days talking with Oren. I don't want to get busted now.

"Did you ever celebrate anything before you linked?"

>Are you seriously asking me more questions when I just said I wouldn't give details?

"Yes."

>Fine. I'll give you one little thing. Then you have to stop annoying me about this, okay?

"Yes! Deal. I'll stop bugging you about this particular topic for at least twenty-four hours."

>I'll believe it when I see it. I remember when I was little, we had a big community party to celebrate our independence.

"Independence? From what?"

>From the Communities.

"What? Why would you celebrate that?"

>I was young, remember? All I know is we'd wave flags and eat whatever food we could get our hands on, and I was allowed to run through the streets with my friends.

"What did your flag look like?"

>Red, white, and green stripes. A golden eagle in the middle.

I think for a moment. "I've never seen a flag like that—where did you live?"

>Southwestern Quadrant, but I think this flag was old. My dad kept it folded and hidden underneath a floorboard in their bedroom.

"Wow. Thanks for telling me that."

>You're welcome.

I yawn and stretch my hands over my head. "I think I need to sleep. Up too late the last two nights."

>Gotcha. When do you link? Do you know yet?

"No. I doubt it will be anytime soon."

>Well, I've got a spot on my team for you when it happens.

"You sure you're going to want me? I'll be a total newb."

>It'll make the rest of us look better.

"Great. Thanks for that."

>No, thank *you*.

I laugh again, and push my face into my pillow. "Talk to you tomorrow," I whisper.

>Goodnight.

Rolling over, I pull my covers over me and motion with my hand to turn out the lights. My mind buzzes in the dark. Guilt niggles at me for cutting Aave off completely for the past forty-eight hours. He's messaged me, and I haven't responded. I didn't even meet up with him last night as we'd planned. I'm a complete jerk of a friend, but knowing that doesn't seem to be changing my behavior.

What would we talk about? How I'm planning to link and he hasn't even been offered a slot for an informational meeting? How we might not see each other again for a long time? It all just seems pointless. Why keep spending time together when we're both going our separate ways? Why go to the celebrations when we already know the result? *Why suffer when we don't have to?*

I pull my covers closer, close my eyes, and hope I fall asleep quickly.

"What!?" I shriek the next morning, partly out of shock and partly out of horror. "How is that possible?" I sit down on the couch defiantly, wishing I'd grabbed breakfast before she sprang this on me.

"I know, I get it. I'm not thrilled about the timing either. I know you're excited about hearing the World Build results, but with so many people signing up for the procedure, we either take the slots we've been assigned or we get put at the back of the line. And that could be a year from now."

I fold my arms across my chest. I couldn't care less about the World Build, but it makes a convenient scapegoat. As much as I'm excited about Cerebrolink, panic pulses through me at the idea of doing it so soon. I instantly regret avoiding Aave and wish I could take that time back. *What was I thinking?*

"That timing is the worst," I say flippantly. "It's like they don't even care about ruining everything. The World Build—basically our entire lives—so who cares anymore? There's no point—"

"I care, Channel!" Mom sits next to me, exasperated. "But I can't handle the unknowns for another year. And I *really* don't want to be the only one on my team still working with archaic technology. It will make my job infinitely more difficult—"

"Why would the whole rest of your team get it before it's your turn? Some of them will probably be waiting too, right?"

The words spill out of my mouth before I can decide whether they make sense or not. I know I'm not making any sense. A few days ago, I gushed about how excited I was to do this. How I felt good about changing things up and jumping in, even though it still felt a little scary. Right now, it feels more like I'm standing at the edge of a cliff and someone's about to push me off.

"I don't want to do this without you," Mom whispers, pulling me out of my thoughts. "But I need to do this now, Channel."

She looks at her hands, fiddling with them nervously.

"You'd get the surgery even if I want to wait?" My tone is biting, and she winces.

"I'm not trying to—"

"No!" I shout, standing up. Hot, fiery anger pulses through me, my chest so tight it feels like it might explode. "This is—selfish!" I splutter. "You're my mom, and you care more about this stupid upgrade than you do about the project I've struggled to work on for the last quarter!"

I ball my hands into fists as tears sting the corners of my eyes.

"And this doesn't even make sense! They gave us—what—a week to come to terms with this?" I know I'm acting like a baby right now, but recognizing it doesn't mean I can stop it. I spin on my heel, rip my mask from the hook, and dash out of the house, slamming the front door behind me. Without missing a beat, I continue down the street to the park, pumping my legs faster and faster, giving the frenzied energy inside me somewhere to go.

By the time I arrive at our bench, I'm gasping for air. Leaning over, I press my hands into the hard surface and let my head hang as my chest heaves. My skin vibrates, and my heart feels like it might burst out of my chest.

I place the mask over my mouth and nose, drawing in a crucial breath. As my panting slows, tears finally spring free and blur my vision, wetting my eyelashes before they drop to the bench, creating dark splashes on the wood. Slowly standing straight, I wipe my eyes and turn, slumping to a seat out of sheer exhaustion.

What's wrong with me? I've never talked to my mom like that before. And over what? Something I actually want to be a part of?

I lean my head back and stare at the sky.

I'm scared. I'm so scared.

Tears begin to flow again down my cheeks, streaking across my flushed skin. Everything is going to change tomorrow morning. I want it to, and I don't want it to, all at the same time.

Suddenly, I think back to my conversations with Oren. How free he was. *He did this, and he's fine.* I'll be fine, too. The people I care about will still be there with me, even if it does take Aave a bit longer. We'll all still be together, so who cares if I do this now or later? This thing is going to change our world whether I want it to or not.

Knowing that doesn't stop me from grieving. Turning, I inspect the letters on the bench. Lifting my finger, I cross out my name. None of this is mine anymore, and it's time to let go.

I take another deep breath and close my eyes. I need to tell Aave. Oren, too. But first, I need to apologize.

CHAPTER 12

"HEY," I say nervously as Aave approaches.

He gives a small wave, walking the last few steps to our bench. "Why is no one ever sitting here?" he asks, motioning around us.

I laugh, grateful for the ice breaker. If he notices the alteration I made to his sign, he doesn't show it.

"Probably because we chose this bench for the exact reason that nobody ever sits here," I say.

"Not because I'm scary?"

"Nope." I shake my head definitively. Aave laughs and sits next to me. The evening sky is rich with the warm hues of sunset. Whether it's real or not, I don't care. It's beautiful.

"So," Aave starts. "You sounded a little upset in your message."

"How could you tell?" I grin.

"You didn't use nearly enough exclamation points."

I smack his arm, and he feigns injury.

"Seriously, though. Are you okay?"

"No?"

"You want me to tell you if you're okay?" he teases.

"That'd be great."

"Lay it out for me then. I'll do my best to tell you how you feel about it."

I take a deep breath and let it out slowly. "I'm sorry I haven't been around. I had a lot to think about, and I convinced myself that being alone would be easier."

"Was it?"

"Sometimes."

Aave nods.

"They scheduled a time for our implant." As soon as the words leave my lips, his eyebrows shoot up.

"I know," I continue. "I didn't think we were anywhere close to that point, but I guess with the sheer number of people on the list..." I pause, looking down at my hands. "I didn't even know we were officially *on the list*. My mom kept telling me that we were 'just getting information,' but clearly that wasn't the case."

"So you're feeling confused and betrayed, got it."

I smirk. "Very intuitive."

"I try."

I look back at the sky. "It's confusing because I feel everything at once. Excited to move on to something better. Sad to leave this life behind, even if it is a trash fire at the moment."

Aave snorts.

I rest my head on the back of the bench. "It's permanent," I say softly.

"I know."

"What if I hate it?"

"I'm sure you won't hate it. What's to hate? Everything will be blissful."

I turn to him, propping my arm on the top of the bench. "Then why am I so conflicted? Shouldn't I be thrilled? Am I terrified of change?"

Aave laughs, "Channel, you're completely normal. This is a massive life adjustment, and you have no reason to want to jump ship on your life right now."

"That's debatable."

"Okay, sure. There are a few obstacles in your way currently, but you've got everything going for you. You're smart, funny, beautiful, strong, an incredibly good problem solver—"

"Hold up, did you just call me beautiful?" I laugh, but Aave doesn't join in. I clear my throat, and once again, I'm incredibly grateful he can't see me blushing. "I was kidding," I say.

"I wasn't." He looks at me intently. "The problem with all this is that our Community is changing so fast. We don't really get a say."

I nod. "Why not? Why don't we get a say? Isn't that the whole point of P3? It's supposed to be what we want, right? So what, maybe people back then wanted pretty scenery and beautiful faces. Maybe we want...not change."

"I think you should give that speech."

"Yeah?"

"Mmhmm, right now. Stand high on a box in the middle of town and rally the people around you."

"Don't tempt me," I laugh.

His hand brushes mine, and heat explodes up my left arm. I do a terrible job of pretending not to notice. Slowly, he interlaces his fingers with mine, and we sit there. Staring at each other.

"You'll be next," I say, my voice a whisper.

"I've got issues, remember?"

"Not enough of them."

He raises an eyebrow, and I hold his gaze. I like the way his hand feels in mine. Aave is my best friend, but right now, I wonder if I know anything about him. His face seems suddenly brand new. Not just because he's changed his profile settings, but because of the way he looks at me now. No longer just acknowledging my presence, but really noticing me—like he can't get enough. Those eyes that always held a joke or a question are now more centered and sure. He's no longer the little boy who chattered with me about imagined escapades in the Real world, though his sense of adventure has never left him. Somehow, I wasn't paying attention when he grew up.

I take in the curve of his cheek and the strong line of his jaw. This is how he wants me to see him, and it's suddenly obvious. He's trying to erase that little boy from my mind, too. Trying to wake me up to a new version of himself that wants more than collaboration on primary projects.

His thumb caresses the top of my hand, and my stomach flips. That's when my body takes over. I don't care that he's my best friend. I don't care that this might make our relationship awkward—because after this week, who knows what life will be like?

I don't care about any of it anymore. This new awareness and attraction that's been twisting within me is desperate to find out what happens next. To know how it feels to take the next step. My free hand shakes as I lift it to his cheek.

All I want is to have this experience for the first time and know it's *really happening*. My lips against his. His hand wrapped around the small of my back. My fingers in his tousled hair. Our bodies pressed against each other.

I gently lift his mask from his face, and his breathing quickens. Taking mine off, I lean in—the air between us electric. I kiss him. And he kisses me back.

"It's going to be just fine," Mom says, squeezing my hand in hers.

I stare at the silver tile on the floor, counting the squares from the wall to the door on our right. We've been here since the early hours of the morning to complete our testing before surgery. I've been scanned, poked and prodded, and given an injection that is slowly making my brain activity slow to the speed of sludge.

As my vision begins to blur, I lean my heavy head on Mom's shoulder.

"I feel weird."

Mom rubs my arm. "Me, too. They said we would."

"I know. But I don't like it."

"This should only take an hour, and then we'll be in a recovery room together."

"Will they give us good food?"

"They better," Mom laughs.

A wave of sadness crashes into me, and I scrunch up my face to stave it off.

"Oren said it hurt at first," I say.

"Oren?"

"That guy that's already linked. Remember? I've been talking with him?" My tongue feels thick, and my speech is sloppy. But it's so much work to make each sound...

"What were you saying?" Mom asks.

I don't have a chance to process her question because a woman in a white coat steps into the hall, followed by two other Community workers.

"Quin? Channel?"

I try to shift my head, but my muscles aren't responding.

"They're pretty far gone," the woman says. "Please help them in."

Someone puts their hands under my arms and lifts me from my chair, then supports me as my leaden legs slowly move one after the other toward the room.

"She'll be on the left," the woman says, pointing to a table behind the door. "Carefully, and let's put a blanket over her legs. She looks cold."

A blanket sounds lovely. Someone turns me around, and I sit. Then I feel myself being lowered to the table, and it feels so good to be horizontal. Luxuriously comfortable.

My skin feels...fuzzy. Like it's blurring into the air—blending with molecules and particles. Soft voices echo around me; then a slow buzzing sounds next to my ear. Something cold brushes against the base of my skull. Up and down. Up and down. Then the buzzing stops. But I liked the buzzing and the way it hummed against my skin. I want to hear it again.

The voices get louder, and I want to scan my surroundings—discover where they're coming from—but my body isn't listening to me anymore. Something crashes against the table, and the harsh sound echoes around the room. I should be startled, but it doesn't bother me in the least. I don't move a muscle. I wonder if I'm floating and why I can still feel the cold from whatever touched my skin.

Someone lifts my head and covers my face. This should make me panic, but again I lie motionless. Is this what surgery is like? I should open my eyes and see what's going on. I should look...

My body is pushed upright and slipped off the table—then I'm lying down again. Yet somehow still moving. There's a scrape against the floor underneath me.

Is it over? Is this what Cerebrolink feels like? It doesn't hurt. Oren said it would hurt, but it doesn't. The scraping sound seems to fade, and I drop lower into...something. Something thick and deep. And dark. And still.

PART 2
MILA

MARCH 8, 2161 - APRIL 1, 2161

CHAPTER 13

My name is Mila, and I'm Real. Before you judge me, let me give you some perspective. I didn't get any choice in the matter, and neither did my parents initially. *Their* parents chose to opt out of the Communities, and as far as I know, we haven't been given the chance to transfer since then. To be honest, though...I doubt my parents would opt-in even if we were.

Let's just get this out there: my parents are complete conspiracy theorists. Which, come to think of it, is probably why we've never been offered a spot in Paradise 1. It's not like they're quiet about their beliefs, and we know there's always someone watching.

But that's where *I* want to be. In the Communities. I think? I'm not really sure, to be honest. I just know I don't want to be here. And it's not even like my life is *that bad*. Sure, the masks are annoying, but it's not like those would magically be gone in P1. It's more the fact that I miss my friends. Almost every single one of their families has transferred to a Community over the past two years, and I basically live in a ghost town—

"Hey!" I yell, reaching for the notebook that was snatched out of my hands.

Alek flips the pages, trying to read what I've written as I grab onto his arms.

"My name is Mila—"

"Stop it!" I spit, finally gripping the book and ripping it from his fingers. "Mom! Alek's messing with my stuff again!"

"Alek!" Mom calls from the kitchen.

"Wow, stop being such a baby," Alek says, readjusting his shirt. His dark hair is longer than usual, and it falls across his eyes.

"That's *my* journal. Stop being such a jerk." I stare him down, hoping he can feel the full force of my current disdain.

"I didn't know—"

"Get out of my room!"

Alek holds up his hands, a patronizing grin on his face that I want to smack right off. He backs up into the hall and sweeps the hair off his forehead.

Alek is a year older than me, and even though he can be incredibly annoying, I mostly love him. Except when he acts like he knows better than me. Or takes credit for my ideas. Or eats more than his share at dinner. Brothers are the worst.

"Dinner time!" Mom calls.

I shove the book under my pillow and stomp down the hall. Alek is already taking dishes from Mom and setting them on the table. I glower at him, and he winks.

"When's Dad getting home?" I ask.

"Any minute now. Can you grab the filtered water from the fridge?"

I nod, but wait until Alek makes another pass so I don't have to get close to him. Our home is simple. A kitchen and open room on the main floor, three bedrooms upstairs. There are bathrooms, too, but we don't use them. Well, that's not totally true—they make great pantries. The pipes for our indoor plumbing broke down years ago, and with no support from the Communities, there's no way to fix them.

The front door opens, and a sense of relief washes over me. Something inside of me feels complete each day my parents return home from work, and we're together as a family for dinner.

"How was your day?" Mom calls, rinsing out a bowl and setting it in the stainless steel sink. She dries her hands on a faded towel, then turns to greet him as he walks in.

Dad trudges down the hall, and the first thing I notice as he enters the room is how deep the circles under his eyes have become.

"Good. Long," he answers with a wan smile.

Mom slides past the edge of the countertop and wraps her arms around him. I watch as they both seem to expand and then collapse into each other. I wonder what it would be like to feel that connected to someone. To be that safe.

Mom whispers something in Dad's ear, and he nods.

"Alek, Mila," Dad says as he steps back. Without finishing his thought, he puts an arm around me and squeezes my shoulders. Alek tries to skirt past, but Dad catches him and pulls him close. "We only have each other, right?"

My eyes flash at Alek, but as I try to summon the fire of indignation I expected to be burning within me still, I can't seem to find it. Dad's hugged it out of me.

"Okay then, time for dinner," Dad says cheerily, dropping his arms and walking to the sink to wash his hands. Case closed.

"Something smells delicious," he says, running his hands under the water as Mom pumps it from the plastic drum.

It doesn't. It smells exactly the same as every meal, and I know Dad's aware of that fact.

"Palm tonight," Mom says, "but I added a bit of heat from the peppers."

"Mmm, and mustard greens. My favorite." Dad smiles at me, and I roll my eyes. He knows I dislike anything with the word 'greens' attached.

We take our seats at the table and load up our plates.

"Did you hear that Kina and her family are joining Paradise 3 this week?" Alek says casually as he lifts meat to his plate.

Mom purses her lips.

"No," Dad says, "I didn't realize. I guess we'll be down a man at the gardens."

"We can't really grow anything anyway," I say under my breath.

"What was that?" Mom asks, her eyes hawk-like as she observes me leaning over my plate.

It's back. The indignation.

"Mom, what are we even doing? I know you feel like we're standing up for something—for freedom, for independence? But seriously, we're going to be all alone! My friend group has been gutted—I spend all day reading through antiquated information because we don't have access to the Edge—"

"Mila—"

"No!" I say, cutting Dad off. I clench my fists, but my arms still shake. "You can do what you want with your life, but what about us? When you're gone, what about Alek and me? What about when our filtration system dies? Do you think someone from Paradise 1 is going to come fix that for us? Do you just envision us wasting away our lives by ourselves? Uninvolved in *literally the entire world* around us?"

Mom and Dad stare at me, their eyes wide with surprise at my outburst.

"First of all, it's not the entire world," Mom says sternly. "Barely half of the world's population lives in Communities—"

"And the other half are buried under ash."

"You know that's not true. Most of the world's population wasn't directly impacted—" Dad says.

"Then where are they? Not here! Not in Europe," I say, shoving a forkful of soggy greens into my mouth and almost choking from the acrid flavor.

Mom glances at Dad.

Tears threaten to spill over my bottom eyelids.

Dad sighs. "Mila, Alek, obviously you've both been thinking about this again, so it might be time to remind you—"

"About what happened in 2130, yeah, we know, Dad. Our people fought for independence at great cost, blah, blah, blah."

Dad stares at me, a hurt expression on his face, and my stomach drops.

"I'm sorry," I mumble. Hot tears sting my cheeks, and I refuse to look up from my plate. *What's wrong with me?* I never speak like this to my parents, even if I'm thinking it on the inside. Alek's eyes are on me, and I sink deeper into my chair.

Dad clears his throat. "It's okay. I've repeated it enough times, I guess that story is getting old?" He chuckles, but his heart isn't in it. "We fought against the Communities at great cost, yes, and we assumed that the families here with us in California territory—that gave up so much to remain independent—would continue to fight with us."

"But we were wrong, Mila," Mom says softly. "They're bone-tired, and living in a Community is so much easier—"

"Then why are we still fighting?" Alek asks gently, his mouth full of food. "Haven't we had enough time to see that nothing terrible has happened? The world hasn't spontaneously combusted because of the Communities."

"Well, that's just it, Alek," Dad says. "We don't really know what's happening in the world. Instead of building a community of our own and keeping our way of life, we've essentially been cut off, like Mila said."

I take another bite and swallow.

"Our way of life was taken anyway," Alek says, and we eat the rest of our dinner in silence.

Later that night, I walk the mile and a half to the edge of the water and sink my toes into the soft sand. The waves are gentle, and the rhythmic sound of them landing on shore pulls my body into a state of much-needed peace.

I still can't decide what bothers me more—spending my time isolated, unable to join one of the Paradise Communities, or the fact that my parents seem to be thinking of giving up. I've spent so much time being frustrated with their incessant commitment to their ideals, that I didn't realize how much I've come to rely on that strength and surety.

I back up and sit down on the dry sand past the surf, burying my feet. My hair swirls around my face in the breeze, dark strands cutting across the pale blue shallows. I pull it behind my head and tuck it into the back of my shirt.

Do I actually wish I could join the Communities? I thought I did. But now that I might be able to, I'm worried I only wanted to join them because my parents said I couldn't.

"Hey," Alek's voice sounds behind me, and I turn. "I thought I'd find you here."

"Yeah. Just thinking."

"I'm sorry I took your journal earlier—"

"I'm really sorry I was so rude!" We speak over each other, and both laugh. I adjust my mask.

"No, you were right to get mad," Alek says. "I'm your older brother. I'm supposed to look out for you."

"Well, you got off easy on that one," I laugh. "There's nobody to protect me from at this point."

He sits next to me, giving me a playful shove that yanks my foot out of its soft, sandy tomb with a slurp. I quickly re-bury it.

"I didn't know you were thinking about all this, too," I say.

"How could I not be? I'm eighteen. A brand new adult with nothing to do or look forward to," he chuckles. Reaching into his pocket, he pulls out a strip of cloth and ties his hair up into a knot.

"Nothing to look forward to?" I say dramatically. "But there's fruit that's about to ripen up, and ground to till, and—"

"Laugh it up! You'll be right here with me in another year and a half."

My grin fades. "I know. I'm kidding." I sigh, leaning back in the sand on my elbows. "Our future looks bleak."

Alek shrugs. "Maybe not."

My eyes narrow, and I sit back up. "Do you think they're actually considering letting us join Paradise?"

"Seems that way. What else are they going to do?"

"Is it sad that that scares me? Mom and Dad giving in like that?"

"No, it scares me too. It's like everything we've ever known about them is suddenly—"

"Gone."

"Yeah," Alek says, stretching out and laying his head on the sand. His dark skin seems to shimmer, golden against the bleached shore.

"But what if they're right?" I ask softly. "What if they've been right all along, and the Communities are terrible, and now we're just going to give up like everyone else. It's not like we can come back from that."

Alek is silent, his chest rising and falling slowly. I watch the surf ebb and flow near my toes, mesmerized by the consistency of it.

"There *is* another option," he says finally, sitting up and wrapping his arms around his knees.

"What do you mean?" I ask, my brows furrowed.

"Mom said only half of the world's population is in Communities, right?"

I nod.

"So what if *we* go and find *them*?"

"Who?"

"The other people. There have got to be other groups—maybe cities even —that exist somewhere. The world isn't big enough for all of those billions of people to be scattered and alone like we are."

Something lifts within me. Is it possible? Could we do this? Could we leave our home and somehow find other people like us?

"But where would we even look? Is there any information we have access to? Could we find out where the Community territory has expanded?"

Alek turns to me, a mischievous look on his face. "I need to show you something."

CHAPTER 14

"Wow, I haven't been here in forever," I say, taking in the brick walls and empty hallways. "What made you think to come here?"

Alek grins. "When you've got nothing exciting to do all day, you explore."

"Why didn't I think of that?"

"Because up until the last few months, you still had friends." Alek walks past me toward the front office of the school.

When was it that his last good friend left? A year ago? Two? The fact that I can't remember makes me feel awful. I've been so focused on myself, I never even considered how lonely he must have been.

"I remember Oren and I were teacher's helpers in first grade. One time we came to the office with a sick student—to drop her off in the nurse's office—and Oren tried to race me back to the classroom." He walks to the edge of the wall, pointing. "Check it out. The brick is still chipped." He laughs, clapping his hands together.

"From what?"

"From Oren running into it! He slipped and hit the wall. He was carrying a hard drive—remember those old, thin ones that looked like metal plates?"

I nod.

"He put out his arms when he fell, and the hard-drive got absolutely crushed. He hit the wall so hard that he broke off part of the brick."

I laugh. "I don't think I remember him."

"No, you wouldn't. You were so young. He was..." Alek trails off.

"Did he leave?"

Alek nods. "His family was in the first group to go." He kicks the brick gently with his shoe. "But I'm getting distracted," he says, turning and plastering a smile on his face. He motions me forward.

I follow him into what used to be the main office, and somehow even now, I feel like I'm breaking the rules by walking around the front desk.

"What are you doing?" I ask, watching Alek crouch down next to the wall.

"Checking for something."

"For what?"

He grunts, and I decide to be patient.

"Yes!" he says jubilantly, standing and backing up. "There's a connection."

I look at him quizzically, but then something appears in the air in front of us. My eyes widen.

"Who knows when this was synced last—it's probably in need of a massive update—but we might be able to find some information, at least."

"Wait, is this—no, how could that be—"

Alek laughs. "It's the Edge, Mila. A primitive version of it."

"We had it *in our school*?"

"What did you think it was?"

"I don't know! Not something that was running our entire lives!"

"No," Alek grins, putting a hand on my shoulder. "The Edge is only code. It can't run anyone's life. Only the people who put it to work can. The people who put it to work in our school were only using it to access and share information, not to change our reality."

Still. The hovering blue light makes me queasy.

Alek waves his hands, attempting to tap the menu button at the top, but the projection doesn't respond.

"You have to have one of those things," I say.

"Huh?"

"Remember? One of those wand thingies."

Alek's face lights up. "Right! Yes. But where would it be?" He mutters to himself as he scurries around the room, ripping open drawers and peering inside. Glancing around, my eyes land on a cabinet in the back corner.

"Try there," I say, pointing it out to him.

He walks quickly and swings open the doors. "Aha! Great find, Mila. Now let's hope it isn't dead."

Running back, he presses his finger over the sensor and points it at the menu. A cursor appears immediately, and we both cheer excitedly. Alek searches until he finds what he's looking for. Maps.

Selecting the North America territories, he points the sensor one direction and the map zooms out even further. Correcting, he moves the opposite way, and the image responds.

I suck in a breath as he zooms in over the Southwest Quadrant. "That's *all* Paradise?"

Alek's brow furrows as he uses the cursor to open another image. "This *was* all Paradise."

"What do you mean?"

"Look," he says, pointing with the wand. "This was last updated in 2156. Five years ago."

"So...it might be bigger now."

"It's definitely bigger now. How could it not be?"

"Whoa," I breathe. "I didn't even know the numbers went up that high." I stare at the small boxes on the screen. P9, P10, and P11. "What's over there?" I ask, pointing to the right.

Alek scans east.

"There aren't any Communities there. Or there weren't, I guess."

"It's a surprisingly large area."

"Even in five years...they couldn't have taken the entire thing, right?"

"Who knows."

He scans the rest of the map. Paradise Communities as far as the eye can see in every direction.

"Wait, what about on other continents?"

Alek hands me the wand, and I push it left, crossing the Atlantic Ocean and stopping over Eurasia.

"They have Communities, too," Alek says.

"Not as many."

"Five years ago," he reminds me.

"It's worldwide." I hand the wand back to him and gently lower myself into the worn office chair behind me.

Alek sighs, leaning against the desk and rubbing his face with his hands. "It was worth a shot."

"What do you mean 'it was worth a shot'?" I ask.

"I'm sorry, Mila. I thought maybe we'd find an option—an area we could travel to—"

"We did."

He looks at me, and immediately I'm transported back to when we were little kids. That look says 'Seriously, Mila? How dumb are you?' and I hate it.

"We did find it," I assert, standing with renewed energy. "There's a huge territory out east that's still Real as far as we know."

"Yeah," Alek says with a wry laugh. "As far as we know. And, by the way, let's ignore the fact that that 'huge territory out east' is over twenty-five hundred miles from here."

"So, what? How far can people walk in a day? Probably three to four miles an hour—let's say four since we're young and healthy—so maybe thirty miles a day? With breaks for meals—"

"Maybe if the entire path was completely flat! And there were zero complications—"

"It would average out!" I say, my body tensing.

"Even with those best-case calculations, that would take—what, like eighty-five days to get there? Mila, listen to yourself. Eighty-five days of hiking eight hours a day. *Through* Paradise territory."

"Possibly. It looked like there was a narrow stretch—"

"Not getting caught. Taking care of all our necessities. Finding water, shelter, food—"

"I know, Alek. It sounds insane. But what's our other option? Sit here by ourselves? Waste away, never having the opportunity to do anything with our lives, or sell out and join Paradise?"

Alek shoves his hands into the pockets of his pants and stares at the floor.

"Mom and Dad could come with us," I whisper. "We wouldn't have to do it all on our own."

"They wouldn't. They'd never give us the okay to do this."

"What are you talking about?" I say, beginning to pace. "They know something needs to change, and they *hate* the idea of joining the Communities."

"But they're not going to sign up for a death mission."

"You don't know that. Maybe they're keen on death missions."

Alek stares at me, unamused. "Fine. Let's go ask them."

"Not now," I hedge. "They'll probably be in bed already. Tomorrow. After we help at the greenhouses."

Alek shrugs. "Doesn't matter to me—I already know what their response will be." He brushes past me, and my nostrils flare. He's wrong. Mom and Dad have to see that our current way of life isn't sustainable. They have to.

CHAPTER 15

ALEK REPLACES the mask on his face after stepping outside past the glass and resealing the door.

"You're not supposed to take off your mask in there," I say.

Alek shrugs and walks past me.

"Alek, seriously," I say, following him. "You can't mess up the CO_2 balance."

He doesn't answer, and frustration builds within me.

"Alek, stop!" I grab onto his arm, and he whips around.

"What's your deal?"

I step back. "I'm trying to talk to you, and you're ignoring me."

"Mila, I know I'm not supposed to take my mask off, okay? I was just sick of it, and I was only in there for a few minutes."

I nod. "I know, I get sick of them, too, but the plants will die if—"

"Yes!" he says, obviously annoyed, "I'm not stupid! I understand the reasoning behind airtight greenhouses, Mila—I've worked here since I could barely walk." He sighs in frustration and sits on a stump next to the path.

My palms are sweaty, and my heart pounds nervously. I hate confrontation like this—especially with Alek.

"I'm sorry, I didn't mean to yell." He runs his hands through his hair and looks down at the ground. "I'm over this," he mumbles.

"Over what?" I move closer now that the edge has left his voice.

"All of this," he says, motioning to the glass structures around us. "It's like we're not meant to survive here, and we're forcing the issue. We spend every second of our day removing poison from the air and water, forcing things to grow in less than ideal conditions just so we can sustain life—for what? So I can wake up and do it again tomorrow?"

My face screws up in confusion. "But last night—everything you said— we still need to talk to Mom and Dad. Don't you believe that something will change?"

"I mean, maybe? It seems like a lot to hope for."

There's nowhere else to sit, but I take a step closer and lightly kick his foot. "There has to be something, Alek, because you're right. Now that we're not receiving any Community support, it won't take long before we're out of masks, or the greenhouses break down, or—I don't know, something worse. Then what? We'll all be left for dead."

Alek looks up at me. "That was the most depressing thing I've ever heard."

"Whatever! You started it!" I smack his arm, and he laughs. "Actually," I say, "I think I am pretty depressed."

His eyebrows furrow. "You are?"

I sigh. "Yeah. I don't think I can help in the cricket house today."

Alek's face breaks into a broad smile. "Ha, ha, nice try." He shakes his head. "You're really trying to get out of that?" He stands, stretching out his back.

"Alek," I whine, "it smells horrible in there."

"Yeah, which is why there's no way I'm taking your turn! C'mon, let's go fertilize house number sixteen," he says, pointing past the house he just exited. "I promise I'll follow the rules this time."

"I'm not holding my breath," I say. Which is funny. Because these days, I always am.

"Hey!" I call, running out the back door on tiny legs.

Eight-year-old Alek looks up from the board he's working on and smiles.

"I'm not finished yet, Mila—I can't play."

I stop next to him to catch my breath. "Mom said you'd be finished after lunch."

"Well, it's taking me a little longer. Look how tough this wire is," he says, motioning to the spool sitting next to him on the workbench.

At six, I know nothing about wires and tools, just how bored I am without Alek to play with. I pout, and my shoulders slump, but before I can present my case, a man I don't know walks into the backyard. I hide behind Alek, carefully observing the stranger. A boy follows closely behind him, and I recognize him immediately.

"It's Zayn," I say, tugging on Alek's arm.

"Go say hi, then," Alek says, pushing me out into the open. Zayn spots us immediately and runs our direction.

"Hi," he says.

"Is that your dad?" I ask.

He nods proudly. "He's working with the Communities now."

"But the Communities are bad," I say, and Alek taps my arm, shaking his head.

"But they are bad, Alek," I insist. "Mom said—"

"Mila," he hisses. "You don't say stuff like that."

Zayn's friendly smile disappears.

"The Communities are building a better life for people," he says, puffing out his chest. "My dad's helping them."

Dad suddenly appears from around the greenhouse and waves, walking toward Zayn's dad. Our conversation stops abruptly as all three of us turn to watch the two men.

"Sorry to interrupt your work," Zayn's dad says, and Dad smiles, waving him off.

"Not a problem—I was just about to take a break anyway."

Dad just took a break for lunch. He never takes a break right after taking a break. Why did he say that if it wasn't true?

"I came by to let you know that since our numbers are down, only a few Edge upgrades are going to be available in a couple of weeks. Our power allotment is also decreasing another twenty percent—"

"But why?" Dad asks. "Our hydroelectric plant produces more than what we need—"

"But there are Community needs that aren't being met."

"So they're taking our power now?" Dad says, attempting to keep his voice calm.

"The number of people here don't justify—"

"Alejandro, you are a member of this town. You haven't joined the Communities."

"I'm a Community liaison."

"I'm aware of that, and we're all grateful for the work you do. But doesn't this concern you? Don't you wonder if they're going to continue pulling resources for Paradise and leaving us with nothing?"

"They wouldn't do that," Alejandro assures him. "This is fair and proportional to our population. It's not up for debate. This is a courtesy announcement so everyone can prepare accordingly."

Dad's jaw clenches, and he nods slowly. "Thank you," he says. "I'll be sure to make arrangements."

I don't realize I've been clinging to Alek's arm until Dad begins to walk back to the greenhouse. I let go, hoping Zayn didn't see the fear in my eyes.

"It doesn't seem like your dad's helping," I say. "My dad looks sad because of him."

"Maybe your dad should've done more to help the Communities. Then you'd be getting one of the upgrades," Zayn says arrogantly.

"You're getting one?" Alek asks.

Zayn nods. "Of course we are."

"Zayn, time to go," Alejandro calls.

"See you later," Zayn says, smiling smugly. "If you want to come over to get premier access, let me know."

"This is unusual," Dad says, settling into the wooden rocking chair later that evening while Mom sits cross-legged on the floor next to him. Alek and I returned from the greenhouses an hour ago, but we took time to clean up and look especially presentable. That hasn't escaped Mom's notice.

"I hope you're not giving us bad news," Mom says, her eyes pleading. "No bad news, right?"

"I don't think so," I say hesitantly, and it clearly doesn't inspire confidence.

Alek starts. "Mila and I stopped by the old school building on our way back from the beach the other day. Mila had a great idea she wanted to run past you—"

"Hold on," I stop him. "It was *your* idea, I only wanted to—"

"It was not my idea! I shut it down after seeing the first map—"

"Okay," Dad says, lifting his voice and holding up a hand. "One at a time. And we don't actually care whose idea it was."

Taking a deep breath, I glare at Alek. "I was at the beach, and *Alek*," I say pointedly, "had the idea to stop by the school to look at territory maps."

"There's still an Edge connection that's working there?" Mom asks.

"That information has to be outdated, don't you think?" Dad adds.

"That's what I said," Alek mutters under his breath. Crossing his arms over his chest, he shifts his weight and stares at the floor to avoid my eyes.

Frustration builds within me, and my chest feels tight. "Alek and I don't want to live alone for the rest of our lives!" I blurt out.

Mom's eyes widen, and Alek visibly stiffens. My words hang in the air, then seem to settle over the room with tangible weight.

"I thought you loved it here..." Mom whispers.

"We do," Alek assures her, "but almost everyone we know is gone now."

"What are we going to do for the rest of our lives?" I say. "What are we going to do when you're gone? Not that I think you're going to be gone anytime soon, but you know what I'm saying," I fiddle awkwardly with a torn edge of my fingernail.

Mom sneaks a sideways glance at Dad, then stares at the wall between us.

"I understand," Dad says calmly. "We understand."

My shoulders slump, and I walk over to sit next to Mom. She reaches an arm around me and squeezes.

"There's also not much we can do," Dad continues.

"But what if there is?" I ask.

"Mila, we will never be okay with you two joining the Communities. I know it seems inevitable, and maybe it is?" Mom looks anxiously at Dad. "But we decided a long time ago that we'd never go without a fight."

"We've done everything we can to keep you safe, to provide a good life, and—"

"Dad," Alek cuts in, "You have provided a good life. And I don't think Mila is suggesting that we need you to do more."

"No," I agree, "I'm not. I'm suggesting that it's time for Alek and me to do something."

Mom starts to cry next to me.

"What is it?" I ask, suddenly feeling guilty for upsetting her.

"We didn't sacrifice this much to have you two sign up—"

"Mom, no!" I laugh with relief. "I'm not talking about us signing up to join the Communities without you!"

She sniffs and lifts her eyes.

"No," I laugh again. "I mean, I'm not going to pretend it hasn't been on my mind, but that was before Alek—"

"That was before she got a crazy idea in her head."

"Alright. Let's hear it," Dad says, leaning back in the chair and closing his eyes, rocking slowly.

"Well," I say, "it seems to me that there are only two ways to solve our problem. The first option is to join the Communities, which—as we've seen just now—will send Mom into a deep depression from which she's unlikely to recover."

Mom wipes her eyes and laughs, nudging me lightly.

"The second," I continue, "is to find more people like us. If we are alone here, why don't we leave and find another group somewhere else?"

The room is silent. Alek looks between our parents, waiting for a response.

"It sounds great in theory, Mila, but we don't even know—" Mom starts.

I sigh in frustration.

"No, wait," she says, "let me finish."

I don't look at her, but I don't argue either.

"We don't even know where these people are, nor do we know much—if anything—about the weather, the terrain, and therefore what provisions we'd need. We'd be walking in blind."

"Based on the maps we saw, it looked like our best bet for finding non-Community controlled territory is out east," Alek says, and the seriousness of his expression makes me wonder if his interest level is increasing.

"I know it's outdated information," I say, hedging their criticism preemptively, "but the maps show a large section of land. Even if the Communities have grown, I highly doubt they could've taken everything."

When nobody responds, I continue. "The southern territory—which I know isn't exactly habitable—would allow us to cross without having to risk traveling through Community territory. At least for the first thirty days or so."

"Thirty days?" Dad says letting out a low whistle.

"Mila calculated eighty-five days total. With optimistic calculations," Alek says.

I roll my eyes. "Sure, yes. It's a really long trip. Could we die? Yes. Could we be caught? Yes. But would it give us a chance to find our own community again? Yes. And I think that's worth it."

Alek sits next to Dad on the floor and hugs his knees to his chest. "Here's the thing. If we're willing to risk everything to go on this insane trip you're presenting, why don't we just—Mom, I'm sorry—join the Communities? How is this risk somehow better than that?"

Mom and Dad are silent.

After a few moments, Dad clears his throat. "Joining the Communities is high risk, but more than that, it's a different kind of risk. When you join the Communities, you are saying 'Here, you manage my life for me' and I —we—can't get on board with that. I can't hand over my life to someone else. I can't allow someone else to dictate the very images that are coming into my brain. And I can't let that happen to my children either."

"But what if they're good images?" Alek argues.

"It doesn't matter!" Mom says. "If you turn that over, you can't ever get it back. What if it becomes *not good* at some point? You'd never even know."

Alek nods, and a shiver goes down my spine. Mom leans back and stretches her legs, then leans her head to the side, loosening up her neck.

"I want to go," I say softly. "I know there's a risk, but I want to see if we can find other people like us. A place where we could thrive. As a family."

Mom glances at Dad, and his brows furrow. I scrutinize their faces, attempting to somehow gain access to their silent communication.

"Alek, how do you feel?" Dad asks.

Alek takes a deep breath. "It terrifies me."

Dad laughs, and a grin threatens to break out on Alek's face.

"As it should," Dad says.

"But so does living here alone forever," Alek continues, his eyes fixed on an imaginary point on the floor. "I think we should try. Worst case, we abandon the trip and come back here, right?"

Tears begin to form in Mom's eyes, and she turns her face.

Dad nods. "I agree. Which is why Mom and I can't join you."

My eyes widen. "But—"

Dad holds up a hand. "None of us have any idea what you're going to encounter. You may travel a few days or weeks and come across something—a border, a threat—and have to turn back. We can't put all our hopes and plans into this trek. If you need to return, there needs to be something here to return to. Food. Water. Shelter. We can't leave you without a backup plan."

"But what if it works! What if we get there and—" my voice catches in my throat.

"Then you'll be right where you need to be. And we," he says, reaching out to hold Mom's hand, "will still be together. Waiting."

My face flushes, and tears spill onto my cheeks. This isn't what I wanted. I'm ready to say goodbye to this place, but to my parents? A heaviness weighs on my heart, and I'm not sure if I can bear it.

"We'll come back for you," Alek says. "If we make it and find something better, we'll—I don't know, find a way to get a message to you. Contact you somehow and bring you out."

Mom nods. "I need to know that you're safe. And then we can find a way to make it to you."

"You'll need to track your path. Gain as much information as possible," Dad says. "I know you won't be able to connect with the Edge, but take one of our old life watches. And a solar charger."

"We still have those?" I ask, wiping the moisture from my cheeks.

Dad nods.

"Mila, we should talk with Zayn and Kaye. They might want to join us," Alek says.

"I doubt it," I mutter.

"Hey, I know you don't like Zayn, but he's about as anti-Community as Dad is. And he's strong—"

"Yeah."

"He's changed a lot over the past two years," Alek cajoles.

I ignore him. "What about Kaye? I have no idea where she stands. She hasn't said two words to me since Paul's family left."

"She's kind. And lonely, just like us."

I take a deep breath. "Fine," I sigh. "We can talk to them, but it will be a lot easier to avoid notice and make decisions if it's just the two of us."

"Take your time," Dad says. "Get as much information as you can from that console at the school. We'll help you plan supplies. I'm sure families that left for the Communities didn't take their emergency equipment with them."

"You're going to go through their stuff?" I ask, incredulous.

"They don't have any use for it," Alek says.

"Still—"

"I'm sure they'd be more than happy to know it was going to good use," Dad insists.

"You said you think it will take three months?" Mom asks, again folding her legs underneath her.

"That's our best guess," I say.

"Then you'll need to leave by the end of March at the latest. You don't want to go south in the middle of summer."

I nod. That gives us about twenty days to prepare. Again, my chest tightens. Twenty days to gather everything we'll need to survive for three months. Twenty days to say goodbye to the only home I've ever known. Twenty days to say goodbye to my parents—

"Mila?" Mom asks, putting an arm around my shoulders. "Are you okay?"

"Yes," I sniff, "this is just a lot."

"Let's eat something," Dad says cheerily, though his smile doesn't reach his eyes. "We need to celebrate our two courageous children." He stands, and the rocking chair swings back, almost hitting the wall.

"Or incredibly stupid," Alek says, and Dad reaches down to rustle his hair.

"Not stupid," he says. "Never stupid."

CHAPTER 16

"Hey, Zayn," Alek says, waving a hand as I trail reluctantly behind him.

Zayn stands, his shirt tied around his waist and his skin slick with sweat. He holds a hand up to block the sun and squints in our direction.

"Alek, what's going on?" he asks, reaching down to pick up a metal canister. He lifts it to his lips and takes a drink.

"Can you take a break for a minute? We had something we wanted to talk with you about."

"Oh, hey, Mila," Zayn says, appraising me. "I didn't see you there."

I look away, shoving my hands in my pockets. He motions toward a shaded area next to the house. We follow him past the garden rows and sit on a couple of stumps set haphazardly in the sand.

"What are you planting today?" Alek asks.

Zayn raises an eyebrow. "Doesn't matter. Just get to the point, man."

I glare at him. He can't even force himself to be amiable for two seconds? I know Alek says he's changed, but I still see that haughty ten-year-old telling us about how his dad was better than ours.

"Fair enough," Alek says, but his jaw flexes. "Mila and I are sick of being forced to choose between living here in a dying town or jumping ship and joining Paradise 3."

Zayn's face hardens at the mention of the Communities. He has good reason to hate them. After his dad spent years doing their dirty work here, they completely cut his legs out from under him. Told him he had to join up or lose everything they'd given him access to. Alejandro—though opportunistic and conceited—has never been one to bend to manipulation. He called their bluff. The only problem was they weren't bluffing.

Zayn sniffs. "Yeah, you and me both. But it's not like we have another option."

"Well," Alek says, "that's not completely true."

Zayn's gaze intensifies. Without blinking, he sweeps his dark hair across his forehead and takes another drink from the canister. His hair isn't as long as Alek's, but it's getting there.

I speak up. "Only half the world's population is in Communities, right? So where is the other half?"

Zayn shrugs, still surly.

"They've got to be somewhere, and we're going to try to find them," I say.

"How?" Zayn asks skeptically. "What if all the free people live across the ocean? You going to row there, Mila?"

My chest tightens, and a knot forms in my throat.

"We're going to travel east," Alek says. "Try to find another free community like ours."

Zayn laughs out loud. "East? How do you know there's anyone east? The Communities are taking over everything, and I don't—"

"Oh enough, Zayn!" I shout, and he looks taken aback. "You don't know anything about this, so don't pretend like we're dumb for bringing it up.

You're right. We don't know exactly where the Communities are at this point, but from the information we've gathered, there's a chance they haven't taken everything out east. We think it's worth a shot."

Zayn stares at me. My heart pounds in my chest, and I can already feel my eyes stinging. It's not like me to get so hot-headed, but with him? Just once I'd love to hear him say we knew better than he did. To admit that we might be a step ahead.

I stand up and brush Alek's shoulder. "C'mon. I told you this was a waste of time."

Alek stands hesitantly, then gives a courteous wave before following me back to the path.

"Mila!" he yells, "Slow down!"

I march forward, wiping the tears from my face before he can see them. Conflict makes me weepy, and I don't want to give Alek yet another reason to view me as his weak baby sister.

"Why did you jump all over him like that?"

"Are you serious?" I say, slowing slightly. "He wasn't willing to listen to anything! He's never willing to listen to anyone but himself."

"You don't know that, Mila. You gave him approximately two seconds before you shut him down."

"Yeah, because I knew where it was headed."

"Is that you, Mila?" a voice calls, and I look up. Zayn. I didn't even know he remembered my name.

"I'm fine," I say, but the fact that I'm sitting on the ground with my hand wrapped around my ankle doesn't breed confidence in my statement.

Zayn walks closer, and I can't help but notice how much he's changed in the past year. Being two-and-a-half years apart didn't feel that different when he was eleven and I was nine. Now at twelve and ten, it feels like we don't even exist in the same universe. I turn away from him, suddenly feeling self-conscious in my small, spindly body next to his more developed frame.

"Can I help?" he asks, and already my defenses are up. The last time he and his dad offered to 'help,' we were left without any electricity.

It was years ago, yes, but it hurt my parents deeply—which meant it left a gaping wound in my own heart. You can't watch your family suffer and not begin to feel resentment toward the people who caused it. I'm not naive enough to believe Zayn's dad was the root of it all—I know the Communities are the real villain here. But he was a part of it. And he has a face I know.

"You're not going to answer me?" he asks, scuffing the dirt with his right foot.

"I'm just letting my foot rest."

"Did you fall?"

"Landed funny," I say, pointing to a tree.

"You were climbing that?" he asks skeptically.

I jut out my chin. "I like climbing."

"Mila, you know we have limited medical supplies, right?"

I nod, and my heart begins to pound.

"So as much as you like climbing, it's probably not smart."

I swallow hard, unable to speak. I'm already sitting in the dirt wishing I didn't have to tell my parents what happened. The last thing I need is to have someone rub my nose in it.

"Thanks for the tip," I spit.

Zayn puts his hands on his hips. "I'm not trying to—"

"Got it," I say, cutting him off. "I'm fine, thanks."

Zayn stands there, and I silently plead for him to walk away and leave me alone. Eventually, I hear his footsteps retreating. That's when the tears begin to fall.

Alek raises an eyebrow. "You're psychic now?"

"No," I sniff, "but it's always the same thing with him. He has to be right. You'd argue our points, and he'd continue to tell us how ridiculous it is. I didn't feel like listening to that today."

"Hey," a voice calls gruffly, and Alek spins around. Zayn jogs up the path toward us, his obnoxiously well-formed chest muscles jolting each time a foot hits the ground.

I cross my arms protectively in front of me and roll my eyes.

"Keep me in the loop," he says, coming to a stop in front of Alek.

Alek nods.

"You could say you're sorry first," I say under my breath.

"For what?" he asks, throwing his hands out. "For pointing out the obvious?"

"Hey," Alek says, holding up his hands between us. "Mila, you need to apologize, too. *Both* of you need to apologize. Zayn, don't be rude to my sister. If we're going to work together, you need to listen and share your opinions in a way that doesn't make her feel attacked."

Zayn stares at him, his face blank.

Alek turns on me. "Mila, you're going to have to get rid of whatever weird negative feelings you have about Zayn's family and the Communities. We don't have many people left here. We need each other."

. . .

"Everyone, please, quiet down," Dad says, standing at the front of the room. It's May of 2160 and my birthday is in two weeks, but right now it doesn't feel like we have much to celebrate.

"We don't know how long this drought will last," Neia says as people settle into their seats. She's older than most adults here, and people tend to listen to her opinion. "We need to petition the Communities for irrigation support. That or food stores, one of the two."

Dad runs his hand across his bald head and sighs. "We've tried that before. I don't expect to get a different result this time around."

Dempsey—one of the men who works with Dad—speaks up. "We could try getting the word out to leaders higher up. Go above P3 leaders."

"Alejandro," Dad says, turning to Zayn's father. "Do you think that would be possible? Do you think it would make a difference?"

The way Dad speaks to him makes my blood boil. I'd never say it out loud, but Alejandro in no way deserves our calm words after hitching his wagon to the Communities like he did. Taking their handouts and upgrades— watching the rest of us suffer while he pretended to be advocating for us. Who knows. Maybe he really thought he was doing the right thing.

Alejandro grunts and shakes his head.

Dad nods slowly. "That's what I thought."

The rest of the meeting is filled with ideas, counter-ideas, and expressions of frustration without anyone ever reaching an actionable conclusion. Pretty much how every meeting like this goes these days. And yet some- how, we're all still here—what's left of us.

When people begin to stand and stretch their legs, I follow suit. "Is it over?" I ask Alek as he rises next to me.

"What, you weren't paying attention?"

I shrug. "For most of it."

Alek shakes his head. "No, it's not over. We're just taking a small break."

My body deflates. I wanted to go to the beach after this. "Do you think Dad would notice if I snuck out?"

Alek grins conspiratorially. "Not if you pretend you're sick or something. Do you need me to come along? Just in case you get sicker?"

"Definitely," *I laugh. We make our way to the back of the small room just in time to hear Neia talking to Alejandro who's standing in the doorway, blocking our exit. Zayn and his friend Tam stand to the side looking disinterested.*

"I'm saying we're not going to survive," *Neia says, her hands gesturing emphatically.* "At this point, I believe we're down to the people who are going to stay. I don't think there are any more deserters, would you agree?"

Alejandro nods, his eyes darting to the side, looking for the same escape we are.

"Once we figure out a solution for all this—and I have no doubt we will—we're going to need to discuss procreation."

Alejandro snorts, then chokes on his spit, coughing into his elbow for almost a solid minute.

"What are you talking about?" *he says finally, his voice hoarse and his eyes watering.*

"If we don't start increasing our population, the Communities won't have to do anything to keep us out of their hair. We'll be doing it to ourselves."

"So...you're suggesting we force people to—"

"Encourage, Alejandro. Not force. Before the industrial revolution, people were marrying and having babies by the time they were fifteen," *Neia says, and my face blanches.* "If our life expectancy continues to go down, we're going to have to adjust or the Real world won't exist past the next few generations, if that."

Alejandro, looks to his son, his face reddening.

"Can we just sneak past him?" I whisper, becoming impatient. I know the meeting's about to start up again soon, and the sand and waves are calling my name.

Alek nods, and we walk forward quickly with our heads down. We pass Neia and are just about to skirt past Alejandro's right arm when I hear my name.

"Like take Mila for example," Neia says.

I turn reflexively and immediately regret it.

"You're how old now?" she asks.

Alek isn't next to me anymore, and I see Dad beginning to make his way to the front of the room.

"Seventeen," I say hastily.

"Seventeen," Neia repeats, "and she's got wide birthing hips—a strong disposition. We don't have many young women still capable of repro- ducing here, but if they're fit as a fiddle like her—"

Zayn and Tam snigger, and my cheeks redden. With Neia still going on about the theoretical logistics behind this life-or-death proposal, I finally take my exit. But not before I hear Tam whisper, "It's too bad she'd never be able to find someone who'd want to get with her. Even if we are the last Real people on earth."

I freeze, and my eyes flash their direction. Just in time to catch Zayn laughing along with him.

"Mila?" Alek raises an eyebrow, and I close my mouth. "Can we be adults and start fresh, please?"

Turning to Zayn, I take a deep breath, refusing to let him see the hurt welling up inside me.

"Why do you even want to know more if it's such a terrible idea?" I ask.

Zayn stands stock-still, watching me curiously. I stare him down, and eventually he looks away, shuffling his feet in the dirt.

"Because everything's terrible here," he growls. "Living here is terrible. Joining the Communities is terrible. This idea *is* terrible, but at least there could be a slight chance of...I don't know, something."

I bite my lip.

He continues, "I don't have anything left here, anyway, so if we all die, it's no skin off my back."

"Your *dad* is still here," I say sharply.

Zayn lifts his head, and his nostrils flare.

"We'll keep you updated," Alek says quickly. "Thanks." He grabs my shoulders in frustration and turns me back toward the path.

The words 'I'm sorry'—soft and low—float on the air behind us, and I whip around to see if I heard what I thought I did. But all I see is Zayn's back as he jogs toward his house.

Twenty minutes later, we're walking down another street I avoid regularly. The houses are run down and mostly abandoned. Except for this one.

"She's home," Alek insists, walking up to the door of Kaye's house. "Where else would she be?"

"I don't know. The place just looks...completely abandoned," I say, taking in the dilapidated porch and broken front window. "She's not alone, is she?"

Alek shrugs. "Shouldn't be. Her parents are still in good health as far as I know."

We walk up the sagging steps and Alek raps his knuckles against the door. No answer. Something catches my eye, and I gasp. A small, heart-shaped leaf is standing at attention, as if reaching for pure rays of sunshine through the hazy atmosphere.

"How—?" I whisper, reaching out a tentative finger to brush the brilliantly green stalk.

The door creaks open, and I quickly stand up. Kaye stands in the doorway, looking even thinner than when I saw her last. Her hair hangs limply against her cheeks, and her eyes look almost vacant. She steps out onto the porch and closes the door, not wanting the good air to escape.

"Kaye," Alek says, his voice hushed. Even through his mask, I can see his mouth open slightly. I know the thoughts running through his head because they're the same ones running through mine. *Have you been eating? Where are your parents? Are you sick?*

He clears his throat. "Mila and I came by to talk to you about..." he searches for the words, "—about leaving. Traveling to find people outside the Communities where we could be a part of a societal group again."

I scrutinize Kaye's face, but she gives nothing away.

"We don't really know what we're getting into," Alek chuckles. "It's going to be an adventure." He looks down at his hands, resting on the splintered porch railing. "With everything that's happened, we thought —" he stops short, and his eyebrows furrow.

"We thought you might want to come along," I say, stepping closer to Alek.

Kaye's eyes shift to mine, and she blinks.

"If you're interested, come by anytime, and we can talk more, okay?" I say. Flashing her a smile, it's my turn to flip Alek around and walk down the steps, completely forgetting to show him the miracle I'd just witnessed in the dirt next to us.

CHAPTER 17

"It was growing," I say with excitement. "Right there with no help from anyone."

Dad's smile is wide. "You saw this yesterday? At Kaye's?"

I nod.

"Want to show me later?"

"Absolutely." I reach past him to pull a cup from the shelf. "It's probably just a weed or something."

"Doesn't matter—life is life. And for a seed or root particle to remain dormant for this long? And grow without human intervention? Incredible."

"We knew things would start to come back eventually, right?" I grin.

Dad sits at the table and takes a long drink of water, wiping his forehead with the sleeve of his grey work shirt.

"We knew conditions would eventually improve so plants could naturally grow again, but as far as I know, nobody has predicted whether they would this soon. Think about it Mila," he says, leaning forward. "We're over six thousand miles from Campi Flegrei, and our plant life was still wiped out completely."

"But that was caused by ash distribution, Dad, not being buried in lava flow. Wind patterns carry that stuff over the whole planet. It doesn't matter how far away we were when it went off."

Dad nods thoughtfully. "True. And that eruption changed the temperature of the planet, which then also changed the wind patterns—the ongoing ramifications are nearly impossible to calculate."

"Especially without the Edge."

Dad nods. "Someone out there probably has very helpful information that would tell us what to expect over the next decade or so." He grins mischievously. "And I think you and Alek are going to find them."

My heart beats faster. "You do?"

He smiles sadly. "You two are right, Mila. We can't stay here and bury our heads in the sand until we get desperate enough to do whatever the Communities tell us."

I sit next to him, and clench my hands into fists to warm my fingertips. "I'm scared, Dad."

"You should be!" he says with a guttural laugh. "If you weren't terrified by this, I'd be worried about you."

"Well, that's...comforting?" I laugh with him, grateful for the distraction from my thoughts.

I don't know how Dad can look at these things so positively, but I'm certain that's been the key to our survival. As a kid, I didn't have a clue we were struggling. Dad had a smile on his face when he walked into the house after finding out our support from the Communities was ending. When Alek ranted about how unjust the situation was, Dad had calmly replied it was 'an opportunity' to problem solve. To hear him say he doesn't have a solution for this and he now needs my help? The weight of it nearly bowls me over.

Most of the time, this adventure of ours seems like a fantasy. Most of the time I can pretend that things are going to get better on their own—or Dad does have a solution—and we won't need to hike across unknown territory virtually blind. Most of the time.

It's day two of twenty, and Mom's already gone through four houses on our street. So far she's found an extra life watch, three bags of various nutrition packets that likely reached their expiration years ago, plenty of water filters, and two different solar lights.

Dad's working on retrofitting used materials from the gardens into backpacks so we can carry everything comfortably. They've both put their regular responsibilities on hold for now, but I know that can't last. Which means Alek and I need to step it up.

I walk around the back of a house down the street. I don't even remember who lived here—it's been that long. Mom probably does. She seems to have an entire catalog in her brain of all the people who've left, and it seems purposeful the way she brings them up in casual conversation. 'Do you remember Caius? He had the most obnoxious laugh,' she'll say fondly, and I'll read the subtext. *Do you remember Caius? Really remember him? Because he's theirs now, and his family history and legacy has been erased—mashed into something small and insignificant so he can integrate. His Realness lies with us now, and we have a responsibility to keep him alive. To keep all of them alive.*

It's exhausting.

Not seeing anything useful in the backyard, I move to the house itself. I try the handle on the back door, and it swings easily—if creakily—on its hinges. Right now, I'm looking for anything that could be used for shelter, which is a tall order. Something that's lightweight, waterproof, large enough for both of us to sleep comfortably under—or I guess possibly four of us, I realize and groan. The last thing I want to do is sleep anywhere near Zayn.

It's barely mid-morning, and I'm already sweating. Maybe it's just because I'm getting older, but I don't remember spring ever feeling this hot before.

Opening the back door, I walk in and begin searching the closets. The first bedroom is empty. The second one has a couple of beat-up pairs of shoes. They're much too small for either of us, and the soles are worn down enough that even if they were, we wouldn't want to take them. But seeing them makes me think: we should probably have Dad make us each an extra pair in case ours wear out. He's probably already thought of that.

Moving to the main living space, I spot one more door near the entrance. I look inside only to find a few ratty coats hanging on wooden hooks. Above them on a shelf, something catches my eye, and I reach up to retrieve it. The external material is slippery—probably waterproof—and excitement sparks within me. I open up the folded square, and it crinkles. The interior fabric is shiny—almost metallic—and the whole sheet is slightly longer than my body and almost twice as wide. I have no idea what this was used for, but it's got to be perfect for a shelter. As long as I can find more of them.

I rush excitedly out the door, silently pleading for this not to be a one-time find. I methodically search the next house, then the next. By the time my stomach begins to rumble around midday, I've found three more of the metallic sheets, and I couldn't be more thrilled.

I run as fast as I can with contraband in tow down the street to our house, and Alek sees me coming.

"What's all that?" he asks as I get close.

"I have no idea," I laugh, breathless.

He reaches out and opens the folds in the material. "These are perfect." He looks surprised, and I smile smugly.

I yank them out of his grasp. "Yeah, I know. That's why I grabbed them."

"Do you think they'll be big enough?"

"Not on their own, but if I sew them together, I think they'll work. It would be nice if I could find two more. I'll check back behind Kaye's house after lunch."

Alek nods, impressed. "Good job."

His praise is hard to come by, but when it does come, it feels richly deserved. I grin, then rush past him into the house to show Dad my finds.

CHAPTER 18

WE'RE AT DAY TEN, and—as expected—we've hit a few bumps in the road. The solar chargers are ancient, and the panels are inefficient. That's on top of the fact that the amount of sunlight penetration through the ashy air these days is still only at about fifty percent. I say 'only,' but that's quite the incredible number. The fact that I can be outside and not freeze to death like my ancestors? Mind-blowing. But it still doesn't improve our charging situation.

Even after cleaning the panels and tuning them up the best we can, they're still taking an exorbitantly long time to charge. Which means we won't be able to track our progress as expected. We can charge them all day while we sleep, then use them during the night as we travel and hope they last long enough to give us intelligible data. Mom and Dad don't seem too worried about this, but I'm a nervous wreck. If we can't track anything...we won't have enough information to find our way back to them.

Dad insists that once we find other Real people, they'll be able to point us back here, but I'm not convinced we'll get that far.

"Here, Mila, try this," Alek says, handing me my pack.

I squat and lift it from the floor, laboriously swinging it onto my back and threading my opposite arm through the strap.

"Better?"

"Maybe. Slightly? I still don't see how I'm going to hike in this."

"Well, I don't see how I can get it any lighter. I'm already carrying—"

"No, Alek, I'm not blaming you. I feel bad. I'm weak, and I'm going to majorly slow you down." I slip the strap off my shoulder and carefully lower the pack to the ground.

Alek obnoxiously messes up my hair. "No, you're not. You know why?"

I raise my eyebrow, smoothing my locks back into place.

"Because we're going to work up to it. C'mon."

"What do you mean we're going to work up to it?"

Alek pushes me to the front door, then turns. "Wait here."

He retreats back to our workspace, and I hear him rustling around.

I call out, "Alek, what do you mean by—"

He pops back into the hall before I can finish—easily carrying my pack in one arm—and I put a hand on my hip.

"You don't have to show off, you know," I mutter.

"Here," he laughs, "put it on."

He hands it to me, and his brief disappearance suddenly makes sense.

"You removed almost everything," I say, raising an eyebrow.

"Not even close. There's still plenty of weight in there. Five miles each day. We'll increase the weight by five kilograms each time until you get to the target weight."

"That's a lot of 'fives' in one sentence."

"It felt right," he grins. "You can do it, Mila. And Zayn and I will come with you—"

I grimace.

"Oh c'mon. He's going to be traveling with us. You better get used to it."

"He doesn't even *need* to train, though. Why does he have to come with us? I could at least put off spending time with him for ten more days," I complain.

Alek laughs. "Are you kidding? He might look like solid muscle, but walking long distances with a weighted pack on your shoulders is a whole new breed of fitness. He's used to lifting and hauling, not traveling."

I adjust the strap on my hips. "Tomorrow, then. I'm not ready for that today."

"Suit yourself," he grins. "Have a good solo walk."

I wave, grab my mask, and quickly step outside before he can change his mind.

Cool water from our filtered barrel in the backyard pours over my head and down my body. I quickly rinse the soap off my skin in the ten seconds I have before I need to hit the pump handle again. We haven't had much rain in the past few weeks, so I work fast. I can totally make this a three-pump shower.

My five-mile walk was easier *and* harder than expected. Easier because I didn't really notice the pack after the first mile. Harder because I *did* start to notice my feet about halfway through. Even now, the sides of my big toe throb. Apparently, being on my feet all day is not the same as walking long distances. Point one for Alek.

I close my eyes as I scrub my scalp, then hit the pump for my final rinse.

"No, that's over here. Let me show you," I hear Alek say from somewhere behind me.

My eyes fly open as I peer between the wooden slats that barely cover my body from being seen by the outside world. Alek is walking toward this side of the house. *With Zayn.*

"I downloaded everything I could from that console," Zayn says, thankfully still watching the ground in front of him.

Hurriedly, I rinse the rest of the soap from my hair and wring it out when the water stops, then frantically reach for my towel. I stand still—barely breathing in the hopes they'll pass without noticing me.

Zayn looks up and immediately locks eyes with mine between the boards. Crap. He stops, and I turn, pretending not to have noticed him. I hear Alek's footsteps stop a few meters from the pump house.

His face is next to the boards. "Mila? What are you—"

"I just got back from my training," I hiss. "Why would you bring him out here when I'm washing up?"

"I didn't know you were here," Alek whispers apologetically. "We can go around the other way."

I hold the fabric tight to my chest, shivering.

"Hey, Zayn, I didn't realize Mila was out here. Let's go check out the shelters she just finished."

"Shelters? As in, there's more than one?" Zayn asks.

"Yep, she made two—"

"It'll be a lot safer if we all stay together. Both for warmth and protection. Splitting up into two groups increases our risk."

I step out from behind the boards, still clutching my towel fiercely and my eyes flashing. "That might be so, but it's an even bigger risk for me not to have space away from *people* while we're on this trek."

Alek gapes at me.

Zayn's eyes go wide, but he quickly recovers, folding his arms across his chest. "So. You're willing to risk freezing to death rather than be slightly uncomfortable for the five minutes before you fall asleep?"

My blood boils. "We're not going to freeze to death—"

"You don't know that! I've been looking at maps for the past few days, and there are plenty of areas of elevation gain. Do you understand what happens at higher elevations?" Zayn looks at me patronizingly.

My cheeks flush.

"We'll discuss and figure out what makes the most sense," Alek says, putting a hand on Zayn's shoulder and turning him back the way they came.

I watch them go, my body shaking. Turning on my heel, I stomp into the house.

CHAPTER 19

TOMORROW IS DAY TWENTY. It's *tomorrow*. I've been playing the morning of day twenty over and over in my head for the past two weeks. Alek and I will meet in the pitch-black at three in the morning in the kitchen. We'll eat a big meal that Mom cooks for us. She'll be tired—her hair will be disheveled and she'll yawn and rub her eyes after she sets our food on the table. Because she'll want to make sure we're full, she and Dad will be giving up their meals until dinner time.

Alek and I will put our carefully prepared packs on our backs and meet Zayn at the front door. I cringe, but only slightly at that thought. He hasn't been quite as obnoxious over the past few days, and some of his ideas have been good ones. *Some* of them. Kaye might be there with him. She might not. We still haven't gotten a firm commitment out of her, and I doubt we will until we open the door in the middle of the night.

And then we'll start walking.

After making our last harvest, Alek and I squeeze ourselves onto Mom and Dad's bed, forcing them to sandwich together in the middle. Dad laughs, and Mom smacks Alek as he jostles her while trying to steal some of her pillow space.

"We have to wake up in five hours! Leave us alone!" Mom crows, attempting to shove him off the side of the bed. Alek wraps his arms around her and snuggles close, despite her complaints. She finally relents.

It's much calmer on my side. Dad wraps an arm around me as I lie on his shoulder.

"Heading to bed, you two?" he asks.

"Doesn't look like it," Mom mutters.

"Yeah," I sigh, ignoring her.

"Everything's ready?"

"Mmhmm." I take a deep breath, savoring the scent that is uniquely my dad's. This is where I'd come when nightmares wrested me from sleep, or when anxieties gripped me so tightly, I couldn't fall asleep in the first place. Dad was always there, pulling me close and telling me it would all be okay.

Tears form at the corner of my eyes, and I can't keep them from spilling over.

"We have everything ready to go by the front door," Alek says.

Mom is surprisingly quiet. I glance over at her, surreptitiously flicking a tear from my cheek as I do so.

Her face is pinched together, and she's holding the bridge of her nose with her thumb and forefinger.

"Mom?" I say softly.

She shakes her head. Alek rubs her shoulder gently.

"I can't do this," she whispers, her eyes still closed.

I look at Alek, not sure what to say or do. Watching Mom break feels almost unbearable—I want to call the whole thing off and accept my lonely fate, just so I don't have to endure this one moment.

"I won't be okay until I know you're safe and we're together again," she says, sucking in a breath.

"I know," I nod. "Us either. We don't want to make you sad like this—"

"It's okay, Mila," Dad says, stroking my hair like he did when I was little. "Sadness is a good thing. It shows how much love has been built between us. And it will only make our reunion that much sweeter."

Mom nods, wiping her cheeks. "I thought I could keep you here forever and avoid ever having to say goodbye to my babies." She grins sheepishly.

Alek sits up. "Good thing I'm not a baby anymore." He flexes his arm, and Mom rolls her eyes.

"I don't care how big your muscles get—you'll always be my baby boy."

He scoffs, but the smile on his face makes it less than convincing. Mom sits up and hugs him.

"You, too," she says, motioning to me.

Dad and I sit up and add ourselves to their embrace.

"We love you both. And we're so proud of you," Dad says, and his whiskers tickle the top of my ear as his mouth moves.

"We're going to miss you so much," I say, squeezing even tighter.

Eventually, our arms drop, and I sit down on my knees.

Mom takes a deep breath. "Now, seriously—go to bed. You can't walk all that way with only a few hours of sleep."

Alek laughs. "Okay, okay." He hops off the bed, and Mom attempts to fix her side of the blankets. "See you bright and early."

"Early, not bright," Dad chuckles. "Love you." He kisses me on the forehead, and I slide to the floor.

"Love you, too," I say, then follow Alek into the hall.

· · ·

At three o'clock, Alek shakes me awake. Disoriented, I roll over and rub my eyes. It only takes a few seconds for adrenaline to rush through my body, and I sit up.

"Get dressed," Alek says as he leaves the room. No small talk this morning, I guess. I don't blame him. I've only been awake for a minute, and already I'm on edge.

I quickly pull my long-sleeved shirt over my head, slip on my pants and socks, and tie my hair up. Forcing myself to take a deep breath, I stand and grab my shoes and jacket from the floor.

As expected, Mom is already serving up mashed sweet potato, beans, and chicken. Even more special than I anticipated.

My mouth waters as I sit down in front of the steaming plate. This may be the last meat I ingest for weeks. I highly doubt we'll accidentally run into any animals in the wild, and even if we did, we wouldn't know how to catch them. I assume trapping a hen in a small, airtight shelter is slightly easier than capturing one in the wild.

Mom yawns and leans against the counter.

"Are you going to eat?" I ask between bites.

"Eat as much as you can, Mila," she says seriously. "Don't worry about us."

Dad opens the back door and walks in. "I wrapped these eggs individually. I hope they'll last."

"Thanks, Dad," Alek says. "I'll keep them on top of my pack so they don't get crushed."

Dad nods and claps him on the shoulder, setting the sack on the table.

It's silent in the kitchen as Alek and I shovel forkfuls of food into our mouths. Even though we eat quickly, I savor every bite. It's impossible to imagine not eating Mom's cooking again—at least for the short term. I have to keep reminding myself we're not leaving forever.

A knock sounds at the door, and Alek rises from his chair.

"I'll get it," Dad says. "Finish your meal."

I glance at Alek, but he doesn't look up. I can't believe we're actually doing this. I can't believe we didn't do this sooner. I'm empowered, excited, and so terrified I might pass out.

"Zayn and Kaye are at the door," Dad announces.

"Kaye's here?" I ask, my voice low so it won't carry past the kitchen.

He nods with a smile.

"Thanks, Mom," Alek says, handing her his empty dish. "I love you." He hugs her tightly, then takes one last drink of water from his cup on the table. He nods toward my food. "Taking your sweet time."

"I'm going as fast as I can."

"I'll wait outside with the others. Just hurry up, okay?"

I roll my eyes. If he bosses me around like this the whole trip, I doubt I'll survive.

"Take your time," Mom says gently. "He's just nervous."

I chew and swallow as quickly as I can until my plate is empty, then clear my place setting. Mom waits patiently, leaning against the counter.

"Love you, Mom." I breathe her in as she holds me close. "See you *soon*."

Mom nods, and her eyes shimmer.

Not wanting to make our goodbye more painful than it already is, I smile and walk quickly toward the front door. Dad stands to the side holding my pack.

"Let me help you," he offers, lifting the straps so I can easily slip my arms through the holes.

"Love you, Dad."

"Be safe, Mila. Be strong." He wraps his arms around my back and nearly knocks the breath out of me.

"I will, I promise." I step back and look at our home one last time. I see the chairs Dad built for us when our old ones broke. The bunches of nearly dried herbs hanging from the ceiling. The old filtration unit humming in the corner, louder than it should be. This house provided for us my whole life. I have to trust it will continue to provide until we return.

"I believe in you," Dad whispers.

"I know."

CHAPTER 20

ALEK AND ZAYN walk ahead of Kaye and me. I can't help but feel slightly perturbed by their immediate assumption that they're leading the charge. It's true; they've spent more time examining the maps than I have. And they're older. But still. They could've asked.

"I'm glad you came," I say to Kaye. I can barely see her outline in my peripheral vision. It's dark, and I don't want to tear my focus away from the ground in front of me.

"Me, too," she says, and I nearly stumble on a rock. Hoping she didn't notice my reaction to her response, I clear my throat.

"What made you decide to join us?" I ask nonchalantly.

"There's nothing left for me at home." Her voice is higher than mine and yet somehow more weighed down. I can almost hear her grief in every syllable.

I nod. "Seems like that's a common sentiment these days."

Ahead of us, Zayn's silhouette in the moonlight gestures animatedly, and I immediately tune in to their conversation.

"I really think we should keep a northeastern course," he says. "The closer we are to the Communities, the more likelihood of finding supplies."

"I thought we already agreed on our path?" Alek says.

"We did, but I've been thinking about it the past few days. It doesn't feel right to me."

Alek laughs. "Doesn't *feel* right?"

"Whatever. You know what I mean. It doesn't seem smart. If we get stuck in the desert with no water—" he stops mid-sentence and steps over a boulder in the path.

"I know it's a risk, but being that close to Paradise 1 seems worse. Especially because those boundaries have most likely changed. If we go too far north, we'll run right into it."

"Ahem," I say obnoxiously. "Do you think it might be appropriate to include Kaye and myself in this conversation?"

Alek and Zayn are silent for a moment.

"You're right," Alek says. "You've looked at the maps. What do you think?"

"I think we spent far too long scouring that information and coming up with a plan to throw that away now and change course."

Zayn snorts.

"I'm not saying it's a bad idea," I hedge, sounding more diplomatic than I feel, "but I don't think it's smart to switch things up this early. We need better information."

"So what if that information is 'hey, there's no food or water, you're all going to die a slow, painful death,'" Zayn says.

"We have enough food supplies for weeks. I know we'll have to replace our water, but don't you think we'll have a little bit of a heads up? We can shift course then."

"She's not wrong," Alek says.

"We'll see," Zayn says as he picks up his pace.

"Positive as usual," I mutter, but the fact that he didn't argue with me feels like a win, and I'm claiming it.

The darkness slowly begins to fade a few hours later. I obsessively tilt my mask to check the numbers. If I'm being honest, that's the link in this chain that worries me the most. With only two extras per person, we don't have much margin for error. I have to remind myself that I've used masks for years in the past without any problem. There's no reason to think any of ours will malfunction over the course of just a few months.

Red and orange light bathes the landscape around us. Though hazy, the air isn't ashy at all today—a perfect morning. It feels like a sign.

"How far are we going?" Kaye asks, and I realize she hasn't been included in any of our planning meetings. I watch her—walking along, following people she barely knows without any prior knowledge of our plans—and I'm astounded. Would I have been willing to upend my life for some stranger's crazy idea? Maybe if I was all alone. I shudder, imagining my life without Mom, Dad, and Alek.

Alek speaks up. "We're planning to walk until noon. Then we'll sleep and start again around nine-thirty when it's dark."

"But how far?" she asks softly.

"We're not quite sure," I answer. "Our goal is to cover thirty miles per day, but we have no idea if that's reasonable. Something to shoot for."

Kaye nods, gripping the straps of the backpack Dad made for her. "I've never been this far away from home."

Her statement is heartbreaking. I try to laugh it off. "Me neither. It kind of looks the same so far. Rocks, dirt...more rocks."

Kaye smiles, and for a moment, her eyes seem more alive than I've ever seen them. I don't want to push my luck, but I have so many questions for her. And we've got nothing else to do but talk.

As the boys get a little further ahead of us, I pluck up my courage.

"Why did you always stay inside your house?" I ask hesitantly. "There aren't many kids our age around anymore. It would've been nice to have someone else to get together with."

Kaye focuses hard on Alek's back ahead of us. "Being around people..." she starts hesitantly. "People make me nervous."

"I get that."

"No, you don't," she says, and it takes me off-guard. We start up a slight incline, and my breathing deepens.

"I guess that's true," I say. "I'm around my family all the time. But I do understand feeling stressed by people. I do have Alek as a brother."

Kaye laughs at this, and Alek turns slightly at the sound of his name.

I continue, "And I could see why it would be less than motivating to get to know new people. Everyone leaves."

Kaye's lips purse, and I wonder if she's thinking about Paul.

I change topics. "What do you do during the day? When you're inside, I mean?"

Kaye doesn't answer. She doesn't even look my direction. Great. Me and my big mouth. This won't be awkward at all for the next few hours.

"Alek," I call, "what's our mileage so far?"

We decided ahead of time to only use one life watch at a time, and it's his turn to wear it.

"Oh, I should get out the panels," he says, reaching over his back. "Zayn, hold up a second." He slips the pack from his shoulders and quickly unfolds a slim set of charging panels, affixing them to the top of his bag.

"Might be a good time to get a snack anyway," Zayn says.

Agreeing heartily, Kaye and I drop our packs to the ground and search for something to eat.

"Seven miles," Alek says.

I look up at him.

"That's how far we've gone."

"Wow, that's more than I expected," I say, pulling out a soft corn tortilla and reorganizing the small bags of dried insects below it to make sure all of the perishable items are more accessible first.

"The terrain's been mostly flat," Zayn says, chewing. "We won't always be so lucky."

I sigh. Any hopes I had for a more positive outlook from him once we started our journey are quickly crushed.

"Do you think it'll charge?" I ask, looking to Alek.

"It seemed to work when I tried it at home. It doesn't charge as quickly when the watch is on, obviously, but I figure every little bit helps."

I nod and take a quick sip of water. "Ready?"

Kaye nods, and Zayn has already started along the path. Instead of walking ahead to join him, Alek stays back with us. With Kaye giving me the silent treatment, I've never been more grateful.

CHAPTER 21

THE SUN IS DIRECTLY OVERHEAD when we stop for the day. My legs are appreciative of the break but not nearly as sore as I expected. We hit the twenty-one-mile mark fifteen minutes ago, and that was with some altitude gain in the last hour. I want to rub that little nugget in Zayn's face, but when I see him grimacing as he sits down on the dirt, I think better of it. It's time for dinner. Then we'll put up our shelters.

"Good job, everyone," I say cheerily. "Day one down."

"Only a hundred more to go," Alek grins.

"Thanks for that. Very inspiring," I say, pulling out sliced vegetables and a rice ball with coconut meat in the center. Zayn must be rubbing off on him.

Kaye pulls off her mask and takes a bite of what looks like a deep green burrito, and my curiosity gets the better of me.

"What's that?" I ask.

She chews and swallows. "Seaweed. And palm fruit."

I can't hide my disgust, and Alek laughs. "It's supposed to be good for you, you know," he says.

"Seaweed?"

Alek nods.

"We use it for fertilizer for a reason," I say, wrinkling my nose.

"Hey, it's the one plant we can always count on these days," Alek says, putting a piece of pepper in his mouth.

"Not for long," Zayn mutters, and I flash him a look. "What? It's true," he continues. "As more sunlight penetrates our atmosphere, the earth's temperature is returning to where it was before the eruption. Eventually, the oceans will be too warm for it to grow near us."

I jump in. "When there's that much sun available, that means the air will be cleaner, which means we'll have other plants available to us anyway. Nobody here will have to eat gross seaweed."

"Mila," Alek gives me a patronizing look, "you know entire cultures have used seaweed in their diets, right? For thousands of years? You're being very insulting."

I still can't hide my revulsion.

"Do you want to try a bite?" Kaye asks, holding out a piece.

"Nope, I'm good."

She shrugs, and gratefully keeps it for herself.

My back aches as Kaye, and I carefully clear the rocks away from a two-meter by four-meter area for our shelter. We already successfully attached our sheet between a couple of large rocks, giving us enough room to slide in underneath. My eyelids feel heavy despite the daylight, and I can't wait to lie down.

Kicking a couple of large pebbles aside, I roll out my mat and test it out. Although the ground is hard, there aren't any obvious spots of discomfort. Kaye rolls hers out next to mine, and we situate our packs near our feet. I pull out the small pillow Mom made for me and set it at the top of my mat.

"Good?" I ask, and Kaye nods. We stand and roll out the end of our shelter sheet, using a rock to stake it at the base the best we can. It's not as stable as I'd like it, and we really only have a foot of space above our heads, but at this point, I really don't care. It's covering us and our packs from the elements. As long as the wind doesn't kick up, we'll be fine.

Satisfied, I stand and walk away from our camp, looking for a place to relieve myself before I sleep. I'm still not used to dropping my pants in broad daylight. It felt much more comfortable in the middle of the night. Having no other option, I quickly squat.

Just as I finish and pull up my pants, I hear a sound to my right.

"What is it with you and your complete lack of respect for privacy?" I say harshly, quickly doing up my button.

Zayn blinks at me. "I'm sorry, I didn't know—"

My face flushes, and I stomp past him. I know it isn't his fault, but I'm too embarrassed and too tired to apologize for my outburst. Besides, it's probably a good thing for him to take a moment to think about someone other than his self-absorbed self. At least that's how I justify my rude behavior, and for the moment, it's working.

I don't see Alek when I walk back into camp, and I can't take any time to look for him. My head is blurry—I'm fading fast. Without hesitation, I crawl into my shelter, adjust my pillow, and finally close my eyes.

Something rustles beside me, and I jerk awake, gasping as my face hits the shelter overhead. My breathing regulates as I regain my bearings. The air is calm and cool, and I reach for the jacket I set next to my pillow. Pulling it with me, I cautiously crawl out from under the sheet and brush myself off, then put it on and zip it up.

Clicking on the small light that's clipped to my pants, I look around. Alek's shelter is still. I have no idea what time it is, but at least it's dark. We may need to put a life watch in each tent at night, just so we can make sure we sleep long enough. It's going to take some time to switch our circadian rhythms.

"Hey," a voice whispers, and I jump, whipping my head to the left. Zayn's face looks ghostly in the white beam of my light. He puts his hand up to block his eyes, and I lower it.

"Do you know what time it is?" I ask, moving closer so I can keep my voice low.

"About nine-fifteen." He flashes his wrist.

"I don't think you should be using that before we start. Who knows how long the charge will last."

"I'm only checking the time. I don't think that's going to make much difference."

"I think it might."

He doesn't answer, and I sit down next to him on the dirt.

"Why are you always so contrary?" I ask honestly. "Can't you just once say 'oh, wow, Mila. You're right' or 'that's a great idea,' or even if you can't muster that, you could just nod and disagree internally—without saying it out loud."

"I'm the one who's contrary?" he scoffs. "Okay."

"You are!"

"Speaking of wasting, can you turn off that light?"

My nostrils flare. I click off the light and glare into the darkness. The air is still, besides the sounds of Zayn breathing next to me. I've never been awake to observe the dead of night like this. Without my eyesight, every other sense seems to heighten—straining to find any input in the world around me.

"I'm only trying to help," Zayn says finally. His voice is soft—humble even.

"Help who?" The words tumble out of my mouth before I stop to think about their impact, but I let them stand. I reach my arms over my head and stretch my back as I wait for his answer. I slept soundly, but my bones ache from being on the ground.

When he still doesn't respond, I elaborate. "It's not helpful for me to feel criticized all the time—"

"Wow, Mila. Okay." Even though his voice is barely a whisper, I don't miss the sarcasm.

"Are you serious, Zayn?" I whisper. "I'm trying to tell you how I feel and you—"

"You're attacking me. That's not telling me how you feel."

"I am not! I—"

"I guess we're leaving early?" Alek says beside me, and my head snaps his direction even though I can't see anything.

"No," I say, "I woke up and was waiting—"

"Didn't sound like waiting."

"I was whispering—"

"That's the loudest whispering I've ever heard," Alek says, and I instantly feel guilty.

"I'm sorry—I didn't mean to wake you."

Zayn says nothing, but I can't feel him next to me anymore. Good riddance.

Alek yawns. "Pack up. We may as well get going and end a little earlier in the morning. Eat, go to the bathroom. We'll leave as soon as everyone's ready."

I stand and click the light back on but refuse to look at Zayn. I walk directly to our shelter, and—after making sure Kaye is up—I lean down to pull out the stakes.

CHAPTER 22

I DON'T MIND the lack of conversation tonight. It's day four, and my body still hasn't completely adjusted. Every part of me aches, and it hasn't yet become second nature to be up in the dark. I also didn't fully anticipate how irritated the skin on my face would become from wearing a mask full-time. But we did find a stream yesterday, so at least our water stores are refilled. I'll take a little discomfort over mortal danger anytime.

"Let's stop for a minute," Alek says, his breathing heavy. I stop behind him gratefully, putting my hands on my hips. We've been hiking uphill for hours—my lungs burn, and every inch of me is sticky with sweat. I wipe my brow with the edge of my shirt.

Alek lifts the life watch and taps it. A map hovers in the air above it, and he turns so we can all get a visual.

"We're here," he says, pointing. "We're making fantastic time, which is both a good thing and...well it's a good thing. But we're also getting closer to the potential expansion of Paradise 2 Community faster than I anticipated."

"How close?" Kaye asks. She peers at the map, and I have to remind myself that she's only seen it a handful of times. It probably still seems utterly foreign to her. She hasn't said much the past few days, but was quick to assure me I hadn't hurt her feelings when I asked. It's left us in an uneasy peace.

"Like I said the other day," Alek says, "we don't know if these boundaries are still accurate or if it's doubled in size since this map was made." He taps the watch again, and the image disappears. "We need to be ready for anything. From here on out, we need to be especially cautious."

All of us nod in unison. If we get caught out here and taken into a Community, there's no way we're making it back home. Based on what Mom and Dad have seen, integration for Reals who buck the system isn't optional. Though I'm insanely curious about the Unreal world, that ending feels worse than death at this point. We have to make it home.

I no longer mind that Alek has taken over the role of leader. I'm having a rough enough time keeping myself motivated, let alone trying to motivate and educate everyone else. Alek turns and begins to climb. I groan internally and force myself to follow.

The moonlight is barely visible through the haze, but it lights the land ahead just enough for us to see the remainder of the peak we're heading toward. That ambiguous dark line nearly brings me to tears after the last few hours of strenuous effort. My legs feel like rubber, and my hands have swollen so much, I can barely close them into fists. If I just keep moving, I'll make it. I repeat this in my head as I plod along, slow and steady.

"I can't do this." I hear a low growl behind me. Nearly stumbling, I turn and see Zayn's light—attached to his hip—drop to the ground.

"Hey," I say, staggering back the few paces to crouch next to him. "Did you see the top? We're almost there."

"I can't," he repeats, panting, and I've never heard him sound like this. Not guarded or arrogant, just...broken. Despite the fact that I dislike him —strongly—this is an instance where I find it easy to set those feelings aside. He needs help.

"Zayn, you can. I know how you feel. I don't want to walk another step tonight either, but we have to. It's too cold up here, and the oxygen levels are too low. We have to make it a few thousand feet lower before we can set up camp."

"Just go on without me," he mumbles, resting his head back against a rock.

I squat lower and lift his face in my hands. "Zayn, look at me. We're not leaving you behind—"

"Why not? You didn't even want me here anyway."

He's not wrong. "I didn't want you here because of your attitude, not because I didn't think you were a useful part of the group. Look at you. You're strong, capable. You obviously know how to work hard. I just...wish you'd listen to people sometimes. Or be willing to admit you don't know everything. Or, maybe be kind when people talk about your birthing hips." That last comment I say under my breath, but I doubt Zayn would've caught it anyway. His eyes are closing, and his arm drops to his side.

"Zayn? Zayn! No, it's not time to sleep yet." I gently but firmly pat the sides of his face, careful not to displace his mask. He pulls away from me.

"You're right," he whispers, rolling sideways.

"Okay, nope. Now you're really scaring me. You're not in your right mind."

Kaye runs up next to me, and I look up. "Where's Alek?"

She shrugs.

"Can you help me lift him? We need to get him on his feet."

She nods, and we both reach under his arms. "C'mon," I grunt. "You've got to help us out, Zayn." He's heavier than I thought, nearly dead weight. I shouldn't have been surprised given his height and muscle mass, but still. I gasp with the effort of lifting him from the rock.

"What are we doing?" he mumbles as we sling his arms over our shoulders.

"Walking. We're walking, Zayn. One foot in front of the other. We'll help you."

Kaye and I push slowly up the hill, navigating awkwardly around dead tree trunks and changes in the terrain.

"Everything okay down there?" Alek calls, and I almost laugh. That question would've been helpful a few minutes ago.

"Zayn is struggling," I call, and the effort leaves me breathless.

"On my way!"

Though I can't get a visual, I can hear Alek scrambling back down toward us. I cry out when a rock hits me in the shin, and he changes trajectory, walking more carefully now that he can see our lights.

"Only a bit further to the top," Alek says. "Let me take a turn."

We stop, and Kaye moves readily to the side so Alek can take her place.

"He's probably struggling with the altitude," Alek says. "Let's get him up and over. He'll hopefully recover as we head down the other side."

I nod, unable to answer. We march in silence and don't even pause at the top to celebrate our accomplishment. Without missing a beat, we continue down the other side. I thought it was difficult dragging Zayn's barely responsive body up, but going down is proving to be worse. His weight nearly drags us off our feet—my lower back screams at me as I lean back to compensate.

It's more heavily wooded here, which requires us to slow down and be more intentional about finding a clear path for the three of us. The effort is grueling. Kaye walks in front of us, attempting to lead the way and take some of the mental strain.

Suddenly, the weight on my shoulders seems to lift slightly, and I glance over at Zayn. His eyes are fully open, but his head still lolls with every step.

Almost there, I continue to repeat in my head. You can take one more step because you're almost there. *Almost there.*

I'm not sure exactly when Zayn starts walking on his own, but the second his arm lifts, I collapse to the ground. Crawling toward the nearest log, I take a desperate drink of water—spilling half of it down the front of me—and close my eyes as my body shakes uncontrollably.

It's still light when I wake up. I lift my head, but the sharp pain that shoots through my neck and back forces me to lower it again. This is going to take some effort. Slowly, I roll to my back and stretch my arms and legs in front of me. Blood pounds in my ears as I gradually sit, pressing my palms against the rocky earth to support myself.

As my mind gains clarity, moments from the night before flow into my consciousness. Zayn passing out. Kaye and I carrying him up the slope. Collapsing in the dirt. I scrounge around for my water canister. Finally feeling it against my fingertips, I pick it up and shake. Empty.

"You're up."

My head snaps in the direction of the voice, and I regret the motion immediately. Wincing, I hold my hand to my neck.

Alek hands me a piece of dried meat. "You did good last night."

I take a bite, pulling hard with my teeth on the fibrous strip. "How are you up walking normally?" I groan.

Alek laughs lightly. "I only did one direction."

I take a bite, suddenly ravenous. "Is he alright?"

"Zayn?"

"No, the other guy we're traveling with."

Alek grins. "Sorry. Yeah, he's okay. He's still completely passed out—sleeping. I guess I should clarify."

I laugh, then whimper and press my hands against my ribs.

Alek looks concerned. "I think last night took a lot out of him. And you, by the looks of it. Are *you* okay?"

I nod, swallowing. "I think I'm only partially broken."

Alek pats my back. "At least we're walking completely downhill tonight."

I swallow. "What time is it?"

"Around six-thirty. Sunset should be in an hour, according to the watch."

I take a deep breath and close my eyes until the pounding subsides again.

"Rest up. I can take care of rounding up the others. We'll go as slow as you need."

I want to curl up and sleep for another week. Standing up and walking for hours seems like torture, but as I lift my water canister, I know it's necessary. This amount of water will barely get me through the day, and we can't stay here hoping for rain. We haven't had rain in weeks.

I stand carefully and fold at the waist, letting my head hang as I stretch my neck from side to side. Feeling slightly more like myself, I sit back down and lay my head on my pack.

A short hour later, Alek shakes me awake. "Time to go," he whispers.

Peeling myself from the ground, I force myself to pick up my pack. Zayn and Kaye look nearly as bedraggled as I feel. Surprisingly, that bolsters my spirits.

Nobody says a word as we start down the hill, an orange glow still visible on the horizon. Though it's significantly easier going with gravity—

without carrying an extra hundred-and-eighty pounds—each footfall sends a jolt of discomfort through my left side.

My own body takes enough of my attention that I don't even notice when I pass everyone else. I don't hear Alek calling my name, telling me I'm too far ahead, and I don't stop even when lights appear in the distance ahead of me.

CHAPTER 23

SUDDENLY, I'm yanked backward, and the breath is knocked out of me. I flail around, attempting to free myself.

"Mila, stop!" Zayn shouts, wrapping his arms around me. "Stop!" he repeats, this time in a soothing tone.

I obey, and as soon as I'm still, I see them. Tall, towering lights creating a massive semi-circular boundary in the valley ahead.

"What were you thinking?" he asks, breathing hard. He loosens his grip but doesn't let me go completely.

I turn my head and look at him blankly.

"You ran ahead! Kaye and Alek are still way back there—I had to run to catch up to you."

"I—I did? I don't know..." I step away from him quickly, and his arms fall to his side.

"You're kind of out of it, aren't you," Zayn says softly.

I nod, swallowing hard.

He runs his hand through his hair and keeps them on the back of his head, recovering and breathing hard. There are dark circles under his eyes, and I can see from here that his legs are trembling.

"You, too?" I ask, and he smiles slightly, dropping his hands.

"Is that—?" I look past him, finally understanding what the lights ahead of us could represent.

"I'm not sure which Community it is, but yeah. What else could it be," he says, taking a step and stopping next to me.

"Why would there be lights only around the perimeter? And why is it completely dark inside—"

"It's the middle of the night."

"I know, but even in the middle of the night, there's got to be someone awake. I don't see a single pinpoint of light in there."

"Maybe they're not allowed to use electricity at night. Maybe they have to conserve—"

"You know as much as I do about any of this, so why are you pretending to have all the answers?" I ask, slight annoyance in my tone.

"Why are you asking me your questions?"

I purse my lips. "I was thinking out loud."

The corner of his mouth lifts. "You did say I know everything."

My jaw drops. "I did not! I said you *think* you know everything—"

"Shhhh!" he laughs. "I'm kidding!"

My eyes flash as Kaye and Alek appear next to Zayn.

"I caught her," Zayn says proudly, and I smack his shoulder. He didn't need to say it like I was a rogue criminal.

"I thought you were tired, Mila," Alek pants, hunching over and resting on his knees.

"I'm sorry, I really wasn't trying to take off. I was just in my own world, I guess." I didn't mean to cause a problem, but I'm also kind of impressed with myself. Beating all three of them down here in less-than-ideal circumstances? It feels good. Pulling my water canister out, I take a sip.

"I'm almost out," I say, leaving one last drink in the bottle for emergencies. My brow furrows as I remember my canister was empty when I woke earlier. How did—?

"Me, too," Kaye echoes.

Alek looks at Zayn. "What about you?"

"Drank the last of it this morning."

Alek doesn't offer his water status, and my heart drops. That explains my good providence.

"We need to find water," I say.

"Obviously." Zayn quips.

I roll my eyes, ignoring him. Here I thought after helping him last night, he'd be more reasonable. More...grateful. And those high expectations make comments like these even more obnoxious than usual.

"There's got to be a water source in these hills," Alek says, scanning the dark landscape.

"We could cross in a grid until we find something," Kaye offers. "We've got plenty of time until sunrise."

"But what if we don't find anything? Then we have to spend the entire day with no water," I say.

Alek nods. "If we don't find something by five o'clock, we could dig—"

"Or, we could go straight for a sure thing," Zayn says.

Alek's eyes narrow. "What do you mean?"

"I mean, that Community has to be diverting a water source. If we track along the edge—"

"No way, too dangerous," Alek says, shaking his head. "We have no idea what sort of security measures they have in place."

Zayn argues back, and I watch them go back and forth—both making solid points to support their stance.

"I agree with Zayn," I cut in, surprising even myself.

Both of them turn to me. "What?" they say in unison.

"Alek," I say apologetically, "we don't have enough information to make either of these decisions. We could search all night and not find anything. Even if we dig," I add as he tries to jump in. "We don't know if the Community has any security measures in place, and you're right—it might be a complete suicide mission. But the fact is, we're going to be running into Communities from here on out. If we don't know anything about them, we're definitely going to make a stupid mistake somewhere along the line. Wouldn't it be better to take a small risk and possibly learn some things that could help us?"

Alek ponders this. Kaye stands next to him, her arms crossed over her chest.

"I agree with Zayn that there has to be a water source for the Community," I continue. "I also agree with you that it's risky. But I think it's worth it if we can also learn about what to expect the next time we hit one of these." Now I'm repeating myself, but the silence is killing me.

"And if we're spotted, and they take us?" Alek says.

I shrug. "It's not like I'm going to find anyone to be with anyway, right Zayn?"

Zayn's eyes widen, and he looks at me in confusion. I stomp past him to get a better look at the lights.

"Ummm, okay. Not sure what that's about, but what do you think, Kaye?" Alek asks, obviously hoping for reinforcement.

She shrugs. "It's risky either way, right?"

I nod.

"Then I'm up for trying."

Alek sighs in defeat. "If anything happens—"

"It won't be your fault. We made this decision together," I say, but deep down, I know he doesn't believe that one bit.

The tower lights loom ominously in the sky ahead of us. Now that we're at ground level, we can see the rays of light pointing away from the ground, shining up into the night sky. Alek thinks they're indicator lights —letting others know where the Community boundaries are. Who they'd be communicating with, I have no idea—but knowing somebody might be watching from the sky terrifies me.

We turn off our own beams as we approach. It takes a few moments for our eyes to adjust to the blue glow of the waning moon, but eventually, we begin to make our way forward. We walk from one tower to the next, staying close to the foothills. Zayn is convinced any sort of water storage could only reasonably exist on this side of the boundary due to runoff. I have no idea if he's right or not, but at the moment, I don't have any better reasoning to go with.

We pass the fourth tower, and my body feels weak. I drink the last of my water, but it isn't enough to satisfy my thirst. I can only imagine how Alek feels.

"Hold up," Zayn says, raising a hand. We stop immediately behind him, and my senses heighten as adrenaline surges through my body.

"Listen."

I close my eyes and search for what he's picking up on. And then I hear it. The soft sound of waves crashing on the shore in the distance. But this isn't in the steady rhythm of the ocean I'm used to. It's consistent and intense.

"Water," I breathe. Zayn nods, and we cautiously make our way forward toward the sound.

Over a small ridge and around another bend, we see the source of the sound. A handful of lights closer to the ground illuminate a vast, low waterfall churning into a river that snakes its way around a formidable, grey compound.

"That's it," Zayn says, and though I can't see his face, I can hear the exultation in his voice. I can't even be mad this time.

"What is it exactly?" Kaye asks.

"It's a dam," I say. "Look." I point to the edges of the water where a metal structure barely peaks out from underneath the deluge. "Hydro-electricity."

"The water winds that way," Alek says, pointing.

"Wait. Follow me," I say, walking up the hill and motioning for them to follow. We walk for a few minutes, weaving through dead tree trunks and large boulders. I scour the blackness for any indication of the clearing I'm hoping for when all at once, the trees thin and shimmering spots of light flicker in the distance. I nearly weep at the sight.

"Wow," Kaye says next to me.

"A reservoir. Good call," Alek says excitedly, and without missing a beat, begins to strip off his clothing.

I laugh. "Alek, seriously?" Grabbing Kaye's hand, I pull her far enough away that we have a little privacy. We drop our packs excitedly in the dirt, and I pull a cleansing tab from one of the exterior pockets.

"Do you need one?" I ask.

"No, I've got some," she answers. Away from the lights, I can barely see a foot in front of my face, but I hear her undressing next to me. I follow suit, and soon we're stepping carefully across the rocks and dipping our toes into the lake.

Even the frigid cold can't dissuade me from getting clean. I feel my way across the smooth rocks, sinking deeper into the inky blackness of the water and gasping as the cold rises above my stomach. Without allowing myself to think, I plunge under the surface, careful to keep my lips sealed so I don't get any in my mouth. Who knows where this water has been.

Surfacing, I quickly rub the foaming tablet into my hair before it completely dissolves in the water. I use the suds to wash every part of myself, breathing in the scent of lavender. When my toes begin to numb, I quickly rinse and walk back to the beach, wringing out my hair and shivering as the air hits my dripping skin.

I didn't think about this part. There's no soft towel to dry off with like at home. Goosebumps prickle my skin, but thankfully the temperature is warm enough in the valley that it's not overly uncomfortable to be standing there air drying.

I flick my hair over my head and let it hang while the water evaporates from my skin. Brushing my fingers through it, I swing gently from side to side to increase the airflow.

"Mila? Kaye?" I hear from the trees, and I freeze.

"We're not dressed!" I hiss. "Give us a second."

"Oh," Alek mumbles, "sorry. We're just filtering the water and filling up our canisters—then we'll be ready to go."

"We'll come your way when we're done," I say, shaking my hair one more time. Pulling a tie out of my bag, I wrap it into a tight bun on top of my head. I wait a few moments before moving—thoroughly enjoying the sensation of cleanliness—then feel for my dusty clothes on top of my bag. I can smell the days-of-hiking-funk when I pull my shirt over my head. There's no way I can wash this tonight, but if we follow the river, maybe

I can do it in the morning. I've got no clean clothes left, and I know I'm not the only one.

"Hey," Kaye says beside me. "Do you have an extra pair of underwear?"

"I'm not sure," I say. "Is everything okay?"

"I've gone through all of mine. We haven't taken frequent enough stops for me to—" She stops short. "Well, to keep everything down there clean."

I'm puzzled for a second, but then it clicks. "Kaye, are you menstruating?"

She sniffs. "Started yesterday."

"Why didn't you say something? You've been dealing with that all night?"

"I have a cup, I just—"

"No, please say something next time. I'm so sorry, Kaye," I say, rummaging through my bag. "We shouldn't have been pushing so hard, and you should've been drinking more water." I rustle through my bag and pull out an absorbent rag I'd packed for just this purpose. It's not as good as a replacement pair, but it will help.

"I didn't want to be a burden," she says, taking it from me.

"You're anything but a burden. I'm going to be in the same boat in a couple of weeks. Don't be embarrassed."

I can barely see the outline of her face as she nods.

"I was thinking we could do laundry at the stream in the morning," I say. "We can let everything dry while we sleep. It won't be as clean as at home since it will be in the open air—"

"I don't even care at this point," Kaye says, and I grin.

"Our standards have lowered slightly—is that what you're saying?"

We laugh, and she steps away to finish dressing. Leave it to bodily functions to break the ice. It's hard enough trudging miles every day without having to worry about staying clean. I can't believe she didn't say anything.

I still don't have a bead on her. She's quiet but thoughtful. I have no idea how she's feeling about all this or what she thinks about us in general. With everything she's already gone through, I feel a responsibility to make sure she doesn't have to 'go through' anything else. Her life thus far doesn't seem fair, and I don't want to make it worse.

I meet Kaye at the water's edge with my filter, and we slowly fill our canisters. After drinking as much as we can without making ourselves sick, we fill them again and replace the tops. Putting on our packs, we hike back into the trees to look for Alek and Zayn. Kaye doesn't say a word.

"Taking your sweet time," Zayn says as we approach, but the bite in his tone is absent for the moment. A bath and plenty of fresh drinking water can put even him in a lighter mood.

"Where to?" Alek asks.

I frown. "Are you asking me?" We're closer to the lights now, and I can see everyone clearly. Zayn's damp hair is tousled and wild, while Alek's is slicked back neatly.

"I am," he says.

I give him a skeptical look. "Why?"

"Because you made some good points. We need to find out more about the Communities and all that. Remember?"

I ponder this a moment. "Yeah...I think if we spend a day or two here—especially since we have a water source—we could scout things out. See if we can observe anything. It might save us time and energy in the long run. But I could also be completely wrong."

I watch his face closely for any indication of his feelings on the matter, but he doesn't react. Standing here alone in the dark suddenly feels more ominous than traveling, and I'm not sure I want to make camp before the sun comes up.

"I don't know," I backtrack. "Maybe we do want to keep moving. We know nothing about their security. For all we know, we may have already been spotted."

Alek looks behind him toward the building. "Seems pretty calm out here. And why would they need security anyway?"

"For people trying to sneak in illegally," Zayn suggests.

"They'd need an implant. The Community would be literally nothing for them without that," Alek points out. "And everyone else is too afraid of them to walk right up to the doors."

Kaye looks around nervously, running a hand through her short, wet hair.

"It's a risk, like we already talked about," I say. "We can get as far away from here as we can, or we can find a protected spot to hunker down and observe at first light. I'm fine with either." Because I don't want to make a decision and be responsible for something terrible happening. I leave that part out.

Alek nods, lifting his wrist and inspecting it. "Honestly, I don't think we have a choice. The life watch is already dead, and I'd rather not travel much further without having some sort of heading."

"Decision made," Zayn says and begins to walk up the hill.

"No," I stop him. "We need to be on the other side of the dam. So we have access to the river."

"Why?" he asks flippantly, but then softens when he sees my pleading expression. "Doesn't matter," he shrugs. "That could be better anyway."

He turns the other direction without complaint, and Alek and I exchange baffled glances. We need baths and fresh water more often.

CHAPTER 24

I CAN BARELY KEEP my eyes open when the sky finally begins to brighten. It's only been an hour or so since we set up camp, but even sitting still for a few minutes is enough to make my eyelids droop.

I force myself to stand and scoop up my dirty clothes.

"Hey," I say, motioning to Kaye. "Ready?"

She nods, wadding up her garments and tucking them under her arm. We walk carefully down to the edge of the river, stopping where the water fans out and looks more shallow. Working together, we move a few good-sized rocks into a semicircle, creating a small, protected pool where we can soak our clothes without worrying about them washing downstream.

"I'm glad you came," I say, plunging my hands into the cold water.

"I was nervous."

"I was, too." I flick the water from my hands and open my pack. Finding the soap disc easily, I pull it out and begin to scrub one of my shirts. With how chilly the water is, it doesn't create much of a lather, but I trust it's working.

I hand the bar to Kaye. "I know you might not want to talk about it—and it's totally fine if you don't—but I've wanted to ask you about what happened. After Paul's family left. We didn't see you anymore."

Kaye continues to scrub, not acknowledging the question. The water laps and burbles at our feet, reflecting the red and orange hues from the rising sun, and I soak in the stillness. For a moment, I can almost imagine how the world would look without the haze and the ash. With green leaves on the branches of these old trees, a pale blue sky with wispy white clouds, and wildflowers blooming in the stream bed. I sigh. Almost.

"Paul's parents raised me," Kaye says, snapping me out of my imagination. Her candidness takes me by surprise, but I try not to show it.

"My parents..." she hesitates, "weren't very present."

I nod as if this is new information, but it isn't. Everyone in our area knows about Kaye's parents.

"You're it!" six-year-old Kaye says shrilly, bouncing in the opposite direction.

"I was on pause!" I say, throwing my hands out to the side for added drama.

"No pausing," Alek taunts, skirting past me and easily dodging my outstretched arm. Tag is our favorite game after group lessons in the morning, but we typically have more players. Today it's just the three of us, and I'm easily the slowest.

I amble toward the edge of the playground, then quickly dart toward Kaye. She shrieks with laughter and runs full-tilt, escaping effortlessly. I'm just about to whine about how the game isn't fair when we hear him.

"Kaye!" a man bellows angrily, and all three of us freeze, whipping our heads toward the school building.

"It's my dad," Kaye whispers, and her face blanches.

"When I call your name, you better run!" he screams, and Kaye's eyes widen. She gives a small wave and runs as fast as her legs can carry her. As soon as she's within arm's reach, her dad snatches her by the hair.

Alek and I watch in disgust as she yelps, and he turns, dragging her along after him.

My stomach twists at the memory, and Kaye's voice again pulls me back to the present.

"Tara and Allen took me in as if I was one of their own," she says as she scrubs with more vigor.

"I didn't know that," I say softly, rinsing a shirt and wringing it out. I lay it on a clean rock next to me to dry. "I'm sorry, Kaye. I...well, your dad scared me. I didn't want to think about how that must've been for you."

She shrugs. "We were all just kids. I didn't expect anyone to get it."

"But Paul did."

"Paul did," she says softly.

Paul lived next door to Kaye and—compared to him—we only saw a fraction of what Kaye's father was capable of. He saw and heard *everything*.

Kaye wipes a tear from her cheek.

"And then after they left..." I encourage.

"I'd lost my parents and the only good family I'd ever known."

I wring out my last pair of pants and find another rock behind me to spread them on, then set the soap to the side to dry.

"But why didn't you go with them then?" I ask. This part of her story has never made sense to me. Why stay by yourself? There's no way I'd stay behind and go it alone if everyone I cared about was moving on.

"I didn't want to see them."

"Paul's family?"

She shakes her head, squeezing a shirt and watching the water drip into the pool. "My parents."

My eyebrows furrow. "But I thought—"

"They died?"

I nod.

"No. They joined the Communities before Paul's family did."

My jaw drops. How did I not know this? "Are you serious?"

She turns and begins her own drying rock opposite mine.

"That doesn't make any sense," I murmur. "I thought you had to qualify? How could your parents—?"

Kay laughs mirthlessly. "Apparently, they aren't as picky as we thought," she says. "But I was honestly grateful. With them gone, I thought my life would finally be the way I'd always dreamed of. I could finally breathe."

"But then Paul's family left, too."

She takes a deep breath and lets it out slowly. "I couldn't make myself go with them. If I did...the Community would've made me join my parents. Paul tried to convince me we could work something else out, but I knew. I just knew. And I couldn't do it."

"Kaye, I'm so sorry," I breathe. "I had no idea."

Her shoulders lift and then fall slowly. "It's okay." Turning, she begins to walk back up the slope, indicating the topic is closed for now.

A mixture of guilt and sadness wells up inside me. She had to choose between living with her parents again—but keeping her best friend close—or solitude and loneliness. I could've made that easier for her. I could've been a friend. Instead, I kept my distance. Why? Because I didn't think she wasn't putting forth any effort? Because she was quiet and odd?

I follow her back up to camp and mentally berate myself for being so selfish and superficial. How could I not have seen what was going on behind the scenes? I'm caught in my thoughts when a splash of green catches my eye, and my breath catches. Doing a double-take, I stop and scan the ground until I find it again. There it is. A brilliant burst of spring color peeking out behind a boulder to my right.

"Kaye!" I shout excitedly, and she turns immediately. I scramble over the rocks to get a better look. A fresh green shoot—almost four inches tall—stretches toward the sky. Three healthy leaves protrude from the thin stem.

"It's—it's growing," she whispers in awe.

I nod excitedly. "It's *alive*."

Suddenly, a shower of rocks and dirt spray up from our left, and I gasp, standing and spinning toward the disturbance. Kaye folds forward, and I reflexively grab for her before she hits the ground. I catch her in time, but her weight knocks me off balance, and I fall hard, hitting my head on the rocks behind me.

As my vision fades, a dark figure hovers above me. Alek? Zayn? I open my mouth to tell them about the plant, but my voice catches in my throat. My arms go limp, and I remember the sound of the river splashing along the rocks. The sound gets louder and louder until it's all I can hear, just as my circle of vision begins to shrink. The orange haze fades—becoming fuzzy and distant—and then I'm gone.

PART 3
CHANNEL

APRIL 2, 2161 - APRIL 14, 2161

CHAPTER 25

I STARE at the inside of my tent, blinking slowly. The thin, neutral fabric is pulled into a steep peak, held by two poles on either end, and staked to the ground in three places along each of the sides. The fabric is strong enough to block sun and rain but light enough to ripple slightly with the breeze. More than slightly sometimes.

I've stared at the inside of my tent for three days now. Well, technically just two since the first day I attempted to escape. If you consider getting tranq'd in the neck a success, then it went really, really well. Regardless, this view is getting old fast. Wearing masks full-time is getting old fast. Everything is getting old *really* fast.

It doesn't help that my bunkmate hasn't said a word since I woke up in the back of a vehicle lying next to her. The only thing I know about the girl taken from P3 the same day as me is that she has reddish-blond hair, she's a few inches shorter than me, she might have blue eyes—she stares at the ground so often, I'm not entirely sure—and she sleeps a lot. That's about it.

She's presumably close to my age based on her height and development, but it's impossible to know if we've met before. Impossible because I've only seen the Real form of a few people in P3. And, if you remember, she *refuses to talk about it.*

Annoyed, I stand from my cot. Hunching over until I reach the front of the tent, I flick the flap to the side and step out into the twilight. The sun hovers low on the horizon, making everything glow a deep red. I'm still not used to the bare earth and thick haze, but tonight the angry, ominous sky suits my mood perfectly.

"Channel, hey," I hear to my right. "It's not safe to be out—"

"I need to see Kenna."

The woman who I've run into regularly—but not often enough to remember or care about her name—clenches her jaw. "Kenna isn't available at—"

"Thanks," I say dismissively, walking past her with an unapologetic smile on my face. I should be nicer, but at this moment, I just can't. These people tore me away from my home with zero explanation. 'Be patient,' they continue to say, but that isn't my strong suit. And it's time I had some answers.

Over the past few days I've seen Kenna coming and going through a shelter in the middle of our camp. I stomp toward it and tear open the flap. Kenna looks up, her body stooped over a table with a stylus in her hand, hovering above a tablet. A man and woman dressed in all black stand next to her. All three of them stare me down, yet their looks aren't antagonistic, surprisingly. They look more exhausted than anything. It almost makes me think twice about what I'm going to say next.

"Where's my mother?" I ask, my breath stilted. I'm shaking despite my best efforts to look composed.

"Channel, we've told you. We've had some unexpected issues arise, and your debriefing—"

I cut Kenna off. "*I don't care if you've had some unexpected things come up!* You brought me here without permission, and I deserve an explanation."

Kenna sighs, standing to her full height. She has to be almost two meters tall. Her chopped hair and athletic build only add to her already intimidating presence.

"You've been recovering," she says crisply.

"I've been recovered," I say, emphasizing the 'd,' "for at least twenty-four hours at this point."

"You were heavily sedated."

"I'm fine."

"Great. Glad to hear it. But it's not all about you, Channel. There's too much," she says, shaking her head. "I have fifteen people needing 'an explanation,' along with two active missions to oversee. It will be more efficient for me to fill everyone in at once."

"Fifteen? I thought there were only eleven of us."

"Well, that's the unexpected part." Her eyes flash as she puts her hands on her hips.

"It isn't my fault you happened to be so busy after my kidnapping."

Kenna purses her lips. Her nearly jet-black hair is pulled into a tight knot at the base of her skull, and her grey t-shirt reminds me of my own.

"Give me the short version," I say, setting my jaw.

Her gaze hardens. "Alright, Miss P3." She walks closer. "I normally sugar-coat this, but based on the fighting attitude I've observed from you, I'm beginning to care less and less about whether you go into shock. So here's the short version, as requested."

She stops directly in front of my face, and I have to look up to meet her eyes. I force my expression to remain blank, though my heart hammers so hard in my chest, I'm positive she can hear it.

"Your whole life in the Communities?" she says provocatively. "It's a lie. It's been a lie for years. The *Real* world is healing. We have proof that Community life will no longer be necessary in the next five to ten years, and yet World Builders are continuing to push their narrative. They're blatantly refusing to transition. That implant they were about to attach to your brain? It would've stripped any autonomy you had." She scoffs. "Though you didn't have much to begin with."

My mind flashes to my Mom and Aave. I shiver.

Kenna continues, more gently this time as if reading my thoughts. "With regards to your mother. We weren't able to bring her along. She's likely been implanted, and we have no idea of her current whereabouts. I'm sorry about that, and we're working on it. Things don't always go as planned on these missions."

My lip trembles, and I bite it. Kenna inspects my face, gauging my reaction.

"Why would the World Builders do that?" I spit. "And how would you magically have access to this secret information that somehow has been so brilliantly kept from all the rest of us? It sounds like a conspiracy theory to me—"

"*BECAUSE I USED TO BE ONE OF THEM!*" she shouts, and I flinch. Her nose is so close that it nearly touches mine. We stare at each other, unblinking, until she slowly retreats back to the table. "Now, please, go back to your tent. And I'd appreciate it if you kept this information to yourself until we hold our official debriefing."

I nod, tears stinging the corners of my eyes. Not wanting to give her the pleasure of seeing me break down, I spin on my heel and exit the tent.

Kicking a rock, I march back to my area of the camp. I'm suddenly disgusted with the world around me. Tan. Grey. Blah. Everything is washed out and plain, including every person I've come in contact with.

From what I've gathered, my implant lost connectivity with the Edge shortly after leaving Paradise 3. Where am I now? No clue. And nobody's given me any indication that I'll be able to sync up again anytime soon. That means no messages and no information. It's killing me.

Movement catches my eye, and I look up, angrily wiping a tear from my cheek. A girl with dark hair who looks to be about my age sits on a rock, reaching out for a water canister from a tall, bronze-skinned man with hair down to his shoulders. Her head is heavily bandaged, and I'm curious if she attempted to escape, too.

I catch myself staring at the pair, and her eyes lift to meet mine. The man turns around, following her gaze, and my eyes widen. His face is young— not agreeing in the least with the strength and maturity in his stature. Embarrassed, I drop my eyes and quickly walk the last few paces to my tent.

Well, those two are definitely new. Flopping onto my cot, I kick my feet up and lie down. Were those the unexpected people Kenna mentioned? But she said there were four. I sigh, not wanting to spend any more time thinking about my conversation with her.

I glance over to see strawberry-blonde girl still curled up and supposedly sleeping. Maybe she's dead. I don't want to have to explain a dead girl in my tent.

"Hey," I say, and the girl shifts on her cot. Not dead. That's good enough for now, I guess.

I roll over and stare—again—at the tent next to me. Lights grow and shrink as people walk past, casting shadows across the shelter. Though I can hear the low hum of voices in the tent across from us, I can't make out what they're saying.

A million questions swirl through my mind. *Your life is a lie.* Kenna's words play on repeat in my head. What does she mean, 'a lie?' The Real world is *healing*? First of all, if that were true, then why am I still wearing a mask full-time? Wouldn't the air have to be better before anything on this planet could heal? And World Builders pushing a narrative? What narrative? We all know *the narrative.* The Communities were necessary to maintain any sort of standard of life. And even if the world is healing— which of course is the end goal for all of us—it would take generations for things to return to normal. If normal's even possible at this point. A new normal, I guess.

I sigh and close my eyes, pressing two fingers against my temples. So much for not thinking about our conversation.

None of this is making any sense. I want to go home and make sure Mom is okay. I want to talk with Aave—to see him in Real life again. I want to meet up with Oren and go on adventures. I want to be anywhere but here.

"Debriefing now, mid-camp," I hear through my tent wall and bolt upright. It takes me a minute to remember where I am, but when I do, my stomach sinks. Yawning, I throw my legs off the cot and plant my feet in the dirt. I have no idea how long I slept, but my tent is bright—I'm assuming through context clues it must be morning already.

Surprisingly, Strawberry is already up and gone. She must've gotten enough sleep over the past few days of never leaving the tent.

"Lex, load—" I start, then stop myself, gritting my teeth. No, Lex. No loading anything. Ever again, apparently.

My stomach grumbles just as I notice a small bowl of food on the ground near the front fabric flap. Tent delivery. That's new. I gratefully pick up the offering and don't even inspect the food before slurping down the strange stew. The food here looks absolutely disgusting, and the taste isn't much better. It's not *that bad,* I guess. Just different enough to be off-putting. But it's incredible how not picky you get when you're hungry, terrified, and alone. Still. What I wouldn't give for a joy tendril right about now.

I take my empty bowl with me to throw in the compost pile at mid-camp. My compliance is making me sick, but I figure I can't cause problems before I get more information. This debriefing is what I've been waiting for. Then I can find a way to get back home.

My heart hammers in my chest as the conversation from last night lands in my brain. What Kenna said...it can't be true. But then I wonder. What *will* happen when the world heals? What will happen when we can be self-sufficient without the need for Community help? Fear sets in when I realize I'm not cut out for a world like that. If the world were to become liveable during my lifetime, I wouldn't be ready to live in it. The only world I know is coding. I've learned nothing about surviving on my own, nor would I want to. It sounds...hard.

After disposing of my bowl, I join the group of people from the camp. I recognize Tabor and Erin from my first day here. They're from P2. We spent a very uncomfortable day in a vehicle together—all of us still hopped up on whatever they gave us before our non-implants. Tabor is tall and wiry with a shaved head. He made sure to tell me his form in P2 looks much more appealing. Erin's face is beautiful—large, dark eyes with long lashes and perfectly symmetrical—but her voice is obnoxious. High-pitched and nasally. If sitting in a cramped vehicle was terrible, listening to her commentary made the entire journey worse.

Though not ideal, they're the only people here from the Communities who I'm on a first-name basis with. Kenna hasn't arrived yet, and it doesn't look like we'll be starting immediately. I have time to move.

Weaving through the group of people to my left, I make my way over. Both Erin and Tabor stand stone-faced and don't acknowledge me when I walk up next to them, leaving me to wonder if I imagined the whole first-name basis thing. Perfect.

Scanning the rest of the crowd, I find the two people I saw last night. The girl's head is still bandaged, and again, I can't help but watch them. Their clothing sets them apart from the rest of us, but even without that, they look *different*. Rustic and almost wild. There are more people in their group tonight—a girl who looks like she might blow over in a gentle breeze and a guy who looks...well, who looks like he might kill someone. That could come in handy. And now that I see four of them, I'm more convinced than ever that these are the unexpected visitors Kenna alluded to. My curiosity is piqued. Who are they, and where are they from? Why would they be here in the middle of nowhere?

Two actual adult men—no young faces this time—stand on the other side of the new group with their hands behind their backs. I can only assume there's something holding their hands behind them in such an awkward position. Noticeably, two of Kenna's crew are watching them closely. They definitely pulled something crazy to be restrained like that, and they don't look thrilled with their punishment.

The entire group is rag-tag and ornery. None of us want to be here. People shift on their feet, clear their throats, and look awkwardly at one another. If any of us had an inkling of how to get around without the Edge, there wouldn't be enough of Kenna's crew to stop us. The realization that I'm useless without my Edge connection sinks deeper, and I begin to panic.

I freeze when I see my silent roommate Strawberry staring at me from across the clearing. As soon as I make eye contact, she looks away. Her light hair is pulled into a tight bun on top of her head, and she holds herself as if trying to sink into the landscape and become invisible. Maybe I do know more about her than I thought. I get that body language. I don't feel especially awesome at this moment either. Without the Edge, every second in public feels like I'm completely naked in front of strangers. Totally vulnerable. No code to hide behind. No wonder we're all jittery and antisocial.

The Reveal was worse, though. Seeing it all for the first time. Being seen for what I thought was the first time. Remembering that night makes me think of Aave. And my mom. The scar on her cheek. Despair washes over me. She must be worried sick.

Or not, I realize. If she was implanted, she might not even realize I'm gone. Though the thought of her distress makes me want to vomit, the possibility that she might not even be aware of my absence feels infinitely worse. They couldn't do that, could they? Withhold information? I shiver and rub my arms with my hands, wishing I could bolt back to my tent.

"Alright, everybody, listen up," Kenna says, walking into the middle of our haphazard semicircle and keeping me rooted to the spot. "I know it's been a long couple of days, and I know a few of you—" she looks pointedly at the two men I'd spotted earlier, "—are feeling less than excited to be here, so let's cut to the chase. We're not here to force you to leave the life you know. We're not even here to convince you that our cause is just. It probably feels that way, but we're not. We've named ourselves The Coalition for Ethical World Transition. If you attempt to use the acronym CEWT, I promise it will not be 'cute' when I choke you out. The group we are fighting against is anything but adorable, and we will match them with equal ferocity."

The group is silent and still. Kenna continues. "We're in a unique situation tonight. We've never had a group quite as diverse as this for a debriefing, so please be patient with me as I try to accommodate everyone. We are privileged to be in the company of true soldiers." She looks directly at the group across from me. The wild ones.

"These four youth are from Southwest Territory," she says, and her announcement causes a stir. I wrack my brain, trying to understand why that information is noteworthy. Southwest Territory. That's where our communities were built. I thought it didn't exist anymore.

Kenna continues. "Their families held out and have been surviving on their own with limited support from the Communities—especially in the last five years. Their pilgrimage here, though misguided and incredibly stupid, is worthy of our admiration." She scans the crowd, scrutinizing our faces. "Their lack of information and Community involvement is to their benefit. They've been spared the indoctrination that the rest of you Paradise members have been force-fed your entire lives. So let's get to it."

She holds a thin silver plate in front of her and presses the top lightly. A projection bursts into the air between us, and seeing something familiar sends a burst of relief through my entire body. I stare at the electric blue globe swirling in front of me. The streamlined, simple code makes me want to cry.

"These red areas indicate Community boundaries five years ago. This," she moves her finger on the plate, "is where the current boundaries are."

The red areas expand to cover over half of global landmasses. It's staggering. Beautiful, even.

"This expansion has happened as these numbers have been coming in," she says, and a series of charts replaces the spinning sphere. I analyze the data as quickly as possible. Temperatures are increasing, but we've all been told to expect that, so no surprises there. Air quality is slowly improving, yes, but still quite toxic. Oxygen levels are increasing. Sure. Makes sense. I don't see how any of this could be cause for the accusations Kenna spouted earlier.

Kenna clears her throat. "For you living in Paradise Communities, these numbers probably aren't surprising. You've been taught that these shifts will happen, but that it will take thousands of years for any sort of recovery to happen, yes?" She waits for an answer, but none of us gives one. She knows she's on point.

"Well," she continues, "that is simply false."

She zooms in on the oxygen and carbon dioxide columns. "Do you see this?" A bright yellow line swoops around the numbers as she manipulates the stylus on the plate. "These rates are exponential and inversely related. We believe—and when I say 'we' I'm not just talking about our coalition, I'm talking about some of the most experienced and well-educated scientists in the world." She pauses to let that sink in. "*We* believe this is evidence of weathering. Does anyone know what that is?"

She's again met with silence. Nodding, she explains. "When the earth was created, we know there was a great oxygenation event. For much of earth's history, people believed this was due to plant life, which could've been part of it, definitely, but there is much more evidence to support a process called weathering."

She minimizes the projection. "Volcanic activity is never simple. Each process is extremely unique, and the levels and variety of gases spewed into our atmosphere is impossible to predict, which is why it's so difficult to understand the ramifications. After the fact, however, we get a much clearer picture. During that first series of events, there is evidence for large amounts of CO_2 gas entering the atmosphere. As we know, this causes the earth to warm significantly, which in turn causes more rainfall. That in turn erodes and weathers rocks, sending large amounts of minerals into our oceans." She pauses, visibly struggling to quell her excitement on this topic enough to speak at a reasonable pace.

"Do you know what loves minerals?" She smiles, and her obvious passion makes her harsh appearance appear almost childlike. "Cyanobacteria. Our oceans are booming with it. And do you know what they produce?"

"Oxygen." The girl from Southwest Territory with dark hair and a bandaged head speaks up.

"Exactly." Kenna smiles at her, and I suddenly wish I'd been the one to produce an answer. "Our oxygen levels are growing exponentially, and as I mentioned earlier, we don't know exactly what to expect. We're in another period of substantial change. But we do have proof that Earth is healing. These bacteria are only one small piece of that; we've also seen increased insect populations and even the beginning of unassisted plant life."

One of the detained men shouts out, "Even if that's true—which I have no reason to believe what you're saying—if we assume this is correct, that still doesn't mean we'll suddenly be able to rip our masks off and run off into the sunset. We still need the Communities."

"I agree one hundred percent," Kenna says. "In fact, I've worked most of my life to improve the efficiency of Community life. However, I began to take issue when Community leaders pushed forward with Cerebrolink."

She throws another projection up into the air. "We've had the technology for Cerebrolink for years. Not as sophisticated as it is now, but it existed. Nobody was comfortable with adopting this as a general standard-of-living improvement. It was only to be used in specific situations where citizens were failing to thrive with the retinal implants. There are significant risks—and I'm not talking about the risks inherent to surgical intervention. I'm talking about massive ethical questions that nobody has done their due diligence to answer. We don't have any systems in place for basic human rights and the moral use of this technology on a global scale."

Kenna reaches out as a woman hands her a water canister. She takes a long drink and clears her throat. "Which begs the question: why now? Why are we all of a sudden moving forward with widespread implantation? And by 'moving forward' I mean, we are really *moving forward*. You were likely told that you were special, right? That you were 'chosen' to test this new technology that would allow the whole world complete freedom in how they wanted to live their lives." She laughs loudly. "I hate to burst your bubble, but that's what every single Community was told. Around the entire world!"

She throws her hands up for added effect. "This is a global takeover. Why? Because our leaders have realized that if they give up their power now—when the earth is slowly becoming more habitable without the need of their help? Well. That would mean there would be billions of people running around making independent choices, completely destroying their meticulously crafted elitist Community."

I begin to sweat. *Could this be true?* I definitely had reservations about how quickly they were rolling out the Cerebrolink...and Aave did mention these same ethical concerns. But how could this be happening without someone stepping on the brakes? And how much can I really trust Kenna? She could easily have some sort of ulterior motive. I know nothing about her besides the fact that she has no qualms about kidnapping.

"I've seen it," a voice pipes up. It's the girl again. "I've seen plants growing independently, with no human intervention."

Kenna nods. "It's happening. World Builders don't want to admit it. I even have reports that people do not have to wear masks full-time on the European continent." She looks pointedly at the man who shouted out. "Though getting that verified has proven difficult."

She takes a deep breath and lets it out slowly. "So, you're probably all wondering what this has to do with you." She folds her arms across her chest and looks at the ground. "I helped develop the current Cerebrolink," she says softly. "I bought into the narrative. But when I found out about all the data we were ignoring as a collective, I couldn't remain a part of that system. We couldn't stay." She lifts her eyes, and a steely resolve has replaced any regret.

"All of us," she says, pointing at the other members of the coalition, "decided to do something about it. We attempted to lobby within the Real and Unreal Communities with very little success. We were left with no choice but to go to the people themselves. You. We attempted to hack into the Edge and were successful a few times," she laughs, and the man in black next to her nods knowingly. "That didn't last long. At which point our only option was to try and prevent as many implants as possible."

That's it. That's who all of us are, then. Besides the Real's, we were all going in for implants when they pulled us out.

"I'm not going to force you to stay," Kenna says. "This is simply an invitation. We've extended this invitation to over two thousand Community members at this point. Some have chosen to join us, some have opted out. It's completely up to you. Between now and then, I'd like you to think about how many times you've seen or heard of a World Builder with an implant. Of any kind." She picks up the plate and stylus. "Tomorrow morning, if you'd like to return to your Paradise Community, we'll have transport available." Kenna brushes a lock of hair behind her ear. "We obviously can't take you directly in, but we can take you to the edge of their boundary surveillance. From there, it would be about a three-hour walk. For everyone else, this is a temporary camp. Once our mission tomorrow is complete, anyone who wishes to join us is welcome to travel to our permanent location."

She nods resolutely, and without saying another word, turns and ducks into her tent.

CHAPTER 26

I STAND THERE in the clearing, stunned. Over the past four days, they've attempted to flip my entire world on its head. I run Kenna's words through my mind but can't fully process them. I can't process anything at this point. I'm completely numb and knowing that only adds a level of frustration to the soul-sucking emptiness. I should be raging right now. I should be *running* back to Paradise 3, not standing stock-still staring blankly like a complete idiot.

"This is a load," Tabor says next to me, and I start. Apparently, now I exist.

"Hmm?" I say, making sure he was talking to me and not just Erin.

"All of this. I'd heard there were extremists—people holding out for life to go back to how it used to be. People afraid of AR. It's a complete load."

I nod.

"I don't know," Erin says. "What if things are getting better?"

"Who cares?" Tabor says. "What do you think that's going to look like? If you're telling me I have to choose between an implant where I can do literally whatever I want or a life where I have to deal with this mess? That's a no-brainer."

I resonate with his words and immediately feel guilt well up inside me. What was it Aave was saying? Make the harder choice? But what makes the more painful choice the right one?

Tabor and Erin head back to their tent without a goodbye, and I find myself staring after them.

"Right?" A voice sounds beside me, and again I jump. "Sorry, didn't mean to scare you. I just recognized that look on your face."

It's Southwest girl with the bandage. She smiles at me, and the wrap around her head prevents the right side of her face from lifting so it squishes instead.

"You know nothing about me," I say, and my voice bites more than I mean it to.

Her eyebrows furrow slightly, but she doesn't look away. "I don't know anything about living in the Communities, that's true. But I do know what it feels like to have your entire world rocked. We came out here looking for other people like us." She hesitates, looking over her shoulder to find her friends. They slowly make their way over.

"You left your home?"

She nods.

"I guess that's not surprising."

"And why is that?" Man-boy from earlier walks up next to Southwest girl, flicking his hair out of his eyes. He's obviously offended by my comment.

"Because. You're outside the Communities," I say factually.

"And?" he says, not missing a beat.

And everyone knows your life is awful. That's what I want to say, but I don't. Despite the situation, I still have some sense of social decorum. Plus, it's four to one in this discussion, and somehow I don't think that type of comment would go over well with any of them.

"Why did you leave?" I ask instead.

"Because the Communities have basically left us for dead," Man-boy says. "No access to information, outdated technology—we needed to find other groups like ours so we could band together."

"Why wouldn't you just join us?" I ask, and he laughs out loud.

"Right. After listening to all that, you're wondering why we haven't marched on in?"

"We don't even know if 'all that' is true. How am I supposed to believe some rogue vigilante group over the life I've lived for the past seventeen years? The Communities have been good to me."

"I'm sure they have," he says. "That's the point, right? Be really good to people so they'll stay in line."

"It wasn't like that."

He shrugs. "You would know, I guess."

"I would." My cheeks are burning.

Killer-boy stands behind them, engrossed with whittling a piece of wood. I still haven't gotten a good look at his face up close. Waif-girl is nowhere to be found at the moment.

"C'mon, Mila. We need to get packed up," Man-boy says.

"You're going with them?" I ask reflexively. It's a stupid question, and I regret it as soon as it leaves my mouth. Of course they are. How could they do anything different?

Mila smiles graciously. "We don't have much of a choice. It turns out there were a lot of things we didn't understand about Community boundaries." She laughs nervously. "It wouldn't be possible for us to go on our own at this point."

Man-boy turns to Killer, nudges him, and together they walk back toward our end of camp.

"That's Alek, my brother," she says.

"Which one?"

"The one who was talking to you. Kind of rudely. I'm sorry about that—he's on edge with all this."

"What about Kil—the other guy?"

"Oh," she snorts. "Be glad he didn't talk to you. That's Zayn. He's even worse. Kaye is with us, too—she wasn't feeling well."

"Who is," I mutter, then fidget with my fingernails when I realize that thought was audible.

"This is probably worse for you," Mila says, then hesitates. "I'm going to be honest. I've wanted to talk to you since I saw you last night. I've never met anyone in the Communities, and...well, everyone else here doesn't seem very approachable."

"And I did?" I ask, raising an eyebrow.

Mila laughs. "More so than the others! At least you're my age."

"How old are you?"

"Seventeen. You?"

"Seventeen."

"Ha, see? I knew it."

I laugh, then stop myself. Somehow, over the past few minutes, I'd forgotten I wasn't projecting my form—now that I've remembered that detail, I'm immediately self-conscious. I don't like the fact that someone could know so much about me just by looking at my face.

"Can I ask what it's like?" Mila asks, seemingly oblivious to the stress I'm suddenly feeling.

"The Communities?"

Mila nods, and I motion for her to walk with me. Standing outside of Kenna's tent is making me nervous.

"They're...the only thing I've ever known. I don't know." I search for a way to describe life in P3 to someone who's been living in the Real world, and I come up empty.

"What does a typical day look like?" she asks.

"Ummm, well, under normal circumstances, I'd wake up and check my console—"

"Okay, stop. What's a console."

"It's where I get all my messages and upload my preferences for the day."

"Preferences?"

"Yeah, like how I look, what my hair looks like."

"Wait, you get to change that?" Mila asks excitedly. "So you don't look like this?"

"Nope, never."

"What do you look like?"

I laugh, "I don't know. It changes every day. Sometimes I have short hair, sometimes long. I like purple, so sometimes I go all out."

"Wow. That would be so fun."

"It is, actually."

"What did you mean by normal circumstances?"

We reach the end of the path between our tents and stop.

"When I left, we were doing what's called a World Build Competition. It's kind of a celebration."

"Got it. So under normal circumstances, what would you do after checking your console?"

"Then I'd go out and eat something with my mom. Then I'd head to the Grid."

"What's that?"

"It's where we do all of our assignments."

"Like education? School?"

"I've never been to school, but from what I've read, it's nothing like it. It's more like training."

"For what?"

"To prepare for our placements. When we turn eighteen, we're placed into permanent assignments in the Community."

"That's awesome."

"If you get the one you want."

"What did you want?"

My hands start to sweat. "To be a World Builder." I wait for an accusatory look, but it doesn't come.

"Why did you want to be that?"

Do, I think. Why *do* I want to be that. As far as I'm concerned, it's still the plan.

"Because I love coding. And I love the creativity of it. I think I could make our Communities better." Why am I telling her this? She doesn't understand anything about the Communities, and what she does know is condemning, based on that presentation.

"I don't know anything about coding," Mila sighs. "We don't even have access to the Edge anymore."

My eyes go wide. "How do you survive?"

Mila laughs. "That's the question, right? Not very well at the moment."

"Hence the leaving."

"Hence the leaving," she agrees.

"Strong play."

"Well, when you're basically the last people left, it's the only play."

"You were the last?"

"I'm being dramatic. But pretty close."

I nod, not sure what to say next.

"Mila!" a voice calls from their tent, and she turns.

"I should probably go." She smiles apologetically and begins to walk away, then quickly flips back around. "I didn't catch your name."

"Channel."

"Nice to meet you, Channel."

I wave. Mila is nothing like I expected someone in the Real world to be. I don't think I had a fully-formed idea about Real people in general, but I expected them to be more...plain. Simple-minded and ignorant. Definitely not bubbly and sharp-witted.

I open my tent flap, but hesitate. If I go in there, it means I'll be alone. Worse. I'll be sitting next to Strawberry and still feeling completely alone. With absolutely zero distractions besides the shadows on the wall of my tent. Nope. That's not happening right now.

Without looking back toward camp, I walk past the tent and off into the barren wilderness. Kenna's crew is so preoccupied with their plans, they don't notice me leave. Not that they'd be that concerned at this point, anyway. Tomorrow I won't be their responsibility anymore, and I'm sure they couldn't be more thrilled.

My breathing quickens, and moisture collects on the skin around my mouth as I walk up the hill. Stupid masks. How do people live like this?

After a few more minutes, my body forces me to stop and catch my breath.

Scanning the horizon, I spot something shimmering in the distance. My eyes widen at the sight—a veritable oasis in the middle of the rocky ground. Water. It's got to be only a kilometer or so away. Without thinking, I immediately start off in that direction, carefully taking stock of my surroundings so I can find my way back.

Now that I have a destination, I decide to walk and not think. I can't think about the fact that I've never met a World Builder with an implant. I've only met three of them in person, but I knew they weren't synced the second they opened their mouths. They talked about 'us' like we weren't 'them.' I always assumed it was because they were the decision-makers, but after what Kenna said...

See? I can't think about that. Because then I can't think about Mom. Or Oren, or Glyn, even though I'm still disgusted by what she did. I can't think about the fact that some of what Kenna said made sense. That Mila exists in the Real world and corroborated parts of her story. Tears sting the corners of my eyes, and I walk faster, pounding the dirt and rocks with my footfalls.

How am I supposed to make sense of this? What am I supposed to do now? Go back and pretend I never heard anything? *If I have to choose between getting an implant or dealing with this mess...* Tabor's words echo in my head. He's right. Even if I go back, I'll know that there are people out here fighting us. Fighting me. And if I stay here, I'll be fighting...them. The World Builders. Community leaders. The people who built my entire, blissful existence. And every single person I care about.

I'm sweaty and out of breath when I see him. Skidding to a stop, I grip a dead tree trunk and yank my body mostly behind it, hoping he didn't notice me. Man-boy, or Alek—I guess I should use his real name now that I know it—is directly in front of me. In the lake. Stark naked.

CHAPTER 27

How DO I know he's stark naked? Because his clothes are in a pile on the rock between us, and his tanned skin seems to glow in the reflected light off the lake. The water is thankfully waist-deep, and his back is turned as he wipes the water from his eyes and throws his wet hair back from his face.

Seeing him now, it's much more apparent that he's young. The way he dresses—it threw me off initially. His shirt has a collar, and his pants are held up by a belt. In P3, that would be considered a more than foreign retro look.

No time to ruminate on that, though. I need to get out of here now. My brain screams of the embarrassment and possible danger of being caught spying. My body, however, isn't in the mood to be obedient. I'm glued to the tree, staring at this strange, beautiful creature. Trying to figure him out—peering at what he's holding in his hand to scrub his skin. His dark hair clings to his neck, and the muscles in his back flex as he lifts his arms to wash his shoulders. My face feels suddenly hot, and I swallow hard.

GO! My mind screams, but I'm frozen with indecision. I've stayed too long. If I walk back the way I came, he could see me and assume I was spying on him. Super awkward and embarrassing. There's no way he *won't* see me if I continue to hide—the tree trunk isn't thick enough. I could make my way farther up the edge of the lake. Again, there's the risk he might see me, but at least then I could plead ignorance. Or—

He plunges himself under the surface to rinse, and I launch my body forward. No 'or.' This is my only viable plan. Staring straight ahead, I navigate through the tree trunks staying parallel to the water. When I've gone a reasonable distance, I step through the trees to the rocky beach. I walk out at the lapping waves and realize my mistake immediately. Though I couldn't see Alek from my vantage point through the trees, our small jetties are completely visible to each other. He looks my direction, and I suddenly become very interested in picking the pebbles from the underside of my shoes. I slip them off hastily and scrape at them.

"Don't drink it," he calls, and I look up. He's half-dressed and in the middle of pulling his shirt over his head.

"What?" I yell back, holding a hand to my ear.

"Don't drink the water. It'll kill you."

"I know that, thanks." I did not know that. It will *kill me?* Is it even safe to touch?

"It won't irritate your skin much—just keep your mouth, nose, and eyes closed if you go under."

I sniff. "I wasn't planning to go under, but again. Thanks." I was totally planning to go under. This guy is a complete know-it-all, and it irks me.

He sets his shoes on the ground and slips his feet into them. They're like no shoes I've ever seen before, and I squint for a better look. Apparently, he takes this as an invitation to walk toward me.

"I guess you'll be fine, then." He stops close enough for me to see his features clearly. His messy hair drips on his shoulders, leaving dark spots on the shirt with a collar. Everything about him is foreign and mysterious, and as much as I don't want him to know I'm intrigued, I can't stifle my curiosity much longer.

"What kind of shoes are those?" I ask before I can stop myself.

He looks amused. "These?" Lifting his foot, he takes a look.

"I've never seen anything like them."

He shrugs. "I don't think they're a 'kind' of shoe. My dad made them for me."

"He made them?"

Alek laughs at my look of astonishment. "Yeah, we make everything. We don't have a Community providing everything for us, remember?"

"Right," I say awkwardly. He must think I'm so entitled and weak. After meeting them, *I* might think I'm entitled and weak.

"Are those the clothes you wear in the Communities?" He points at my grey shirt and pants.

I nod. "Nobody ever sees them, though."

Now it's his turn to look confused, and I grin.

"I was telling your sister about that earlier," I say. Realizing I'm still holding my shoes, I set them down on a log near my feet. "Since our implants are connected to the Edge, we choose what we want everyone else to see. We can change our appearance every day—every hour—if we want."

"Sounds like a lot of work."

"Nobody really does it that often."

He walks closer, and my heart races.

"Can I see it?"

"What?" I ask, my voice catching.

"Your implant." He continues moving toward me, and I clear my throat.

"I don't think you can see anything from the outside. That's the cornea," I say, pointing to the front of my eye. "The implant is inside on the retina—"

He stands directly in front of me and reaches out, placing his fingers under my chin and tipping my face upward.

"I know my anatomy," he says, his voice low as he stares intently into my eyes.

My heartbeat quickens. He's so close. Though I try to shut it down, my body remembers how good it felt that last night with Aave. But this is *not* Aave, I remind myself. He tips my face from side to side, and his eyes narrow as he scrutinizes me.

I pull away, my cheeks hot.

"I'm sorry, I didn't mean—"

"I'm not a science experiment, okay?" I turn back toward the lake and reach down to pick up a pebble.

"I know, I was just—"

"Thanks for the information about the water," I say, cutting him off. "I'd like to bathe now if that's alright with you. I need to get things ready to go home tomorrow."

He ponders this a moment, not retreating like I'd hoped. "You're going back?"

"Of course I'm going back."

The silence is palpable. I sift pebbles in my hand until I'm sure he must be gone.

When I turn, I'm relieved to find myself alone again. I quickly pull off my clothes, walk back to place them next to my shoes, and freeze. On the log is a small, round disc.

Carefully setting my clothes down, I pick it up. The scent of lavender and—oranges? Lemons?—fills my nostrils. Sighing gratefully, I grip it tightly and step into the inky water.

Clean and mostly dry after the walk back, I cautiously make my way to my tent. Surprisingly, I find myself getting used to this odd landscape. There's a macabre sort of beauty between the fiery sky, gnarled wood, and glittery granite. Lifeless, barren, but poetic nonetheless. I bet an artist like Carole Marine could find some story to tell in all this. With my coding brain, I'm coming up short with words to do it justice.

The camp is humming like a nest of bees with everyone loading up and making preparations for the next day. I spot Tabor and Erin sitting on a boulder near their shelter. Tabor nods my way, and I walk toward them out of perceived obligation.

"Got your walking shoes on?" he asks, rubbing his hand over his shaved head.

"Always," I grin. "Those are going to be the best few miles of my life."

Tabor laughs and motions for me to come closer. "I'm not talking about tomorrow," he says in a hushed tone. "I'm talking about tonight."

I look at him questioningly.

"Okay, fine," he shouts. "I'll show you that rock I found. It's inside." He stands abruptly and walks to their tent, opening the flap. I follow hesitantly.

"What's going on?" I ask as soon as Erin joins us.

Tabor puts a finger to his lips and begins to talk. "I know, isn't it a beauty? I found it right along the edge of the trees."

"Wow," I say, playing along. "So colorful."

He gives me an odd look, and I blush. Blushing in real life is embarrassing enough that it only makes me blush harder. It's not fair that my body betrays me like this, and I have no way to hide it. Tabor motions for us to gather together in the middle of the tent.

"I got a glimpse at Kenna's map today," he whispers. "If you had to guess, how far do you think we are from the closest Paradise Community?"

"No clue," I answer honestly.

He nods. "On the map, it shows a body of water slightly north and probably a couple of kilometers away—"

"I think I was just there. It's not far at all," I say quietly.

He beams at me. "You walked over there?"

I nod. "I walked up the hill and happened to see it through the trees."

"That confirms it then," he says, celebrating as much as possible with Erin while attempting to remain silent. "That's the water source for P4!" he whispers excitedly.

"No way."

"Way," Erin whispers.

"That means we're four to five kilometers away from P4 boundaries, max."

"But I thought you guys were from P—"

"Right," Tabor shakes his head. "We're not from P4, but don't you get it?" He looks at me expectantly, but I've got nothing. I'm beginning to think I'm not as bright as I thought I was. I stare at him blankly, and he shakes his head in mock disappointment.

"These lunatics are trying to take down the Communities," he says, pointing toward the tent wall. "They're offering to take us home, but as soon as we do that, we've got no way to tell our leaders where the coalition is or where they're headed. This is only a temporary camp."

"So..."

"So we break into P4. Tonight," Erin whispers a little too loudly, and Tabor hushes her.

"Are you kidding me? You want to—"

"Shhh!" Tabor growls.

I lower my voice. "You want to turn them all in?"

"Don't *you?*" he counters, his eyes wide and maniacal. "If we go there tonight, we could lead them right to this camp before anyone even wakes up in the morning. Then *they* could get us all back to our rightful Communities."

"And we'll be heroes. Taking down the opposition," Erin adds.

She's not wrong. If Kenna is the leader of this coalition, I can only imagine what her location would be worth to the Community leaders.

"There's no way it can be that easy," I say softly. "Kenna isn't going to just let us march out of here—"

"You just walked to the lake, didn't you? Did anyone stop you?" Tabor asks.

"Well, no, but—"

"Exactly. They're busy. And they think we're helpless. So that's why we sneak out before everyone settles down for the night."

Erin steps cautiously back toward the door. "I'm going to spread the message to the others—"

I look at her, surprised she's completely on board with this. Wasn't she just expressing some doubts after the meeting earlier?

"What about the Real's?" I blurt out.

"Who?"

"Those other kids our age. The ones from Southwest Territory."

Tabor scoffs, "Who cares? They left their homes because they're dying out. It's time they joined the Communities anyway."

I bite my tongue. He's right; they should join up. But is it our place to force them into it? Something about being even a tiny part of what is sure to be their forced integration feels wrong to me.

"Go back to your tent. We'll send a message when it's time," Tabor says, then looks past my shoulder at Erin. "I'm sure those two dudes from last night would be up for creating a distraction."

Erin grins mischievously. "On it."

CHAPTER 28

BACK IN MY tent later that afternoon, I find Strawberry curled up on her cot, as usual. It's unsettling to know I'm leaving tonight and yet have nothing to do to prepare. No busy work to quell the nervousness. I have no personal items to pack or bring with me besides the clothes on my back. And Alek's soap.

Tabor's idea fills me with dread, but I can't tell if it's because I think it's a bad idea in general or if I'm just terrified of running off into the wilderness with people I barely know.

The kids from Southwest went off on an adventure, so it can't be that bad. Especially just for a couple of hours. From my studies, I know people used to do things like this for fun. I do get the appeal of being in wide-open spaces—I've done plenty of nature hikes back in P3—but this isn't anywhere close to the same thing.

Tabor's head pops through the flap, and I gasp.

He laughs. "Go eat dinner as soon as it's announced. When you hear the yelling, go back to your tent and wait five minutes. Then head into the trees above camp."

His face disappears, and I sit down on my cot. Strawberry—who I'd almost forgotten was there—rolls over and stands, stretching her arms above her head.

"Wait, are you in on this, too?" I ask, inspecting her face.

She nods.

"So you'll talk to Erin and Tabor, just not to me?" This whole time I've been telling myself her silence isn't personal, but now...it feels really personal.

She walks toward the tent opening, but I reach out and grab her wrist. "Did I do something to offend you? We're from the same Community. We should be able to talk to each other and figure all of this out. I—"

She rips her arm away from me and slips outside without a word.

With a pit in my stomach, I follow Tabor, Erin, three other people I don't know, and Strawberry through the trees between camp and the lake. Their plan is to walk straight into P4 territory as fast as possible. The quicker we are, the less likelihood of someone in Kenna's crew recognizing we've all gone missing for the night. The men Erin talked to definitely pulled out all the stops for their distraction at dinner. From the sound of it, they were still yelling and hammering away at each other even after we waited our five minutes before escaping to the trees. So far, so good.

The sun is low in the sky, which means we really have to cruise. We only have three hand lights, but even those tiny beams would be easily noticeable from camp if they were turned on in close proximity once it's dark.

My eyes dart from Erin's back in front of me to the ground below of my feet. I'm in a good rhythm, and I'm keeping up—but with low visibility, my probability of tripping on a rock and biting it *hard* is high. I don't want to be that girl in this group.

"Their plan isn't going to work," Erin says ahead of me through her heavy breaths. "There's no way they'll be able to stop these implants, even with their small disruptions. They don't even understand the tech they're up against."

"Kenna said she used to be a World Builder," I say.

"What?" Erin turns her head in surprise and almost hits a tree trunk.

"That's what she told me. I went to her tent to figure out what was going on, and she told me she used to be in the Communities."

"Huh. Kenna said she worked on Cerebrolink, so I guess that makes sense. That's where I'm hoping to place," Erin says.

"Still? Seems like things are changing fast enough, they won't need us anymore."

Erin scoffs. "They'll still need us. They'll need people to innovate and upgrade. Whatever learning program Cerebrolink is currently running, it's going to have some bugs."

Fair point. I hadn't thought about that.

"She could've been making all of that up," Erin says. "You know, trying to intimidate you."

The image of Kenna's face directly in front of mine flashes through my mind. *Because I used to be one of them.* It didn't seem like a premeditated lie.

"What changed your mind?" I ask between breaths.

"About what?"

"I don't know—after the meeting it seemed like you weren't sure what to think about everything Kenna said."

"It was a lot to sift through."

"True."

Erin pulls her mask out slightly and wipes her face with her shirt. "I got scared. When she talked about all of the Communities being told the same thing about the implants—I thought maybe..."

"Yeah. I'm worried about those numbers. What if the world is healing faster than we thought? And they did move exceptionally fast with this implant in P3."

"Us, too. But then Tabor was saying that of course all of us would've been chosen for the first round. We're in the original Communities. We've all been there the longest, so it makes sense they'd want us to be the first. You didn't see anyone from P8 or P9 in camp, right?"

"True." I hadn't thought of that. Every one of us is from an original Paradise Community.

"Did anyone in your Community freak out about the timing of Cerebrolink?" I ask.

She dodges around a tree, then picks up her pace as our path opens up. The hand lights flick on ahead of us, making it easier to follow the others.

"A few," she says. "But I'm not concerned about that. We've been using AR for far too long. It's about time they figured out how to give a better sensory experience. If they move too slow, everyone complains about bureaucracy. Too fast, and they've got a nefarious motive."

The group ahead of us slows, and we slump together, all of us breathing heavily from our jog down the hill. I didn't notice it earlier, but now that we've stopped, the sound of rushing water is close.

"Did we pass the lake?" I ask, and Tabor nods.

"We're at the base of the dam." He points ahead with his light, and I see the river.

"I found a good option!" someone calls, and Tabor turns, motioning for us to follow.

One of the girls I haven't met points with her light. "Right there. See that rock? I think we could easily jump to it and avoid getting wet. Then on the other side, we can use those logs to get to the bank."

Tabor nods. "Agreed. Let's cross, and then we can all take a breather. Should be an easy walk from there on out."

I follow behind Erin, and just as I approach the bank, something in my vision flickers. My breath catches, and I freeze.

"Did you see that?" I whisper, and Erin nods frantically.

"You guys!" Erin yells exuberantly. "I think we're getting close enough for Edge access!"

Shouts of excitement rise around us, and I laugh.

"Do we know what direction to take after the river?" I ask.

"Nope," Tabor says, "but this proves we're walking in the right direction. I know if we walk in there and sync, someone in P4 is going to find us. There's no way they don't stop us the second their security system picks us up."

"I've never thought about our security a day in my life," I say. "I'm glad you know so much about it."

"My dad's placement. That's the only reason," Tabor says proudly. "Man, they picked the wrong group to mess with."

"Don't they know only top-tier individuals are chosen for Cerebrolink?" a girl chimes in.

Someone laughs. "I can't wait to see the look on their faces."

Immediately my heart stops, and I look up, narrowing my eyes.

"Who said that?" I ask, and the group goes silent. Tabor holds up his light, and I see Strawberry's cheeks flush. Our bodies give us up every time.

"So you thought if you stayed silent, I wouldn't figure out who you were?"

She stares at the ground.

"What's going on here?" Tabor asks, confused.

"Would you like to tell them, Glyn?" I stare at her. She looks nothing like her form in P3. Her fair skin and light hair are exactly opposite.

When she refuses to open her mouth, I step closer. "This is Glyn. I'm not sure what she's told you, but she's from P3, and she's a liar and a thief."

Glyn's eyes flash. "That's not true."

I laugh. "Oh, it's not? Did you or did you not steal my code and pretend it was yours just so you could get the Cerebrolink?"

She glares at me, and that expression I recognize.

"Which is ironic," I continue, "because it looks like you got the implant the same day as me. And look where it got us both."

"There was a delay," she hisses.

"Clearly." Rage mixes with the anxiety and frustration already boiling within me, and I can't keep it contained.

"*How dare you?*" I explode. "How dare you claim our project as your own and then act like a coward sitting next to me in that tent for *three days* and not reveal yourself? We've been friends our entire lives, Glyn, and that obviously means nothing to you." I close the distance between us, and she backs away. "*It's pathetic.*"

"Want to know what's pathetic?" she shouts back, off-balance. "You whining to Erin the entire way about 'what if the world is healing faster than we think?' Same old Channel. Never trusting anyone outside of yourself."

"I trusted you! And Aave!"

"Yeah, 'trusted.' As long as you always got to be the one making final decisions," she says snidely. "That's not trust, Channel. You're controlling and overbearing, and that's why I claimed our project. Because you've never let me do anything to stand out. Or at least ever stand above you."

Her words sting as if she'd slapped me, and I lurch backward.

"Okay," Tabor says, stepping between us, "I get that you have some personal history here, but we really have to get going. We can deal with this later." He turns and begins to walk. The others follow, and Glyn takes one last opportunity to flash a look of complete revulsion before sweeping past me.

"Come on," Erin says, nudging my shoulder.

"No," I shake my head. "I'm out. If she's here, I'm not coming."

"Don't you think that's a bit of an overreaction?"

"Call it what you want."

Erin puts her hands on her hips. "That's the biggest cop-out I've ever heard."

I know she's right, but the weight on my chest won't let me admit it.

"So, what?" Erin throws up her hands, "You're just going to spend the night out here?"

"I'll make my way back up toward camp. When you all bring in the cavalry, I'll be there."

Erin looks at me disapprovingly.

"It could be helpful to have someone there. Just in case."

"Do what you want, I guess." She tosses me her light and turns, jogging to catch up with the group. As she relays the information to everyone, a few people turn their heads. Someone motions for me to come with, but I shake my head and give a small, noncommittal wave. As their lights move further away, I turn and begin the trek back up the mountain solo.

CHAPTER 29

OUR PATH SEEMED a lot shorter on the way down. My breath comes in fits and spurts as I determinedly put one foot in front of the other, continuing the climb back to camp. Passing the lake a few moments ago settled my anxiety over whether I'd chosen the right direction, at least. The very present fear of being lost on this mountain has brought me to tears twice, though I blame my encounter with Glyn for most of my emotional instability.

Even though there's literally nobody around, I find myself desperate for the Edge—especially after that small glimmer of hope back there. I hate that my emotions are glaringly present on my face. The mask helps slightly, but I'm also incredibly over that, too. My skin is irritated, and I've probably got a permanent indentation on my nose at this point. *Why me?* I could be comfortably implanted and hanging out with Oren. Instead, my quads are burning, my face itches, and I just completely blew up at the only 'friends' I had here.

Gasping, I collapse onto the nearest boulder and put my head between my knees. Why do I even care so much about Glyn? It's not like it even matters—I know the World Build and placements are irrelevant at this point. Obviously, there are much bigger things in this world to worry about.

But still. It feels like she keeps shoving a hot poker into my heart. One moment it's nonexistent and the next, something like this makes it molten hot again.

I remind myself it's only been a little over a week since everything went down. It's a lot to process. Betrayal, life-altering medical procedures, world-changing technology, loss, fear...adjectives slam one after another into my thoughts. And I feel nothing. It's too much at this point, and my brain is completely shutting down—not allowing me to bear the weight of it.

I close my eyes and continue to catch my breath. My life is completely out of control. That's why this hurts so bad. I can't *do* anything, nor do I have enough information to make a good plan of action even if I could. I'm entirely at the mercy of the groups around me. The Communities, the Coalition. It's stupid. *All of this is so stupid!*

Pressing my hands into the granite beneath me, I stand and take off running up the hill. I don't care if I can't breathe. I don't care if I pass out and die here in this barren dirt. I don't care—

"Agh!" I scream involuntarily as my body slams into something solid. I'm thrown sideways, landing hard in the dirt. My head smacks against a tree trunk—after my body took most of the hit, thankfully—and for a moment, specks of light sparkle in front of my eyes.

"Are you okay?" a deep voice asks, sounding distant and almost ethereal. "Hey, Channel. Are you okay?"

The words begin to solidify, and I attempt to focus on the face in front of me. Someone's there, but everything is fuzzy—shifting.

"No, don't get up," he says. "Lie back. Just close your eyes and breathe."

I obediently relax my arms and do as the stranger says. The world seems suddenly quiet and almost peaceful. I can still hear the sound of rushing water in the distance. Am I still near the lake? What was I doing after I passed it?

"Can you hear me?" the voice calls again.

"Hmm?" I say, opening my eyes. This time, I see him clearly, but I can't immediately place him. Long hair, concern on his face.

"Hey," he says softly. "I need to put something on that cut. Stay here, I just need a second."

His hand slips out from behind my neck, and my head throbs at the slight movement. I groan, wishing he was still there. I don't want to be alone right now, and he feels safe. My heart starts to pound out of fear, only making the pressure in my head strengthen.

Scuffling noises sound next to me, but I don't trust myself to turn.

"Here," he says, pressing something cool against my forehead. A ripping sound rings in my ears, and his hand gently lifts my head again. A band of something soft touches both ears and pulls tightly against my head. The pressure against my skin somehow centers the pounding slightly.

"You need to keep this tied firmly, okay? I know it might not be the most comfortable thing—"

"What is it?" I ask, my voice weaker than I'd intended.

"Birch bark. And a piece of my shirt. It'll stop the bleeding and help it heal."

I take a deep breath and open my eyes. He's inspecting the bandage, and the look on his face sparks my memory.

"Alek."

"Yeah?"

"You're Alek."

He chuckles. "You must not be too messed up if you can remember that." He adjusts the placement of the cloth slightly, and I wince. "Sorry. That should be better." Leaning back slightly, he meets my eyes. "What were you thinking? Running around out here in the pitch dark?"

My eyes dart left to right, and I point when I find my hand light in the dirt.

"Yeah, that light is tiny. Not sufficient for night jogging."

I laugh and immediately regret it. My hand flies to my forehead.

"Shhh," he says, pressing his hands against my temples. "You need to be really still."

"I have to get back."

"To camp?"

"Mmhmm."

"I know. I'll help you, but it's not happening right this second. We've got time. I promise—"

"No!" I insist. "I need to get back." Panic fills my chest, and with it comes a sudden burst of adrenaline. I press my forearms into the dirt and lift my body slightly.

His hands hit my shoulders. "No, Channel. You banged your head. Hard. You need to take it easy."

He doesn't get it. If I don't make it back before P4 gets there, I could be stuck out here forever. He could be stuck out here forever.

A wave of guilt passes through me, and I stop struggling. He's going to be stuck no matter what.

"We have to get back now, Alek."

His eyebrows narrow. "What were you doing out here?"

"What were *you* doing out here?"

He purses his lips. "Scouting things out."

"Why?"

He takes a deep breath and looks out into the night. His hands are still on my shoulders, and in the stillness, I suddenly become very aware of his touch.

"Because I'm not convinced that Kenna's going to make good on her promise," he sighs. "She needs people, and I'm not here to enlist my family in a confrontation with the Communities. We want to find people on the outside, that's it."

He looks back at me and lifts his hands, rechecking the bandage.

"What was her promise?" I ask.

"To us?"

I nod carefully.

"She said she'd take us past the P4 boundaries and help us map a path out east." He shakes his head. "I don't know why I'm telling you this. I know you think we're crazy, and this probably makes zero sense to you. Don't worry about it." He leans back, resting on his knees.

"I was out here because there's a group heading into P4," I blurt out. I don't know if I can trust him, but I don't know if I can trust anyone. The fact that he opened up to me makes me feel like it's worth the risk.

"What do you mean?" he asks intently.

"Tabor, Erin—"

He looks at me blankly.

"Two other people in the group like me—they're from P2," I explain, "they don't believe Kenna either. They're headed into P4 to give away the Coalition's position."

"And you were with them."

Again, I nod slowly. "I—I didn't feel good about your group getting wrapped into this."

"So you left to warn us?"

"Something like that," I mutter, closing my eyes and lifting my hand to my forehead.

He doesn't say anything.

"It wasn't that noble," I admit, still looking at the inside of my eyelids. "You know the girl from P3? Who shared my tent? I have a history with her."

"I assumed you would."

My eyes fly open. "Well, I didn't until tonight," I say a little too strongly, and the pounding starts up again. Slightly less intense this time, which I assume is a good sign. "She didn't ever talk, and we don't really see each other in the Communities."

"Right, I remember. Still sounds like a lot of work."

I roll my eyes. "Regardless, I didn't know it was her."

"And that matters because…"

"Because she cheated me out of some coding work I did. Before I was pulled into this hot mess."

He nods. "I'm sorry."

"It's fine."

"Doesn't sound like it."

"Well, whatever, it's not important. We're wasting time. We need to—"

"I need to know why you're telling me this."

I stare at him. "Why does it matter? We need to get back—"

"It matters because I'm curious and because I think you still need some time to sit still and rest, so I'm stalling."

He smiles, and my breath catches. This smile isn't guarded or purposeful, and suddenly I can't think straight. To be fair, it could just be the concussion. I swallow hard.

"I just—I guess I don't think it's fair that you get forced into living life in the Communities if you don't want to. You're right. I do think it's crazy that you're living out here on your own. I honestly don't know how you deal with wearing these all the time—"

"We don't have to wear masks 'all the time.' We have filters," he says calmly, still observing me almost clinically as I talk.

"Well, you don't have filters here," I say.

"True. And to your point, I agree. It's annoying."

I smile slightly. "Anyway, I don't get why you're fighting it, but I do think it's your choice. If P4 comes tonight..."

"We're toast."

I raise an eyebrow. "What?"

He meets my eyes, confused.

"What does that mean? About 'toast?'"

A laugh bursts out of him. "You've never heard that phrase before?"

"No. It was weird."

"It's something my parents always say—it means it's over. We're done for," he says, still chuckling.

"How does that make any sense? And does toast even exist anymore?"

"Okay," he laughs, "I get it. It's weird. But *now* we're wasting time. The fact that you're able to muse about regional idioms means you're probably going to be just fine." He reaches behind my neck with one hand and gently supports my head as he grips my right arm and begins to lift.

"Slow," he says, observing me as I begin to rise from the ground.

"Did I hit you, or did I hit a tree?" I ask, distracting myself from the rushing blood in my ears.

"Both. Me first, then the tree."

I breathe deeply, waiting for the pounding to subside as I finally reach my feet.

"It was my fault. I saw your light and came to check it out. I didn't realize you were moving so fast."

"I was."

"Hmm?"

"Moving fast."

"I think we've established that."

I laugh and immediately hunch over as a bright light explodes behind my eyes.

"No laughing," he says seriously. "Just one foot in front of the other. We aren't far."

I cling to him, allowing his body to guide mine through the tree trunks and around the rocks embedded in the hillside. It's comforting and terrifying all at once. It's not like me to blindly follow anyone, let alone someone I just met. Although I guess it is becoming a new habit. Thankfully, the pressure inside my head won't allow me to properly self-reflect.

I keep my eyes fixed on the ground, made visible by the thin glow of my hand light. After a few minutes, though, everything seems to blend together. Alek and I move in sync with each other, our feet hitting in a steady rhythm. My eyelids beg for permission to close, and just as I'm about to give in, my body stiffens.

"Wait!" I shout, and Alek grips me tightly, frantically scanning the area for danger.

"No, it's okay, I just thought I saw..." I trail off, still holding tightly to his waist, pulling him back a few paces. "There!" I point excitedly until he shines the light in the direction of my finger.

I gasp as the small splash of green is illuminated. Together we move closer, and—with Alek's help—I crouch down to investigate.

"What is it?" I breathe.

"It looks like a plant."

I smile wryly. "Thanks for that. I might be Unreal, but I'm not a complete idiot. I meant what *kind* of plant."

He shrugs.

"It doesn't matter," I whisper, lifting the tender leaves and sweeping my fingers along their edges. "It's growing. In the middle of all this."

"Mila found a plant growing like this outside of Kaye's home."

I stare at the thin stem and marvel at how the light seems to make the spring green glow from within. This amount of detail and intricacy is not what I'm used to.

"Incredible."

"I hate to say it, but I think we have to keep going." Alek's voice brings me back to reality, and I nod. Leaning on him again, I stand. This time, the throbbing in my head nearly bowls me over. I forcibly close my eyes and focus intently on putting one foot in front of the other while simultaneously not throwing up. And even in this most uncomfortable moment, the green shoot continues to light up my subconscious. The plant I just saw proves that Kenna was correct about one thing. Which means she could be right about all of them.

CHAPTER 30

"Is she awake?" Mila asks, tentatively peeking her head past the wooden door to my room. Alek, sitting on a small stool next to me, waves her in. She inspects my face, and even in my half-awake stupor, I find myself shrinking. I know I look awful.

"Hey," she says gently, walking toward the bed. "Remember me?"

Alek quickly jumps up from his seat, moving out of the way for her to sit down. Every time I've opened my eyes, he's been somewhere in the room —on the stool, propped against the wall, napping on the floor. I'm starting to feel guilty that he feels so guilty about knocking me out.

"Mila, right?" I say, my voice scratchy from a lack of use.

She smiles. "You got it. How are you feeling?"

"Better," I say, and without thinking my hands lift to my face. There's nothing there. "No masks?" I ask in shock.

Mila waves at the air around us. "Filtered," she says with a grin.

I sigh gratefully and run my fingers over the bumpy rash on my skin. It's in a perfect circle where my mask sat against my face. No way to hide that here, but at least I'm not the only one. Mila has a ring around her mouth and nose, too.

"Your bandage is gone," I say.

"We swapped places," she laughs, and I smile.

"Alek was telling me we're still with the Coalition," I say.

Mila nods. "We're at their home base. At least for now. I guess they move around a lot."

It makes sense. With what they're doing, there's no way Community leaders aren't looking for them constantly.

"What happened to everyone else?" I ask, not sure if I want to hear the answer.

Alek shifts uncomfortably, only confirming my suspicions. He clears his throat. "Anyone who wanted to go back to the Communities stayed."

"At the temporary camp?" I ask.

"Yes."

"They were left behind? Alone?"

Alek nods, and Mila looks away.

Suddenly feeling faint, I press into my pillow. "Figures," I sigh.

"I didn't like it either," Mila says quickly, "but the Coalition was sure they'd either be picked up by P4 and your friends—"

"They weren't my friends," I cut in automatically. I don't remember much of that night, but I do remember Glyn. The way she looked at me as she passed. I shiver.

"Right, sorry," she says. "I mean the people you were with. The group left at camp was given directions into P4 just in case nobody showed up."

I nod, feeling better about the situation. "It's definitely walkable."

"And they have water close by. They were given some food supply, as well," Alek adds.

"So you're saying I shouldn't go on a rampage about this?" I tease, hoping to convey I'm mostly over it.

"I mean, it would be fun to watch." Alek laughs, and I can't help but smile at him. I catch my eyes lingering and reach my hand around to rub my neck as a distraction.

"So," Alek says, clapping his hands together. "You need food. I'll go grab that."

"Wait," I say, just as he turns toward the door. "I know I told you about our group going into P4, but..." I hesitate, not wanting to accuse anyone. "How did it turn into all of this?"

"You mean, how did the Coalition find out?" Mila asks.

I nod warily.

"That was me," she says hesitantly. "I told Kenna."

I stare at her intently, waiting for a more in-depth explanation.

"I didn't feel good about leaving them," she continues, "and I don't think we could've traveled without their help. You were in bad shape—"

"You wanted to take me with you?" I ask, cutting her off. Why would they have taken me with them? They knew I was planning to go back to my Community. Alek had already done everything he could to help me, which was above and beyond given the circumstances. They could've left me there to be found by P4.

"Of course," Alek says simply.

I look at both of them, somewhat perplexed. They don't owe me anything, and yet—

"I know Zayn and Alek—probably Kaye, too—don't agree with me, but I trust the Coalition," Mila says conclusively.

"I don't think we have enough info," Alek says hastily, "I didn't say I completely disagree with you."

Mila rolls her eyes at her brother, and a laugh escapes my lips. The sudden motion makes my head spin slightly, and I press my palms into the mattress to steady myself.

"That just means we need to find out more," I say, and I mean it. I want all the information I can get my hands on. And I think I want to find it with them.

CHAPTER 31

"THAT'S CRAZY," I say. "None of you know what you're doing. The Coalition is going all vigilante and you four—you seriously thought you could cross from ocean to ocean on your own? Without Edge access?"

"What else were we supposed to do?" Alek says defensively. "It was only a matter of time before things started to break down—"

"Hey," I cut in, "I'm not saying I don't get the motivation—I'm only saying it was incredibly stupid." Alek looks at me, brooding, and I have to stop myself from smiling. He's cute when he's mad.

"And maybe a little bit brave," I add. Alek looks away, but not before I catch the corner of his mouth lifting slightly.

What am I doing? Am I flirting with this boy I barely know? Who comes from a completely different background and whose path I'll most likely never cross again in the future? Actually...that doesn't sound half-bad. Until I think of Aave and realize *I'm a terrible person*. Is there something wrong with me? I'm in the midst of a crisis and all I can think about is—

"It *is* crazy, though," Mila agrees. "They seemed a lot more professional when they picked us up."

"I need to know more about how that went down," I say.

Kaye speaks up. "We were down at the river washing our clothes." Her voice is light and airy, consistent with her waifish appearance. She's the one I've talked with least, and I can't quite get a bead on her.

"And they tranq'd you?" I ask.

"Nooo," Mila says slowly. "Did they tranquilize you?"

"Mila had a bandage because she fell and hit her head," Kaye says before I can answer. I'm glad to let the question slide.

"Ah, that makes sense," I say, thinking back to that night in the clearing.

Mila grimaces. "It wasn't as bad a fall as yours."

"You passed out," Kaye says, and Mila shrugs.

"What about you?" I ask, pointing to Zayn.

"What about me?"

"Do you have anything to say? About anything? Ever?"

Zayn scoffs, and Mila laughs out loud.

I look between them quizzically. "I don't think I've ever heard you speak." I wait, folding my arms across my chest.

"I speak plenty," Zayn says.

"Too much sometimes," Mila mutters, and Zayn looks at her, annoyed.

"Fine," he says. "You want to hear my version? These two decided to go down to the river and came within inches of P4 boundaries. A few Coalition members found our camp and—after talking with Alek and me—rushed to find them before they accidentally crossed and tripped security. They risked their lives to keep us undercover and bring us back to camp."

"Wait, the river? That's the boundary?" I ask, ignoring Mila's expression of frustration.

"That's what they told us," Zayn says.

"When you cross a boundary. That's when the Edge is accessible," I say to myself, remembering the glorious flicker of light at the river.

"Explain," Alek says, and I look up to see them all looking at me, confused.

"You know what the Edge is, right?"

They nod in unison.

"I'm guessing for you, though, the Edge is accessible through a port—you have to link up with a device?"

They nod again.

"Well for me, it's not like that. It's linked to me through my retinal implant. Right now it's completely offline, so it doesn't matter, but when I'm inside a Community, I'm connected permanently. That means everything I see is dictated by my settings and whatever program is currently running. The whole time I've been out here, I've wondered where and how I'd be able to link up again. When I walked down to the river that night with Tabor and Erin—the group of Unreals heading into P4—I saw something. A flicker. I'm sure if I would've continued on, the signal would've gotten stronger."

"I wonder why the signal is only available inside the boundaries?" Mila asks.

"Think about it," Zayn says. "Why would they want to use more energy and bandwidth to send their signals out into no man's land?"

"It's more than that," I say excitedly, "it's about purposeful signal interference."

They look at me blankly.

"Because the whole earth has had universal connection for over a hundred and thirty years."

Again, blank stares.

"Okay, let's step back. What do you know about the Edge, exactly?"

"It connects us to information," Kaye says. "I've never actually used it, though."

My eyes widen.

"I know it's a worldwide network, allowing us to communicate and access information. When it's working," Alek says.

"Right, but don't you see?" I say. "This is how they've been cutting you off! You can't just 'turn off' the Edge. It exists everywhere. Ever since 7G became a thing in the early two-thousands, the orthogonal frequency division multiplexing tech became so advanced that high-quality signals existed literally everywhere, and nobody could turn it off or disconnect."

"Wait," Mila says, holding up her hands and blinking rapidly. "*What* is that?"

"What?"

"The orthogonal whatever whatever you just said."

I laugh, forgetting that the tech I live and breathe probably sounds like nonsensical babble to them. "In simple terms, it's the ability to modulate a digital signal across several different channels to reduce interference." I search their faces for some element of understanding. "You send signals out in unique ways so they don't cancel each other out and can reach farther distances."

This gets a few nods. "You've really never learned any of this?"

"Maybe our parents knew it," Alek says, "but there really wasn't a need or opportunity to teach us."

And it's in this moment when I realize how truly divergent our lives have been. They haven't had access to any of the knowledge the rest of the world lives and breathes every day. It's the equivalent of them growing up on a desert island.

"Yeah," I say, "that makes sense. I'll try to explain this the best way I can, but keep asking questions if I go too fast."

I lean over to the bedside table, pick up my cup, and take a drink of water, attempting to gather my thoughts. My moments of clarity come and go, and I don't want this train of thought to disappear quite yet.

"So, we got continually better at modulating these signals, right, but then —of course—people realized this faster speed also gave governments, corporations, and tech companies massive amounts of information, as well as complete flexibility in their bandwidth. Then the question became 'how can we monetize this?'"

Alek's eyes are narrowed, intensely focused. "Smart City explosion."

"Exactly. The internet of 'things.' That's where the Edge was born. That tech allowed us to move applications and services to the *edge* of the network instead of pulling from central data centers. Along with other processes that are too complicated to get into, this basically obliterated the ceiling on what companies could provide to consumers."

"I don't need to comprehend everything, but what exactly are Smart Cities?" Kaye asks.

"Where everything was connected," Alek says. "Imagine billions of devices talking to each other—a whole network of digital communication happening under your feet. Like you'd pull something from the cupboard, and your house would notify the store that it needed to be replaced."

"Exactly. Breakfast is ready when you get up, your car takes you to work, your food is at the door when you get home—you barely have to think about anything."

Kaye nods, impressed.

"Sounds idyllic," Mila says.

"It was. Until it wasn't," I say, thoroughly enjoying the drama of my storytelling.

"Right," Mila breathes. "But don't you think that eruption would've knocked the signals out?"

"I'm not even talking about the eruption yet. I'm talking about privacy. If nobody could disconnect, that meant someone had access to you and your information at all times of day. Not everybody appreciated that."

"Understandable," Alek says.

"Dad would lose his mind," Mila says, her eyes wide.

"Finding ways to hide off-grid became a rich man's game. And to your point, Mila, yes, the eruption unhinged things for a time, but not forever. The new tech and the communication possibilities it created is exactly what allowed us to survive. Getting everything back up and running was imperative to producing filters and managing our food production, for example. The human race would've been wiped out without it."

"But life wasn't running as smoothly as it was before," Zayn says. "I know this part."

I nod. "Right. I'm sure you're all very well versed in the birth of the Communities, but now that you understand the before, think about this: if you created a way for a small group of people to live life at a higher level than everyone else, would you want that signal to be freely accessed by everyone?"

"Definitely not," Alek says. "Someone would want to benefit."

"I don't know about benefiting," I shrug. "In the beginning, this was a group effort between the five major tech companies in the world. It was altruistic cooperation to—"

"Ha!" Zayn laughs out loud, interrupting me. "It was not altruism."

Mila nods as if saying *I warned you*, and I grin.

"How so?" I ask calmly. "The Communities weren't formed by a private company, they were working off of grant money from at least sixteen different governments."

"That's still money," Zayn says. "It doesn't matter who it came from. The owners of those companies were billionaires."

"They were billionaires before they took on this project," I argue.

Zayn shakes his head. "I realize we don't know everything about the Coalition, but I agree with what Kenna said. About how Community leaders are trying to control us. All of us—inside and outside. I think it's been that way since the beginning. Maybe they had the money already. This was about gaining power."

"But the Communities dramatically increased our quality of life," I say, this time slightly more impassioned. "Would you want to continue to live looking at rocks and dead remnants of vegetation for the rest of your life if there was a better option?"

As the words leave my lips, I freeze, immediately regretting them.

"Yeah, actually. We would," Zayn says, standing and walking from the room. Mila smiles apologetically and follows after him.

"I'm sorry," I say as Kaye walks toward the door, but before my words fully form, it's just Alek and me.

I lie back on my pillow and take a deep breath. "I didn't mean it like that."

"I think you did," Alek says, his tone kinder than I deserve. He walks toward me and sits on the stool vacated by Mila.

"What were you saying, though—before we got sidetracked?" he asks, and I have to think for a second.

"Umm..."

"You asked if the Communities would want that signal to be freely accessed by everyone."

"Right," I say, thankful for the reminder. "You were correct that they wouldn't want everyone to benefit, but I guess we disagree on the reasons."

"What are yours?"

I shrug. "It was an experiment. A trial. I don't think they wanted anyone to have access to their information before they did."

He nods. "I could see that."

"Anyway, my point was that they would've had to create a way for their signal to remain safe. They'd already started working on ways to protect individual privacy, right? I don't know any of this for sure, but it occurred to me: just as that technology allowed for removing interference, it definitely could've worked backward."

"Creating it. To hide their signals."

"Exactly." Now he's getting it. "And we're way past 7G at this point. 4iO could easily be precise enough to land that signal exactly on a boundary line."

Alek runs his hands through his hair. "Which would prevent families like mine from accessing the Edge."

I nod, noticing the circles under his eyes for the first time. He looks exhausted.

"I'm not saying that's what they did or that their motivations are nefarious, but I can see how it would work," I say.

"Channel, if any Community leaders wanted to help us, they could've helped. We've petitioned them over and over again. They know exactly what they're doing when it comes to the Reals."

"But we don't know why."

"I think Kenna's numbers give a pretty good idea."

"I don't know," I sigh. "My life was really great there, Alek. I don't see how something good could be as bad as she says."

"Just because something's good doesn't mean it's right. Or that it's not headed in the wrong direction."

"But if it's good...does it matter?" I ask carefully, not sure if I actually mean it or not.

Alek stands, stretching an arm over his head. His shirt lifts, baring an inch of his waist, and I can't help but think about the lake.

"I can see why our way of life would seem very...unexciting to you," he says, shaking out his arms.

"It's not that it sounds horrible, it just seems hard. For no reason. I mean, you could be learning anything you want in the Communities. Not having to worry about where your next meal is coming from or how you're going to keep your air filters running. It doesn't cost you anything."

Alek smiles wanly. "Everything has a cost, Channel. You might not recognize it yet, but I think Kenna may have an idea. You have to pay the piper eventually."

I tilt my head quizzically, and Alek laughs.

"Don't tell me you haven't heard that one either?" He shakes his head, and walks toward the door. "Maybe you have more to learn than you think." Grinning, he turns and walks into the hall.

CHAPTER 32

"You're standing," Kenna says, looking up from her plate. The sun is barely rising, but I couldn't stay in my bed one second longer. Spending forty-eight hours lying flat will do that to you.

"I am. Successfully, I might add."

"And you're up early." She stabs a piece of something gelatinous and puts it in her mouth.

"Am I the only one?"

"So far. Help yourself."

I follow her gaze and see breakfast on the counter. Picking up a plate, I serve up my portion, grab a fork, and walk back to the table without looking at it too closely.

"What is this?" I ask, glancing at the thin, square loaf.

"Don't ask."

"That bad?"

She shrugs. "Not bad, just...nondescript. But I'm sure it's nutritious, and I'm grateful I didn't have to cook for everyone."

I take a tentative bite. Bland, but not repellent like some of the others. "Not bad."

"Like I said."

I smile and put another forkful in my mouth. Kenna's dark hair hangs loosely around her shoulders, and somehow this makes her seem more approachable than when she has it tied back. More of a casual peer rather than the leader of the Coalition.

"Who takes care of the food anyway? And where do they get all this?" I ask.

"Ames."

"Have I met Ames?"

"Probably. You'd recognize her, I'm sure. Thin, shorter than me, curly hair?"

I scan my memory but can't place anyone with that description. "She makes everything?" I ask skeptically.

"No. This is courtesy of the Communities."

My brow furrows. "They gave this to you?"

"'Gave' is a strong word."

"Ah," I say, nodding. That makes much more sense.

"Shouldn't I have to schedule an appointment or deal with a bodyguard or something to talk with you like this?"

Kenna laughs. "We're not nearly that organized."

I can feel her eyes on me as I eat, and it's unsettling.

"What do you think?" Kenna asks finally.

I swallow. "About the food or the Coalition?"

She raises an eyebrow.

"I don't know. About the Coalition," I answer honestly. "I'm still trying to figure out what's true and what's not."

"I get that. But if I could prove to you that everything I've said is true—I can't, by the way, but if I could—what would you think?"

Setting my fork down, I contemplate this. If everything she said was true, that would mean the people at the top—the billionaires Zayn mentioned yesterday—would currently have enough power and technological strength to strong-arm the entire world into Community living. They'd be hiding the fact that Earth is on an upswing, making it possible for us to build our own lives. Outside of the Communities. Seems terrifying.

"I guess I'd ask what you're trying to accomplish? I know you're opposed to Cerebrolink, but why? And if the goal of these Community leaders is to 'take over' as you say, why wouldn't they just kill everyone and get on with it? It seems like they'd certainly have the resources."

Kenna nods approvingly. "Those are the right questions."

She stands and takes her dish to the sink, quickly washes it, and sets it next to the sink to dry. This kitchen looks almost prehistoric, and I find myself gawking at every new-to-me piece of outdated equipment she touches.

"Do you know who is currently the worldwide Community head?" she asks.

"Brin Lee, isn't it?"

She nods. "Right. He's organizationally 'in charge,' so to speak. But just like we have a Coalition? So do they. That's how it's always been, ever since the inception of this dream of a new world order. It started with eight delegates, and there are still eight delegates—each from a different part of the world, each with massive technological backing. You have to remember, Channel, these guys didn't just decide to build a utopia out of the goodness of their hearts. They were hurting. With the world in complete crisis, they were watching their companies—their fortunes—everything they'd built waste away into nothing. Technology wasn't going to save the world. It already had. People were using it to survive, but they weren't interested in innovation when they were scrambling to keep themselves alive."

I hadn't thought about it that way. So much for altruism.

Kenna lifts herself up and sits on the counter, swinging her legs lightly beneath her. "By accepting this delegation, they were evolving—grasping at straws to hopefully solidify their positions of power. And it worked. I don't disagree that a lot of good came out of it, but 'a lot of good' doesn't justify what's happening now."

Just because it's good doesn't mean it's right. Alek's words play back in my head, and I feel myself bristling slightly. Why can't it be right? Why can't the good things—the easier things—be right?

"To answer your questions, I'm against Cerebrolink because it gives them too much power. They aren't functioning like a delegation anymore, Channel. They are *the* world leaders at this point. No governments have any sway when the Communities are literally holding all of the technological cards. I give it ten years—maybe twenty—before countries, territories, and governments as we know it completely dissolve. It's already mostly happened here."

True. I didn't even know territories still existed at all until meeting Alek, Mila, Kaye, and Zayn.

"Once that happens? We're done."

We're toast. Again Alek's words flash in my brain, and I bite my tongue to hold in a laugh. Those phrases make absolutely no sense.

"But what does that even mean?" I ask. "We've all been implanted and have no say in what happens anymore? What about the World Builders? What about the people taking care of the infrastructure, food production, all of it? And again, why not just kill us all instead of carrying out some lengthy world domination charade?"

"Eight people, remember?" She gives a meaningful look, but I'm not following. "Not all of them agree," she continues, hopping from the counter and walking toward me. "I'm sure some of them—Brin included —would be completely fine with killing all of us, no problem. But they're not in the majority. My guess is that the majority—while attempting to live within the realm of morals and ethics—still agrees that we can't go back to the way things were before. You know the stats. Community living has decreased our overall resource usage by seventy percent, with all else equal. *Seventy percent*. We haven't had an innovation in efficiency like that in the history of the world. Well, maybe since the invention of farming, but that's beside the point. And Cerebrolink will most definitely increase that."

She sits on the chair next to me, turning it around backward so she has somewhere to rest her arms. "So what would you do? You know the world is on its way back, much faster than expected, but certainly not fast enough to support our old, inefficient way of life. Up until this point, you've chosen to remain in the Real world, and there has to be a reason for that." She looks at me pointedly. "You don't want to harm anyone, but if there was a way...A way to make sure they were happy—beyond happy —until their dying day, and you got to keep the Real world for you and your family. Your best friends, maybe?"

"You think they *are* killing us off."

"Kindly," she says definitively, standing and replacing the chair under the table. "Killing us slowly and *kindly*."

"So how is ripping people from their homes going to help?"

"It's not. We're stalling. Disrupting things enough to draw their focus. Spreading the truth and hopefully gaining more support—"

"I know who you've been targeting. All of us—we were all hoping to place as World Builders." This is a slight exaggeration, but I don't think it's a coincidence that Erin, Glyn, and I all had the same goals, and we all simultaneously ended up here.

Kenna smiles. "Interesting, no?"

The wheels in my head are turning but not gaining traction. Why would she want us here? She was a World Builder. She should have all the skills necessary for any sort of cyberattack, though she'd already mentioned her efforts weren't entirely successful. So why us? Why me?

Kenna's hand lingers on the back of the chair a moment before she turns and grabs her mask from the counter.

"Think about the plant you saw, growing on its own on the side of the hill," she says, slipping the mask over her head and cinching it into place. "I can't give you much more proof than that."

She opens the backdoor, gives a small wave, and walks into the early morning glow.

CHAPTER 33

LATER THAT DAY, the whole house and property are humming. People moving in and out of rooms prepping equipment, packing up essentials, and an entire group of people on projection screens in the main sitting area. And then me. Doing nothing, just watching in frustration because I have no idea what to think anymore. I know the Coalition's preparing for another raid of some sort, and the business of it is fascinating, but I've been mulling over Kenna's words all day and still can't come to a satisfactory conclusion. I don't know why I'm here. And I don't know why any of this could possibly be worth the trouble.

Out the back window I spot Kaye, Mila, Zayn, and Alek playing some game involving thick pieces of wood placed in the dirt and large sticks being thrown at them. This is almost as strange as their phrases.

Zayn tosses his stick, and it misses the block by inches. Mila turns and taunts him, and Zayn runs at her, tossing her over his shoulder and running across the yard. I can't help but smile watching them. It's not all annoyance between those two.

The back door opens, and I sit up straight. Alek pokes his head in and motions for me to come outside. Hesitantly, I stand and walk to the door. Four masks hang on hooks, and I grab one. Mine is being sanitized, and

I'm fairly sure these ones are available for the taking. If they're not...there's nobody here to stop me.

"I saw you through the window," he says as we walk toward the others. "Spying on us?"

"Don't flatter yourself. I'm so bored—watching you was my best option."

Alek grins. "I have a better one. Want to join us?"

"I'm still trying to take it easy."

"Smart. But this is a no-contact game. That excuse isn't going to work."

"Tell that to Mila," I laugh, watching her chase Zayn with a cup of water from the dispenser.

"Mila!" Alek calls, "Don't waste that!"

Mila groans but slows her gait and drinks from the cup instead of throwing it.

"I'm always the bad guy," he sighs.

"Seems that way. So how do you play?" I ask, and Kaye hands me a stick.

She points at the blocks on the ground. "Your goal is to knock as many of those over as you can before Alek hits his." She motions to another set to the right. "When you hit one, you run and grab it and add it to Alek's line. He'll add to yours, and so on. The first one to knock all their blocks down wins."

"I don't know how fast I can run right now," I say.

"I'll be your runner," Kaye offers, grinning at Alek.

Alek looks between us skeptically. "That seems fair."

Kaye laughs. "Ready?"

I nod, and Kaye counts us down. When she says 'go,' I throw my first stick, and it falls short. Kaye hands me another. This time it goes long.

On the third throw, I at least graze one of the blocks. Alek's already running and putting a block on the end of my line.

"Hey!" he shouts, watching Kaye pass me another stick. "You can't hand them to her, she has to pick them up from the ground like me!"

"It hurts my head to bend over," I say churlishly, and he shakes his head, running back to his pile.

"You got this," Kaye says. I throw and hit a block squarely. Kaye immediately takes off and places the block while I continue to aim and fire. I hit another one, and she laughs giddily, running again to retrieve it.

Alek's head spins toward us, an expression of panic on his face. He throws another and hits one of the blocks Kaye just set down. He runs to get it just as I hit another.

"This two on one isn't working for me," he laughs, but I ignore him, focusing on my last block. I hit it, then notice the one he just set down.

"One more, Channel! Hurry, before he hits another one!" Kaye cheers from between our two lines, and my adrenaline spikes. I can barely hold my hand still enough to throw.

"Stop!" I giggle. "If I'm laughing, I can't aim properly!" I toss a stick and miss. Leaning down I grab two more and throw them together. Kaye jumps and shouts as one of them makes contact.

"Winner!" she says triumphantly, and Alek throws up his hands.

"Did you use two?" he asks accusingly.

I shrug, grinning widely.

"If you threw two, that doesn't count."

"Nobody ever told me I wasn't allowed to do that," I say.

"It's true," Kaye laughs, "I forgot that part."

"Convenient story," Alek says, breathing hard as he walks over. "Beginner's luck."

"No luck about it—I'm just a good aim."

Kaye runs up, and we slap hands. "Good teamwork," she says.

"Thanks for the help."

"When your head heals, I call a rematch," Alek says, and I nod in agreement.

Kaye looks around, but Mila and Zayn are nowhere to be found.

Alek perks up. "Where'd they go?" he asks.

"Probably packing up," Kaye says.

"We don't have anything left to pack," Alek mutters.

I laugh. "She's almost an adult. You can't hover over her forever."

"She doesn't feel comfortable around Zayn," he says, and Kaye and I look at each other. Kaye snorts, and I burst out laughing. I'm really beginning to like this girl.

"What?" Alek says, looking slightly offended.

"I think she's probably just fine having him around," I say, and Alek stares at me questioningly. "I think they enjoy each other's company," I clarify, and his eyes widen.

He begins to stomp toward the house, but Kaye grabs his arm. "I'll go check on them, okay? Don't make her mad again, please. For all our sakes."

Alek takes a deep breath and holds it as he watches her walk toward the door.

He finally lets the air out slowly and puts his hands squarely on his hips. "Want to take a walk?"

"I think *you* need to take a walk," I tease, and he looks at me unamused. "Sure, I'll come. It'll be good to move my legs."

We stride past our game and further away from the house. The air is sticky today, and I can already feel sweat beginning to collect along my hairline and the edges of my mask. My skin is never going to heal.

Alek walks quickly, and I try my best to keep up. Eventually, he slows, recognizing my struggle.

"You okay?"

I nod.

"I don't understand why they're suddenly buddy-buddy, you know?"

I look at him, confused. Then realization hits. "Oh! We're still talking about Zayn and Mila?"

Alek grunts and looks away.

"Alek, he's an attractive guy, and Mila's seventeen."

Alek stops and turns to me. "You think he's attractive?"

"I—yeah, I mean, he's strong, and his face—he has a nice face," I stammer awkwardly.

"You're attracted to him?"

"No, I didn't say *I* was attracted to him. I was simply noting that one—especially a seventeen-year-old girl—*could* find him attractive. If that was their thing." My heart is beating out of my chest, and it doesn't escape my notice that my body often does this around Alek. It's a sensation I love and hate—and want again—all at the same time.

He looks away, crossing his arms over his chest.

"It's not like they're pledging their lives to each other, Alek. They're just having fun," I say. "She's smart. You need to trust her more."

"She said she hated him," he mutters, kicking at the rocks by his feet.

I shrug. "Things can change."

"Have things changed for you?" he asks, meeting my eyes.

"What do you mean?"

"Are you going back?"

I ponder on his question. "I think so."

"Well, you should probably figure that out soon," he says brusquely. "Tomorrow they'll be in P3."

"What?" I say, incredulous. "That's where their raid is? Nobody told me that."

"This morning. They practically announced it."

His tone is brash, and I don't appreciate it. After talking with Kenna, I'd gone back to my room and slept. I must've missed it.

"Seems like that would be your chance," he says. "I think we're moving east later in the week."

"We?"

Alek nods. "We're going to stay with the Coalition until we pass P7. Then we should have a clear shot to the coast."

"Have you looked at any maps to see if the people you're looking for actually exist?"

"Yep. The territory is smaller than we'd hoped, but it's there."

"What about your parents?"

Alek turns as if he can see past the miles of barren countryside to wave to them. "We'll arrive in the Eastern Territory much sooner than anticipated, even with these delays. I want to scope things out there before we go back for them."

"Seems like you have a solid plan, then," I say.

"Seems like it."

I purse my lips. "Why is Kenna helping you?"

Alek shrugs. "We're all on the same team as far as I can tell. We all want the freedom to live in the Real world. She's more concerned with taking power away from the Communities, but I think we'll have to join that effort to protect our way of life."

The dissonance within me clashes harshly and bubbles to the surface. It's like a wall stands between my understanding and theirs, and it's maddening beyond belief.

"I still don't get it, Alek. Why is this worth fighting for? You're risking everything for an opportunity to work and have a more difficult life."

"I don't get why you'd want to live in a society where you have to worry so much about your appearance, and no one can ever see the real you," he shoots back. "That sounds more stressful and less satisfying to me."

"What are you talking about?" The question comes out more confrontational than I'd intended, but I press on. "It's not all about appearance."

"The Communities are literally all about appearance. That's why they exist. So people like you don't have to look at—at this all the time," he says, motioning to the dirt, rocks, and dead trees.

I shake my head. "Yes, it's about making our world more visually stimulating, but not because we're obsessed with it or anything. It's just a better way to live."

"Channel, you said you have to decide everything every day—"

"I don't decide everything—the World Builders do! I get to control my own space—my own image, my own living areas—and everything else is done for me."

"And with this new implant?"

"With the new implant, everything will be even better!" I say passionately. "I'll have complete freedom to do whatever I want with whomever I want! Everything will be beautiful, everything will taste fantastic, and everything will be fun because it will be exactly what I want."

Alek shakes his head. "Are you even listening to yourself?"

"How does that not sound amazing?"

He turns and looks at the world around us, thinking for a moment. "Channel, it sounds completely self-indulgent. Like a complete waste of a life."

"How is that a *waste*, Alek? My brain doesn't know the difference between what's actually happening or what it's being told is happening. It's the same thing! I can learn, challenge myself, innovate, grow—all within a perfect simulation."

He turns and walks closer. "But don't you see?" His eyes sear into mine, and the whole world seems to move slower. "That world might be perfectly comfortable—exciting even. But it will never hold meaning because meaning and deep, sustaining fulfillment come from the imperfections. The mess. When I get a break after working in the dirt all day, it feels better than anything in the world because I *didn't have it* a few minutes before. When I eat a delicious meal after going two days without food, it tastes better than any Community enhanced food I've ever tasted. It's the not having it that makes the having it good."

"Sounds unnecessary," I mutter.

Alek ignores me. "And it's our relationships that help us grow, not exciting new challenges or made-up competitions."

My eyes flash. "I'd still have relationships, Alek."

"Would you, though? A relationship isn't just one way, and the best ones aren't all *good* all the time. Do you really think that after building your brain on convenience and a low level of required effort you're really going to have the mental fortitude to stick it out when things get tough with someone? Because meaningful relationships are always tough, Channel." He takes a step closer, and my heart rate speeds. Everything he's saying, I can't even imagine it. Not having things purposefully? It terrifies me to think of the world he's describing. How could anything possibly be made better by being worse?

"The struggle is what makes them great," he says, his voice low and sure. "That's what makes life *great*. Digging into the hard times and working until you feel like you might break. Hurting so bad that you don't think you can take another breath." He takes another step, and he's so close I can feel his breath on my forehead.

"But in my world, I'd always know what to expect. I could control it." My voice is shaky, and my whole body tingles. Something is happening within me that I very much can't control in this moment, and I want to run. To escape. To make it easy again.

Alek reaches out and slips his arm around my waist. "No," he says. "Because then you never truly know if something's Real. If you let the world go—in all its wild unpredictability—and it comes back to you...that's when you find out. That's when you build something bigger and stronger than any code could simulate."

My heart feels like it might burst out of my chest, out of panic or fear or excitement—I can't tell the difference at this point. Standing here with him feels awful and incredible and anxiety-inducing and like I never want to leave all at once.

"What are you thinking?" he asks, his voice low and rough.

"I—I can't think right now," I say. "I think my head is—" I reach up to my forehead, but he catches my hand.

"There's nothing wrong with you," he says, chuckling. "This is the Real world, Channel. This," he whispers, tracing my jaw with his fingers, "and this," he breathes, leaning forward and brushing his lips against my cheek. "I want to be here. Right now, with you. Not because you coded it. Not because you made it happen. This is Real."

I reach up and pull him to me, crushing my lips against his. His hands press against my back, and I can barely catch my breath.

I know I'm not thinking straight, but his words sink deep into my soul because I'm living them. The last week has been the hardest of my life. The most miserable by far. Being torn from everything I knew, put in a place that's uncomfortable and dismal. Not having any clue what to expect next. Then the pain of my fall and the torture of not functioning at a level I'm used to. Ten minutes ago, I just wanted to get back to what felt good and forget all of it.

But this. This is better than anything I've ever felt before. My hands tangle in his hair as I breathe him in. I don't know if he's doing this purely to prove his point, but right now I don't care. If this is the Real world, I want more of it.

CHAPTER 34

ALEK LEADS me back to the house, and Mila comes running out the back door.

"Are you two okay?" she asks, her face full of concern. "We didn't know where you were, and—"

"We're fine," Alek laughs, still holding my hand. "Just went for a walk."

Mila looks between us, her eyes narrowing. The irony of the situation is not lost on either of us.

"Well, hurry up," she says. "Kenna's in, and we don't know how long it's going to last."

"In?" I ask. "In where?"

We rush through the back door and find a crowd of people staring at a projection in the middle of the room. Kenna is tapping and swiping frantically.

"Did you get that?" she calls.

"Yep, it's in our system."

"Scrolling," she says, and a long list of text begins to move.

"What is this?" I whisper, sidling up to a woman with curly hair who's standing near the back of the group. Ames, I realize. This is who Kenna was talking about.

"It's the list of transplants for tomorrow. We're finding our targets."

Targets. They're pulling people out. And Alek said they're going to P3. I rush forward, pushing through the crowd as considerately as possible until I reach the front.

"Kenna," I call, but she doesn't answer. "Kenna, I need to see that list."

"A little busy," she says, riveted on the projection in front of her.

"I have to know if my friend is on it."

"We all have friends, Channel, please step back—"

"I'm all in, Kenna! I don't need more proof, and I'll help you, but please. Let me find him. He's a coder and a good one. Maybe he can help you, too."

She pauses slightly, then says, "First Name."

"Aave"

"Placement number."

"Seven, six, five, three, one, two." I've remembered that number since Aave first recited it our first year of primary.

"Right here. Nat, put that in," Kenna commands. A man behind her with a projection mirroring her own swipes the line into what I can only assume is a data bank of some sort. Before it disappears, I search the text for information. Relief floods through me as I see his date of implantation is upcoming. Not tomorrow, though. I'm not sure what that means. If he's not going in for surgery, will we still be able to pull him out?

I blink, and the screen changes. Alek stands next to me and nudges my arm, nodding toward the others. I follow him back through the group and stand next to them.

"Who's Aave?" Mila whispers.

"My best friend," I say.

"Do you think they're going to be able to pull her out?"

"Him," I correct, and Alek shifts uncomfortably next to me. "I have no idea," I continue. "It didn't look like his date was tomorrow."

"Do you think they're only able to find people going in for implantation?" Zayn asks, and Mila hushes him.

Kaye joins in, her voice even softer than usual. "You'd think they would need to change things up. They already got you and a few others from P3. Wouldn't Community leaders be expecting them?"

I shrug. "This whole operation seems like a suicide mission."

"I mean, what are the Community leaders going to do if they catch them?" Zayn asks, and his question stumps me.

"I have no idea," I admit. "Nothing like this has ever happened in P3."

"That you know about," Zayn says.

"What happens when someone breaks the law?" Kaye asks.

I shake my head. "I don't know."

"Nobody steals things? Or gets into fights?" Zayn asks, confused.

I shake my head. "Everything's linked up, remember? If someone did that, they'd be caught in two seconds. Plus, there's nothing to really steal or fight about, I guess."

"Huh," Zayn says. "Seems pretty boring."

Alek laughs, and I elbow him.

"We're out!" I hear Kenna call, and there's an audible let-down in the room.

"Three minutes, forty-three seconds," Nat says.

"Less than last time," Kenna sighs, already organizing her equipment. "Okay, people. We have our options. Get on, do the analysis—we'll be heading out at zero-four-hundred."

Not knowing what any of that meant, we turn to head back to our quarters.

"You three. And you five," Kenna points at us. "Come with me."

We walk across the large common room to a wing of the house that's foreign to me. I don't know why I hadn't noticed the doorway here on the other side of the room before, but it had completely escaped my attention. Kenna winds past people sitting on chairs in front of makeshift desks—flat pieces of wood on top of blocks and old furniture definitely not made for this purpose, but working nonetheless—and stops when we reach the back room. The ceilings stretch high above us, and there are open shelves built into three of the four walls.

"You three," she says, pointing at the boy and two girls standing next to us. "This isn't your mission, but I want you to hear this so you'll know what to expect."

They nod, and I try to get a good look at them. I don't think I've seen them here before. But then again, I don't get out much.

Alek starts. "Kenna, we didn't agree to any missions, we only—"

"Save it," Kenna says, "I'm not asking you to do anything you don't want to. I've called you in here because of what Miss P3 pulled in there." She looks at me, and I steel myself.

"These raids are dangerous," she continues. "We target patients entering surgery because they're already compromised, which means it's easier to extract them. We typically only have twenty to thirty minutes within the boundaries before our patch is detected—"

"Is that how you're doing it? Hacking the visual settings in a geographical area?"

She nods. "Obviously they're beginning to catch on. The time on that entry in there was less than it's ever been; however, they still haven't figured out how to detect us preemptively. And that was an attack on their most protected server."

Our conversation this morning still niggles at me. *Why us?* It doesn't make any sense. These 'disruptions' as she calls them, can't be making any significant difference, and I still don't see how we're supposed to come up with anything better than she can. I'm willing to put this all aside, though, with Aave on the line. The more I spend time with the people here, the more I'm beginning to feel different. To feel...more, somehow. And I'm not ready to give that up yet.

Kenna continues. "Their counterattack so far has been to convolute their streams of information. We went into P4 from our temporary camp to find the coordinates we'd gleaned were incorrect. We were more careful this time, but who's to say if we have the right intel." She looks at me intently. "Which means we may be going in blind unless someone who understands the Community is there to lead us."

I suck in a breath. "You want me to go in there?"

"No. You can't go in—it'd be too risky. As soon as you reconnect with the Edge, they'll know you're back, and they'll be looking for you. Too much attention."

I deflate. "So, what do you want me to do?"

"Guide our crew. I need you on deck."

"You don't have a map?"

"I haven't been able to find one yet. I have no idea why that isn't easily accessible, but the only way I've found it is by hacking individual profiles, and it's only in working memory. I can't download it. We've studied it as a team, but we can't be tapped in there and still have the bandwidth to patch."

I nod. "I can do that. And Aave?"

"We'll do our best. We don't have a strict location on him, so it will be a game of chance. I'm willing to try, but you have to know it's risky."

I think back to my life in P3. Was it only last week that I was attending the World Build Celebration? Feels like eons ago. Where would Aave be first thing in the morning? I can come up with a few options—home, the Grid, the bathhouse. That'd be awkward.

Kenna speaks up, pulling me out of my thoughts. "I called you four in here because we're going to need some support getting loaded up. After we high-tail it out of P3, we'll need to be on the move immediately. I'm sending in more of our group than usual tomorrow."

"Just let us know," Alek says. "Whatever you need."

Kenna smiles gratefully and nods her head. "That's it, then. We'll see you first thing."

We exit the office and walk back through the large room to our end of the house. Mila, Zayn, and Kaye walk down the hall first, and I follow them, my thoughts racing. What if I don't know where to go in P3 because I've only ever seen the Real version of it once? How am I going to find everything when it looks completely foreign?

Alek reaches out for my arm, and I stop short of my doorway.

"Are you okay?" he asks.

I look at him and nod.

"I'm here for you if you need anything tomorrow."

"Thank you," I say, and I want to tell him how scared I am to do this. How worried I am that I won't be able to find Aave. How I feel nauseated that I'll be looking at my home and, as far as I know, my mom won't be in it. How I can't think about her or I get so emotional that I can't stop crying.

Instead, I take a deep breath and stand tall. "I don't know what to expect, but if anything comes up, I'll let you know."

Alek looks at me quizzically.

"What?"

"You said that very professionally," Alek laughs.

"I did?"

"Yeah. Like we share a work assignment or something."

I blush. "Sorry. I don't know how to do this."

"Do what?"

There it is again. My heart hammering. "I—I don't know. Life. Me, you. Under these circumstances. It's like moving to a different planet. I'm used to letting people see what I want them to see. Here...I don't know what people are seeing or how to change it. Everything I do means something, apparently, and I don't—"

Alek reaches out and tucks a tendril of hair behind my ear. "You don't have to control it all, remember?"

"I don't know—" I stop mid-sentence and gasp. The world around me suddenly lights up with colors so brilliant, I can barely take them in. My surroundings don't look like a house anymore. The hall is replaced by a series of pathways stretching out in every direction. I slam my hand against the wall to stabilize myself.

"Alek?" I call frantically and feel a hand land on my shoulder.

"I'm here. Channel, what's wrong?"

"I can't see you." I move my head from side to side, but he's gone. All I can see are the undulating, psychedelic patterned lines in front of me.

"What's going on?" he asks, his voice thick with concern.

"The Edge," I breathe. "I'm back online."

"But that's impossible. We're not within the boundary lines like you said—"

"They must've extended their signal. Alek, you have to find everyone else. If I'm connected—"

"They know where we are."

I nod, closing my eyes to keep from seeing the kaleidoscope of colors.

"Stay put," he says, and his footfalls are already sounding behind me.

CHAPTER 35

"It's a localized signal," Kenna says, quelling the hubbub in the room momentarily. "It's currently only affecting Unreals on channels six and twenty-four. I'm guessing that means the signal's coming directly from P3."

"What is she talking about?" Mila asks, though I can barely hear her above the chatter.

"Our implants. Remember when we were talking about signals the other day?" I wait for a response. "I can't see you Mila—you have to say something."

"Oh, sorry," she says, raising her voice. "Yes, I remember."

"My implant is set up to talk to this signal."

"Can you adjust things? Change your settings so you can see?" she asks.

"Tried that already. I'm locked out."

Alek's hand stays firmly planted on my shoulder as Kenna again speaks up.

"We can't wait," she calls. "We have to move now."

"What about the mission?" someone says, and other voices join in.

"Too dangerous. They know we're here. Who knows how long we have before they get here. And, half our crew for tomorrow is now blind until we get out of the signal range."

"What if we can't get out?" someone asks, and the room falls silent.

"We'll find a way to get back off-grid. They've thrown things like this at us before, and we've always figured it out. Don't worry. We'll find a solution. For now, please hurry. Grab only the necessities."

The room comes alive around me, but even if I could see, I wouldn't be able to move. Aave. We're not going in for him, and I can't bear it. My eyes fill with tears, and they bleed into my lashes, eventually falling down my cheeks. Hunching over, I drop my face in my hands and begin to sob.

Mila puts an arm around me, and as much as I want to shrug it off, I don't. At least I can't see their expressions reflecting how pathetic I am.

"Channel," Kenna's voice calls, and I sit up, attempting to compose myself. "I'm sorry about this," she says. "I know this meant a lot to you."

"Isn't there another way?" Mila asks.

"Mila—" Kenna tries to jump in.

"No, there has to be," Mila continues. "We can't leave him behind."

"We have to leave him behind," Kenna says. "Along with the other four we selected. It's simply not possible to wait."

"What if—"

"No, Mila. Anyone I send in there would be at risk. Even the people who haven't been connected yet. What if they switch channels? Every Community runs on their own frequency, and we have no idea what they're up to."

"What if you send someone in who isn't implanted?" she asks.

"That would be me and Nat. Total. Everyone else—"

"I meant me," Mila says softly.

"No," I say. "That would be too risky. If you got caught—"

"It's risking one life for possibly five," she says matter-of-factly.

Though I can't see her, I hear Kenna tapping her foot. "You couldn't get them all out by yourself. And there's no way you can carry patients who don't have full use of their limbs."

"I can," Zayn and Kaye say together.

"I can," Alek says a moment later, and my heart squeezes.

"No, this is crazy," I say. "You'd all be at risk of losing everything—"

"*If* they catch us," Alek says.

Kenna considers this. "I don't see how they would. Unless they have World Builders in that part of the Community—which they never do— there'd be nothing to tip them off. You aren't built into their augmented reality."

"So we could walk around, and nobody would even see we're there?" Zayn asks with far too much excitement in his tone, given the circumstances.

"Not exactly," Kenna says. "Even though Unreals wouldn't be able to see you, they can hear you and feel you. You'd have to be silent unless you're in a large group of people. And you'd have to be vigilant about giving everyone a wide berth."

"Easy," Kaye says.

I want to scream. They can't do this. It's too dangerous. "How would they get out?" I ask. "They'll be with people who are linked to the Edge."

"That's where we'll patch. Since we won't have to worry about that early on, we'll have twenty minutes to take them out before we're noticed," Kenna says. "It could actually work perfectly."

"And everyone else?" I ask.

"They can move on to our next location. We'll meet them there. At that point, we'll know how far the signal reaches—"

"And what if we don't know?" I ask, becoming more agitated by the second. "What if it reaches forever and we can't escape it? What if the people we pull from P3 are homing beacons that lead Community leaders right to us?"

Kenna puts a hand on my arm. "Channel, you of all people know how much bandwidth it would take to project this signal. They won't be able to hold it. My guess is they're sending them out for a certain amount of time, flipping through different channels, and hoping they get lucky."

"Well, they did."

"Which is why we need to move. You especially." She pauses, and I stand. Alek puts out an arm, and I grip on tightly.

"Are you sure you four want to do this?" Kenna asks.

"Yes," they say in unison.

"Then meet me out front in ten. We have to go now. Channel, as soon as we get out of range and you can see, we'll need you to guide them. Can you do that?"

No! I scream inside my head, but I realize no amount of arguing at this point is going to change anything. *You can't control this.* I nod, and Alek leads me out of the room.

Fifteen minutes later, we're in the transport. This time I ride in the front. It takes a few minutes for the filtration system to bring the air quality up to acceptable levels, but once it does, I rip off my mask. The ring around my face is doing better each day, and though I've become much more comfortable with how I look naturally, I'm going to do everything I can to get rid of this particular feature.

Each time I open my eyes, I'm treated to another mind-bending visual reality that makes me want to throw up. I'm relying entirely on others at this point, and that also makes me nauseous. Especially because I can't stop thinking about the fact that Alek, Mila, Zayn, and Kaye are on their way to P3 without me. At least Nat's driving their transport. Since he's the only other person besides Kenna without an implant, he got the job. And he's one of the most seasoned Coalition members by far.

"It's going to work," Kenna says from the driver's seat.

"You don't know that."

"I feel good about it."

"That's comforting."

Kenna laughs softly. "You're a bit of a skeptic, aren't you?"

"You're just noticing this?"

"No, I'm simply continually astounded at your propensity for stubbornness."

"I'll take that as a compliment."

"You should."

We drive in silence for a few minutes. I'm still not used to this kind of transportation, and—mainly because I have no visual cues—my brain is convinced we're moving at nearly the speed of light.

"Alek said we're heading east," I say, trying to distract myself.

"We are."

"How long will we be traveling?"

"Tonight? Only as far as we have to. We can sleep in our transports since I don't think anyone will want to set up camp in the middle of the night."

I open my eyes, hoping beyond hope to see something normal—something Real—but I'm disappointed. I quickly close them again.

"Not there yet?" Kenna asks.

"Nope."

"It's okay, Channel. We're still only fifteen minutes from the borders of P3."

"So if this doesn't clear up in the next five minutes—"

"They'll have to drive fast."

CHAPTER 36

IT'S BEEN FIFTEEN MINUTES, and I'm still seeing colors. At least the rain stopped. Kenna attempted to call Nat, but he'd already gone to radio silence for their approach. There's nothing we can do but keep driving and hopefully come up with some sort of plan to get them out safely. If they actually find everyone. Right now, with me unable to see their location, that's seeming less and less likely.

"Try again," Kenna says.

"No," I whisper.

"It has to be any second now."

"That's what you've been saying for ten minutes."

Little taps begin to sound on the roof of the vehicle. Now on top of everything else it's raining again. I take a deep breath and blink my eyes open. When I see the colors, I slam my eyelids shut again. I pound my hand against the window in frustration. Kenna doesn't say a word.

We drive in silence for what seems like forever, the rain drumming steadily now.

"Channel, can you put a hand on my bag before it falls?" Kenna asks softly. "I can't quite reach it. Next to your left knee."

I look and see it slowly slipping off the side of the center console. Gripping the handles, I replace it on the floor. Kenna slams on the brakes, recognizing my newfound sight before I can process what I just did.

"It's gone!" I shout jubilantly. "Kenna, I can see!"

She's already sending voice messages to the other transports, telling them we're going to find a place to set up and link in to communication with the team on the ground.

I'm amazed at how quickly everything happens and how good it feels to finally be able to help. Within minutes, Kenna's parked our transport behind a large boulder, and I've unloaded the equipment from the back.

Other transports are pulling in around us, and pretty soon our small patch of desert is full of life.

"If their signal won't reach here, how are we connecting to the Edge?" I ask, leaning down to set up the power bank.

Kenna sets up one of the wooden desks she pilfered from the house before we left. "We're not using their network." She sets her projection plate on the table top and turns it on. "The Communities were set up with their own localized networks because it allowed them to transfer massive amounts of data faster and more reliably. They must have taken a major hit in function to send their signal as far as they did tonight." A dashboard appears in front of her, and she swipes to the comm screen. "We're connecting through the iO towers."

"Those still exist?" I ask incredulously.

Kenna nods.

"Wait, if those are still around, couldn't Southwest Territory connect?"

"Absolutely. If they had tech capable of handling it."

"What do you mean?"

"The Communities stopped supporting their upgrades before the transition. Their devices won't be able to receive and interpret those frequencies."

"But iO's been around for, what, forty years?"

"It hasn't been everywhere for that long, but yeah. Sad, isn't it?" She stares at the screen, waiting for Nat to connect.

"If the Communities were already using a different network, why was iO even necessary?"

"Well the technology is used in the Communities, too. But back then, you have to remember there were huge gaps between groups, and Communities weren't covering nearly as much area. When people would travel from place to place—go out on recruiting missions and such—they still needed a way to connect."

I nod. "If the Reals aren't using it now, then who is?"

She grins mischievously. "Only us."

An image springs to the screen, and everyone gathers around. Four more images pop up next to it, and Kenna swipes to turn on the audio.

"Com check, Nat."

"I hear you," he says, waving in front of the small camera attached to his shirt.

"Com check, Mila."

"Here," she says breathily as her camera jolts with her footsteps. She's walking across a landscape that looks shockingly unfamiliar. I can't see any part of P3, and they're supposed to be close.

Zayn, Alek, and Kaye all check in, and I breathe a sigh of relief. We may have zero idea how we're going to get the targets out of there, but at least everyone's earpieces are working and they're safe for the moment.

"We should pull them out," I say, my voice low. "There's no way they'll have enough time—"

"They're already within the boundaries," Kenna says. "They're about to enter the Community proper."

I stare at the screen. How? A blank landscape stretches as far into the distance as we can see. Though it's dark, the light of the moon is enough for the cameras.

"Is that—?" My eyes narrow and I move closer to the screen. The four of them reach the crest of a hill and suddenly, the entire Community comes into view. It looks much larger than I expected, sprawling from one side of the camera to the other.

"There aren't any lights," Zayn says softly.

"Communities don't need light," Kenna says. "Everything is sent directly to the retina without the need of light entering through the pupil."

"Do you think Unreals will evolve to not have pupils?" Alek asks. "Isn't that how it works? If we don't use something, we lose it?"

"Focus, Alek," Mila growls, and I feel guilty all over again hearing her stressed.

They approach the first square building, and I'm frantically searching the screen to gain my bearings. *South edge of town. What is on the south edge of town.* Then I see it. It isn't the look of the building that tips me off, it's the layout.

"The bathhouse," I say. "There. That building with the metal bars in front of it."

"We see it," Alek says, and their cameras move up the street. Everything is dead, as it should be at this time of night.

Please be careful, I silently plead. They walk past the bathhouse and continue up the road.

"Keep going," I say. "You're going to walk straight for a few minutes. Then you'll split off—Aave's house is further up the road and off to the right. The medical center is in the middle of town."

"This is a perfect time, then, to review your assignments. As you know, we've changed our targets based on the time discrepancy. Our team assessed the information we pulled earlier and found three candidates that meet our criteria who also should be small enough for each of you to carry. Fortunately or unfortunately, the Communities are desperate enough to push people through—they've got appointments running all night." Kenna pauses and takes a sip from her canteen. "Do you all understand where you're going?"

"Yes," Kaye whispers. "Nat gave us a rundown of the building."

"Those images are based off old blueprints, but they were correct last time we were here. You're going to have to move fast," Kenna says. "Nat will deploy the Welcome Wagon, and we'll start the patch as soon as you have targets in hand. Please try to be synchronized."

"They all know how to use their tranquilizers as needed," Nat says. "I offered to let them try them out on Ames, but they didn't take me up on it."

"Only because Ames wasn't there," Alek says, and I laugh. "Focus, Channel."

I bite my lip. His attempt to keep the mood light only serves to sober me. There's too much at stake here and too much out of our control. How does the Coalition do this night after night? How are their nerves not totally shot?

"Turn," I say, recognizing the street I used to walk to the Grid each day. The road is wide, and I can see the steps up ahead. "Not you, Mila. You keep going straight." They each obey, and I guide Alek, Zayn, and Kaye up the steps and through the courtyard. The lonely, dilapidated brick building is on full display as they walk, and I can't help but stare at it. This is not the Grid I know.

"Keep going?" Mila asks, and I look over at her screen.

My breath catches. "Stop," I say, and her camera goes still. Centered on the screen is our bench. It has to be. It's plain and washed out like everything else in P3, and I can't look away. No letters. Tears form in the corners of my eyes.

"Mila, Channel, is everything alright?" Alek's hushed voice sounds tense.

"Yes," I say, wiping my eyes. "Sorry. I just saw something and it took me off-guard. Keep going, Mila. You're not far." I look back at the other screens. "When you get to the next street, turn left. Then you'll follow that to the big clearing. The medical center will be on the far side, directly in front of you."

I let my lids fall closed and imagine the way the Community looks in my mind. Pristine. Colorful. Perfect. Even though I can see it, I can't seem to conjure the feelings it used to bring up in me. In my imagination now, it only seems cold and lonely.

"Turn right," I tell Mila, and she turns. I envision walking to Aave's house—remembering how his street looked. It's the fifth house on the left. I look again at the camera and begin to count. "There," I say. "That's it. The fifth house from the corner."

Mila hesitates.

"He'll be sleeping," I say. "You'll need to wake him up without causing a scene."

"Okay," Mila says, and begins walking cautiously toward the door.

"Do you see it, Alek?" I ask, switching my attention to the other images. "Right in front of you."

"Got it," he answers. "We'll take it from here."

Mila stands in front of Aave's door. "Do I just go in?" she whispers.

"Yes, but you need to slip in quickly. If the door stays open too long, someone will be notified of a ventilation breach."

"Okay." She reaches out and turns the knob, then quickly swings the door open and pads inside, closing it softly behind her.

"His room is the first one on the left."

Mila walks forward and turns into the dark room.

"You can flick on your light," Kenna says, and she does so. Immediately, Aave's bed comes into view, and there he is—sprawled out across his sheets, his chest rising and falling peacefully.

Sorry, Aave.

Mila walks toward him and extends her hand. Before she makes contact, Aave rustles and shifts position.

"Aave," she says softly, and he turns his head.

"Mmm?"

"Aave, I need you to wake up."

"M'wake," he mumbles, his eyes still closed. She shakes his shoulder, and he slaps her hand away.

"Aave, it's Channel," Mila says. Brilliant.

At this, Aave stops moving and slowly blinks his eyes open. Pushing up to rest on his elbow, he squints.

"I know, you can't see me, but I'm a friend of Channel's. Here," she whispers, pulling out her earpiece and placing it in his hand. Aave's eyes widen at feeling something he can't see.

"Put this in your ear," Mila instructs.

"What is she doing," Kenna mutters, watching the screen intently.

Aave puts it in his ear slowly.

"Hey," I say, and Aave sits up straight.

"Channel? Is that really you? Where've you been, I've been so worried—"

"Shhhh!" I say, and he stops talking. "Aave, you need to listen to me closely. In a few minutes, you and Mila are going to need to run as fast as you can. I'm waiting outside of P3, and I'll explain everything when you get here."

"Is this a dream?" he says, rubbing his eyes.

"No, Aave. Trust me. Please."

"Prove it's you," he says, and I sigh.

"You told me you wished there were tongue implants so that everything would taste good."

Aave grins. "I've told a lot of people that. Doesn't count. Tell me something only you would know."

I swallow. "Aave, this isn't the time. Please—"

"Tell me what happened on our bench the last time I saw you."

Kenna raises an eyebrow, and I can feel myself blushing.

"You kissed me," I say quickly, "now, please."

"That's a lame description and not really the correct order of things, but okay," he says. "I believe you. Am I leaving P3? I need to tell my mom—"

"Aave," I hiss, "you were right about the implants. You need to leave now. I promise—I'll explain when you get here."

He nods and pulls the earpiece out, holding it out in front of him.

Mila takes it back, and he jumps.

"Alek, Zayn, Kaye—I'm clear." As Mila speaks these words, my stomach sinks. All three of them were on the comm channel as Aave and I were talking. They heard every single word.

Alek clears his throat, and I groan internally.

"I'm in position," he says.

"Me, too." Kaye chimes in.

"Give me a second," Zayn whispers. "Almost there, I think."

I can see his light scanning the hallway ahead of him. "Ready."

"Nat," Kenna calls, "are you ready?"

"When you are."

Kenna swipes across the bottom of her screen and quickly taps in the code. "On my mark. Patch is uploading...and...live. Go now."

A flurry of action erupts on screen, and I can't keep track of who's who. A young girl slumps in a chair next to a man who looks equally out of it. Someone squats down and turns, pulling her wrists over their shoulder and hugging her to their chest, blocking the camera almost completely. Though we can't see much, the screen is moving up and down rhythmically. They're running.

My eyes are drawn to the next screen over, where I can barely see a thing. Something is flashing in front of the camera, and all we can hear is the sound of scuffling.

"I'm clear," Zayn says, panting.

"Us, too," Mila says, and I see her view down the road clear as day, with glimpses of Aave's arm swinging next to her.

"Having a little trouble," Kaye says. "He's heavier than anticipated." I watch as she attempts to throw the nearly dead weight preteen boy over her shoulder.

"Get as far as you can," Zayn says. "When I reach the meeting point, I'll come back and help you."

Where's Alek, I think. His camera must be the one in the middle. Whatever was happening is clearly over, but the view remains dark with no motion.

"Alek," I call. No response. "Alek," I say again, forcing myself to remain calm.

"Welcome wagon is at the meeting point," Nat says.

On Zayn's screen, I watch it come into view, and my eyes widen. A long, flatbed on heavy-duty wheels sits silently on the dirt. Zayn runs toward it and gently lays his target down flat. He turns just as Mila and Aave come into view.

"Get on," he says hurriedly. "Squish to the back. I'm going to relieve Kaye." He sprints back the way he came, and I'm watching the clock. It's been four minutes. Still no word or movement from Alek.

"Alek," I call again, this time my worry evident. No answer. My hands start to shake.

"I have to go back for him," Mila says, and her camera moves to the edge of the wagon.

"No," Kenna commands. "You won't make it."

"I can't leave him—"

"He's here," Zayn says, breathing heavily. "He's here. I've got Kaye, Alek, and their targets. We're making our way to the wagon."

Relief floods through me as I see his face clearly on the screen.

"Lost his camera and earpiece in the room. Two workers in there," Kaye explains, barely able to talk as Zayn pulls the target off her shoulders and onto his own.

All three of them dart as fast as they can toward the meeting point. At six minutes and thirty-two seconds, they're all on the wagon, clinging to the pop-up rails along the edges.

"Clear?" Nat asks.

"Go," Zayn growls, and their cameras again show movement. The wagon starts slow but quickly picks up speed, heading toward Nat and the transport.

I reach over Kenna's arm and tap the mute button on her projection. "They're not going to make it."

"They could."

"They took too much time. They have barely fourteen minutes to get out here, and we're a solid thirty-five minutes away."

"They might have longer. If the patch holds—"

"But what if it doesn't!" I shout. "I'm not willing to bet their freedom on a 'might!'"

Kenna puts a hand on her hip. "What do you want me to do, Channel? Nat knows how close this is going to be. He's doing everything he can to speed things up."

"We need more than that. You're a World Builder! *Think of something!*"

She looks at the screen, her eyes searching.

I keep talking because I don't know what else to do. "In fourteen minutes —possibly sooner—those dots are going to be glaring on P3 Community leader's security logs. Kenna, we have to—"

"I've got nothing, Channel!" she shouts. "I've spent every waking hour planning a very specific mission, and everything was shot to pieces a few hours ago. Your new friends found a way to make this happen for me and for you. *Your P3 friend is in that wagon because of them.*"

Pressure builds behind my eyes, and I pinch the bridge of my nose with my thumb and forefinger. "What does any of it matter if they're picked up in fourteen—thirteen—minutes, Kenna? You didn't listen to me when I asked you to pull them out. You didn't listen back at the house when I said this was too risky—"

"Channel, the only way we've succeeded thus far is by doing everything that everyone said was 'too risky.' You're new to this. I know how scary this feels because I've been living it every single day for the last six months. I've just stuffed it *way* down deep so I can make decisions without obsessing over every possible false move. I suggest you do the same."

The images on-screen begin to shift, and our group watches as my friends move the targets to the transport, then climb in themselves. On Zayn's camera, we see Alek reach out for the now-folded up Welcome Wagon and Nat shoves it in the back.

Tears build in the corners of my eyes, and I blink them away. Twelve minutes. *We have to do something.* We have to find a way to keep Community leaders from seeing—

A thought slams into my brain, and I nearly lose my balance.

"Channel, are you—"

"Lag time," I breathe.

"What?" Kenna reaches out to steady me.

"Lag time. We can change the simulation code."

She tilts her head, processing.

My voice is high and shrill. "*Everything that moves forward can also be used backward.* We can add lag time back into the system! I know how to re-write it. If you can get me in, I can put it directly into their source code. There won't be any hack or patch to find. They won't even know it's there until the morning when people start showing up five minutes earlier than their indicator light."

Kenna blinks at me. "You can do that?"

"It was my World Build project. I obviously haven't seen the P3 source code, but there's not much variation with something like this."

"I don't know if we can get in there while the patch is running. The source code is deep." She taps on the screen and shakes her head. "I don't have enough processing speed."

"I can write it now. As soon as the patch crashes, we can move as fast as possible."

Kenna nods. "Even if they see their actual location for a few seconds, that may even work in our favor."

"It'll look like they've stopped," I say, my voice shaking. As soon as I have an empty screen, my fingers fly across the screen, typing in line after line of instructions.

Kenna watches me, her arms folded in front of her. "You missed a bracket there," she says.

"Thanks." I correct my error and skip back to where I was, typing out the last line.

"It's good," she says approvingly, scanning my work a second time.

"It will give them a chance."

We wait and watch as the twenty-minute mark comes and goes with the patch still intact. Kenna's foot is tapping again, and it makes me nervous.

A red error box appears abruptly on-screen, and Kenna rushes forward. She swipes communication back on.

"Patch expired," she says, and Nat cusses under his breath.

"Nat," I call out, "we're going to try something. Keep driving, and we'll update you as we go."

"I'm almost in," Kenna says slowly, her fingers dancing across the screen. "Yes! Gotcha."

Every second of this wait is torture, knowing they're sitting ducks.

"Upgrading my privileges..."

I close my eyes and breathe. *Please work. Please work. Please work.* I chant this over and over in my head until Kenna calls me over.

"Here it is," she says. "You've probably got less than two minutes."

Jumping over to the code I'd written moments before, I copy it and swipe back, pulling up the search function. *C'mon,* I beg silently, willing it to move faster. The code pulls up, and I hurriedly select the section I was looking for, pasting my version in its place. Looking over everything, I make a few necessary edits and step back.

"That's it. I think," I say, my hands trembling again. "I hope I didn't screw it up."

"You didn't," Kenna says. She excitedly taps the screen to upload my changes, and another red window appears.

My heart stops. Password required.

"Do you know the password?" I ask desperately.

Kenna curses and ignores my question, frantically pulling up another screen I don't recognize.

"Kenna, we're running out of time."

Again, she doesn't respond, still cursing under her breath. She's sending a message—that much I can gather—but to whom? Standing up straight, she crosses her arms, and her toe starts to tap. I'm beginning to dread that sound.

A weight settles on my chest as I stare at Kenna staring at the screen. We're not going to make it. She's waiting for something that isn't coming, and *we're not going to make it.* My head swims, and I drop to a crouch, closing my eyes and waiting for the vertigo to pass.

My friends risked everything to help me tonight, and now they're going to be toast. Is that the correct way to say it? My heart aches, remembering Alek's laugh when I didn't know what the phrase meant. I hate that we let them do this—that *I* let them do this. And for what? Four people—five including Nat—risking their freedom and safety so I can get my best friend back? I'm selfish and short-sighted, and as much as I love Aave, I can't justify this. Tears form in my eyes, and I angrily blink them away. I shouldn't have let them go in. I should've—

"Yes! Thank you, Tara," I hear Kenna mutter, and my head snaps up. Tara? I don't have long to ponder this because something's happening. I stand as Kenna copies a string of numbers, letters, and symbols into the field on the red box. The password. She has the password. How she got it, I have no idea, but the box disappears and my code is accepted.

"And we're out before they kicked us out. Impressive work," Kenna says calmly, but her hands are visibly shaking as she reaches up to tuck a loose strand of hair back into her bun.

I barely hear her—the throb of rushing blood in my ears too loud to process anything else.

"How—?" I start, but Kenna cuts me off.

"You've got time, Nat," she calls into the comm.

"Do you hear that?" Mila whispers, and my eyes are immediately fixated on the screen in front of me. I listen, trying to tune in to what they're noticing. A low hum is audible in the background.

"Nat," I choke out, "we uploaded a slight edit to the P3 system. It should create a good five-minute lag time for you if it works properly."

"Don't stress, Nat, just keep driving," Kenna says. "You still have our coordinates?"

"Got 'em," Nat says, his fingers gripping the wheel tightly. He's turned off the vehicle lights preemptively, and I don't blame him. If they're out looking—even in the wrong places—they're not going to miss a bright light in the distance.

"What's lag time?" Mila asks, and Aave—sitting directly in view of her camera—lights up.

"Who's talking about lag time?" he asks, seemingly unaware of their very present danger.

"Channel."

"That's what we did for our World Build project," he says thoughtfully.

"Tell Aave I have sooo much to tell him," I say, barely getting the words out through fresh tears. The humming through their mic grows slightly louder, and I hold my breath, wiping my cheeks. It has to work. Kenna got the password, and it *has to work.*

Everyone in the vehicle is now dead silent. We watch Aave bounce in his seat. Alek—his face turned from us—holds a boy's head away from the side of the seat so he won't slam into it as the vehicle bucks over the uneven terrain. Nat's knuckles grow white as he clenches and unclenches his hands on the wheel.

I slump to the ground and lean against the bumper of our transport, my eyes glued to the footage. People in our group begin to pack equipment up and stow it. Ames walks around with a tray of what looks like break-fast bars, wearily offering one to anyone who'll take it. I wave her off. I can't do anything but watch, and even if I could bring myself to move, I'm too nauseous to attempt eating anything.

My friends on-screen continue to bounce, and the humming eventually grows quieter. My eyelids begin to droop. I allow them to close for a few seconds, then look up to make sure I didn't miss anything. I close them again, and it feels so good to be sitting here in the dark and still. They're going to make it, I repeat. *I know they're going to make it.*

CHAPTER 37

"CHANNEL."

I hear my name.

"Channel. I've got a spot for you in the transport."

Something jostles my shoulder, and I lift my head. It's Kenna. Turning to look around me, I wince. My neck is so stiff it hurts to move quickly. I slowly stretch it out and take in my surroundings.

"Did I fall asleep?" I yawn.

"You did."

"Did they make it?" I whisper, my stomach dropping.

"They did."

"Where are they?"

"Sleeping."

"But I need to see them," I say blearily.

"You will. Come on."

She reaches for my hand, and I give it to her, allowing her to help me up. I follow her to the back of the transport next to ours, and she opens the doors. Stepping inside, I see the seats have disappeared into the floor.

"The targets are being taken care of. Except for Aave," Kenna says. "I left him here with all of you."

"Thank you," I breathe, and she hands me a thin blanket.

I wake to the orange morning glow outside our windows and stretch my arms over my head. My back is stiff from sleeping on the hard floor of the transport, but I feel surprisingly well rested, considering. As the events of the night before flood into my mind, I sit up. Mila, Alek, Kaye, and Zayn —they're all here. I have no idea how they made it, but they're here. Looking down next to me, I find him. Aave.

His sandy hair seems longer than when I last saw him, now wild from sleep. His long, dark eyelashes stand out against his light skin. I know I should let him sleep, but I can't wait another second to talk to him.

I gently shake his shoulder, and he shifts.

"Aave," I say softly, trying not to wake the others.

"Hmm?" he lazily blinks his eyes open. "Oh, hey!" he says, smiling widely when he recognizes me.

"Shhh!" I say, grinning and motioning to the sleeping bodies piled on the floor around us.

He nods apologetically. "Where are we?" he whispers.

"In the middle of nowhere."

"Were we moving last night?"

"Were we?" I look out the window. "I thought I dreamed that." It makes sense, though. It wouldn't have been wise to stay so close after leading them—albeit slowly—in our general direction. A thrill runs through me as I fully absorb the fact that my plan worked. *My plan.* I helped save my friends with lag time of all things. Eat that, Glyn.

Alek turns over in his sleep, and his face looks totally peaceful.

"Who's that?" Aave asks.

"Hmm?"

He points at Alek.

"Oh, right. You already met Mila last night. She's there, and that's her brother, Alek. Next to him is Zayn."

"He looks like a beast."

"He's a force, but a gentle force, believe it or not. Next to him is Kaye."

"Who are they?"

I watch his face as I answer. "Reals."

He raises an eyebrow. "From where?"

"Southwest Territory?"

"I thought—"

"I know. We thought wrong."

"But how?"

"Their families have been there for generations. They believe in preserving...Real experiences," I say, my eyes subconsciously drifting toward Alek.

"You said I was right about the implants," Aave says, rubbing my arm softly. "I'd like to return to that comment."

I laugh, pulling away. "I'm sure you would."

He rubs his chin with his forefinger and thumb. "Tell me more about how I was right."

I shake my head. "You're the worst. But yes, I'll humor you and explain."

I tell him about Kenna, the Coalition, and their missions, about how I've been with them since I disappeared. I fill him in about Glyn and P4—conveniently skipping over Alek and the lake—and about how I warned them. Aave listens intently, taking everything in.

"Kenna used to be a World Builder. She left because she believes this new implant is being used to slowly take Unreals out of the picture."

"Why?"

"So the Reals—well, not all the Reals, but the ones who have power—can have the world to themselves."

Aave nods, pondering this.

"I saw a plant, Aave."

He looks at me blankly.

"Like, in the wild. It was growing on its own."

Aave's eyebrows shoot up.

"I don't know for a fact that everything Kenna's said is true, but I'm becoming increasingly convinced that some of it is."

"You know, Channel. I haven't felt good about this from the beginning."

"But you were on the list. I saw your name—"

"What was I supposed to do? Everyone was signing up, and you were gone..." he looks down at his hands. "I wasn't especially optimistic about my placement, and with things changing so fast—"

"I know. I'm sorry, I wanted to come sooner, but there wasn't any way—"

"No, I get it."

I take a deep breath. "Have you seen my mom?"

He shakes his head, not meeting my eyes. "Your house was empty for a day or so."

"And then?"

"They pulled everything out. Gutted it."

This hits me hard, and it takes me a minute to speak. "I have to find her," I whisper. "They say it takes three weeks for Cerebrolink to fully bond or whatever, right?"

Aave shrugs. "My parents are signed up for the same time I was."

I nod slowly. "I still don't understand how the Coalition is going to affect any significant change. I know Kenna is targeting Unreals with a high aptitude for coding, but she was a World Builder. I don't see—"

"Wait. Didn't you solve a problem last night that she couldn't solve?"

I blink. "Oh, right. You heard all that."

"I did."

"That was pretty awesome."

Aave laughs. "Here I thought you'd gotten all humble on me."

I hear movement and turn. Alek sits up and stretches his arms over his head, moving from side to side.

"Stiff?" I ask.

"I've gotten soft," he groans, smiling. Then he notices Aave next to me, and his smile dissipates slightly.

I grin, feigning obliviousness. "I'm so glad you made it out. For a minute there—"

"I know," he says. "I couldn't hear anything. I just kept running in the direction I came from." His hair—disheveled from sleep—falls across his face, and he runs his hand through it.

"Smart," I say, now fully distracted from the conversation. I clear my throat, attempting to get back on track. "What happened in there?"

He doesn't respond, but as he turns, I see a dark, angry bruise on the right side of his face.

"Alek, are you okay?" I ask, shuffling over Mila to take a closer look.

He explores his face gently with his fingertips and winces. "That swelled up nicely."

Kaye stirs. "Where are we?" she asks, yawning.

"Middle of nowhere," Aave says, not missing a beat, and I laugh.

"You must be Channel's friend," Kaye says. "Wait—where are the other targets?"

"Kenna said they're in another transport," I answer.

"I'm starving," Zayn groans without even opening his eyes. Alek chuckles, then flinches as his movement tugs on the swollen skin.

"I'm sorry," I breathe.

He meets my eyes. "Don't worry about me. You should've seen the Community workers."

"Did you get to stab them with your tranq's?"

Alek laughs, trying not to move his mouth. "Had to, is more like it. I only got one of them."

"But you got out," I say softly.

His eyes sear into mine. "Had to."

Aave clears his throat. "I'm with that guy," he announces, pointing at Zayn who is still refusing to get up. "What do we need to do to get some food up in here?"

"Mila, get up," Alek says, nudging her with his foot.

She groans, annoyed. "I feel like I got hit by a truck."

"And you didn't even have to carry anyone," Kaye teases and rolls her shoulders, loosening up her neck. "Thanks, by the way." She says, patting Zayn on the back.

Zayn lifts two fingers from the floor, his maximum effort for acknowledging her comment.

"Do we have masks?" I ask, not seeing any near me.

Mila spots a bag near the back door of the transport. She opens it, searches the contents, and pulls out two masks, delighted with herself.

"Brand new," she says proudly.

"They've been holding out on us," Kaye says, reaching for one.

"More like I grabbed a box of them on my way out," Zayn mumbles.

"What?" Mila says, her face scrunched up in confusion. "How would that even be physically possible?"

Zayn finally rolls over, exposing his bare, impressively chiseled chest to the rest of the group. "It was on the counter. I figured we could use them."

Mila's eyes linger on him a little too long before she shakes her head. "You're something else."

Alek clenches his jaw.

"C'mon," I laugh, "I see Ames out there. Aave...I'm sorry, but the food is definitely not going to measure up to what you're used to."

"Set the expectations low—I like it," he says, hunching over as we file one after another out of the vehicle.

CHAPTER 38

AFTER GRABBING OUR PORTIONS, we find a few logs to sit on while we eat. The air is crisp and cool against my skin. I can't tell if there's more humidity because of our location or due to the rain the night before. It's a new sensation, and I love it.

Our mission the night before was a success—best case scenario—and yet, as everyone talks excitedly around me, I can't shake the feeling that I'm still missing something.

What is it? I wrack my brain, running everything over again. What is it that's not sitting right with all this?

Kenna's clearly intelligent and organized. It doesn't make sense that she would jump into something with no plan—no end game. It doesn't make sense that she'd be randomly targeting people with a specific aptitude in the hopes that we'd haphazardly discover something she'd missed.

"Not hungry?" Alek asks, and I look up. We're completely alone on the log, and my breakfast bar is still unopened.

"Where's everyone else?"

Alek laughs. "You've been sitting there staring off into the abyss for at least fifteen minutes."

"No way," I shake my head, looking at him skeptically.

"Everyone else went to set up the blocks." He points behind him, and sure enough.

"Nice. We're staying a while then?"

Alek shrugs. "At least until everyone else finishes breakfast. With the midnight caravan, Kenna didn't want to make the crew start early. Not everyone was as lucky as us—sleeping on the floor while they drove."

I nod.

Alek chews and swallows. "Aave seems cool."

I busy myself with opening the packaging for my bar. "He's a really good person."

Alek brushes the hair from his face. "Seems like he's more than that. More than a friend, I mean."

My heart begins to race. "How so?"

"Last night. You were talking about how he kissed you before you left—"

"I was about to go in for surgery the next day, Alek. Things were a little...unknown at the time."

"So you're saying you don't have feelings for him?"

"I'm saying—" I search my brain for words I don't have. Closing my mouth, I pause and try again. "I've had more *feelings* the past week than I've had my entire life. I don't know *what* I feel. Being Unreal—you kind of just feel the same all the time. This is all new to me."

It's the truth, but from the look on Alek's face, it wasn't what he was hoping for. He smooths his expression over and makes a valiant effort to be empathetic.

"Is that what you've been thinking about? When you're quiet and staring off into space? Feelings?"

"I'm sure it's part of it, but no. There's something else. Something I can't quite put my finger on that's not making sense in all this."

Alek nods, seemingly grateful for the shift in topic even though he's the one who brought up Aave.

"I know what you mean," he says. "That's exactly how I felt back at camp."

"Hence the collision in the trees."

Alek laughs. "Right. How's your head doing, by the way?"

I wave him off. "Fine. I don't even notice it anymore." I glance back toward base camp. "Something happened last night—when we were trying to cover your position. Kenna messaged someone. Do you know if she's up?"

Alek nods, pointing toward the breakfast serving area, and I spot her next to Ames. I stand, brushing the crumbs from my lap and take a few steps. Before I get too far, though, I stop.

"I was worried," I say hesitantly, not daring to look at him directly. "Last night. When we weren't getting any feedback from your camera."

"You mentioned that this morning."

The corners of my mouth turn up involuntarily, and my cheeks flush. I still don't like this whole biofeedback thing, but at least reactions like this aren't sending me into apoplectic shock like they did initially.

"Feelings are a good thing, Channel," he says, his voice low. "Even when they're complicated."

"You mentioned that the other night."

He chuckles. "See you later, then?"

I nod and turn toward the transports.

. . .

"Anything you need help with?" I ask Kenna, watching her pull out another box of food for Ames.

"I think we're good. Almost everyone's up at this point, but thanks." She grunts as she lifts the box and walks back to the table. Setting it down heavily, she adjusts her shirt and takes a deep breath. "We'll need help taking down if you have time then."

"My schedule's pretty packed, but I'll see if I can swipe you in."

She grins, scanning the table to see if any other supplies are running low.

I take a deep breath. "Kenna, I know this is probably the last thing you want to talk about right now, but—"

"You have questions. You're wondering what happens next."

I nod hesitantly.

"We're heading east like we talked about. We'll be meeting another group in about a day's travel, and from there, we'll make assignments for the next few weeks."

"Assignments," I repeat. "Like what kind of assignments?"

Kenna shrugs. "Depends."

"But for me specifically. Or Aave. How are we going to be able to come up with new ways to fight this if we don't even have access to the Edge?"

"We can get you access to the Edge."

"I know, but even then. There are hundreds—maybe thousands—of people being implanted every day, and there's no way we can come up with something fast enough to stop that. Even if you have help—which I think you do because you got that password from someone last night. I'm curious about that, by the way. But even then, no number of missions from this small Coalition is going to disrupt the Communities enough to make more than a ripple. The only way we can possibly slow this thing down is by—" I freeze mid-rant, goosebumps rising on my arms.

"Hey, Channel!" Aave calls, closely followed by the others. "We've only got a few minutes to play—" he stops short when he sees the expression on my face. "What's wrong?" he asks, close enough now to recognize he's interrupting.

Kenna stares at me intently.

"You weren't ever planning to keep us out," I say, my voice barely more than a whisper.

She raises an eyebrow, egging me on.

"You want us to go in."

Aave steps closer, concern written all over his face.

"Do you always make realizations mid-sentence?" Kenna asks, amused.

"She does," Aave says slowly. "It's a common problem."

"But how?" I ask, utterly oblivious to Aave's comment. "We can't alter something when we're inside it—"

"You do it all the time, don't you?" Kenna says calmly.

My eyes narrow.

"What's going on?" Alek asks, pushing carefully past Kaye to the front of the group that's forming around Kenna and me.

"The Grid," I gasp. My eyes widen, and I begin to talk in a rush. "But that's a simulator. It was built for us to be able to alter it—for us to give it input and have it react under the current code, and—" I freeze. "*So is Cerebrolink.* Kenna. It's a simulator! Our *brains* are giving the input, and the code is reacting, and vice versa." I suck in a breath. "Whatever goes forward can also go backward."

"What's going on?" Aave asks, echoing Alek's earlier question.

"Aave," I spin toward him. "I know why we're here. I finally get it! We have to go back in. You and me. And the others from Paradise. We have to be implanted with Cerebrolink."

Aave's eyes widen in confusion and disbelief. Alek turns away abruptly from the group and walks back toward the log he was sitting on earlier. I want to call after him, but my heart is hammering too quickly. My voice dies in my throat.

Mila reaches out and puts a hand on my arm.

"Today, we travel. Tomorrow we start training," Kenna says determinedly. "Welcome to the Coalition."

END OF BOOK 1

Preorder now!

ABOUT THE AUTHOR

 Cindy is first and foremost mother to her four beautiful children and wife to her charming and handsome husband, Scott. She is a musician, a homeschooler, a gardener, an athlete, a lover of Canadian chocolate, and most recently, a writer.

Cindy grew up in Airdrie, AB, Canada, but has lived most of her adult life between California and Colorado. She currently resides in the Denver metro area. Cindy graduated from Brigham Young University with a B.S. in Psychology, minoring in Business. She serves actively within her church and community and is always up for a new adventure.

ALSO BY CINDY GUNDERSON

Tier Trilogy

Yes, And

I Can't Remember

Let's Try This Again, But This Time in Paris

Holly Bough Cottage

The New Year's Party

www.CindyGunderson.com

Instagram: @CindyGWrites

Facebook: @CindyGWrites

Made in the USA
Monee, IL
17 September 2021